BLACK TIDE

Book #5 In The Ironborn Saga
by Andrew Cavanagh
© 2024 all rights reserved

Chapter 1
His Own Home

The Ironbay navy barracks were nestled inside the same stone walls as the army barracks, dwarfed by the army barracks' enormous size. Most navy officers slept on their ships, so they didn't need special accommodation.

Corporal Turner, the man in charge of managing all the navy cottages here, led Crutch past a large building towards a row of smaller houses.

'Got a nice place for you, Lieutenant Crutch. Usually we only give the cottages to captains and higher ranks, but I said to the chief of staff, I said, this isn't any ordinary officer. This is Lieutenant Crutch, double iron cross winner, hero of the Kona Track, siege breaker and the man what stopped these very barracks from being taken over in a bloody coup. If we can't give him a cottage, then no one should have a cottage.'

They came out the back of the navy barracks, and Crutch could see a second stone wall with shrubs and gardens inside. Corporal Turner unlocked a neat iron gate in the stone wall. It swung open cleanly, like someone had come and oiled it every day.

'The last person what stayed here was a retired fleet commander. This is my favourite cottage, truth be told. Fit for an admiral, if you ask me.'

'What happened to the fleet commander?' said Crutch.

'Died peacefully in his sleep,' said Corporal Turner, opening the solid wooden door at the front of the cottage.

Inside was a room with a small chimney, a desk made of finely polished wood, a couple of chairs, and a lounge trimmed with leather.

'This is your bedroom,' said Corporal Turner, opening the single door that led off the main room. Inside was a large double bed with clean sheets, a nightstand on its side, a wardrobe, and a mirror. 'A maid will clean and change your linen once a week.'

'Change my linen?' said Crutch.

'She'll put clean sheets on your bed,' said Corporal Turner. 'Here's the key to the front door and the gate. Is there anything else I can help you with?'

'No. I think that covers it,' said Crutch. 'Thank you, corporal. This is far more than I expected.'

After the corporal left, Crutch sat behind the desk and looked around him. For the first time in his life, he had his own home, a roof over his head, a bed, and two meals a day. The street urchin inside him, who'd slept in alleys and hid in the sewers, was amazed.

Crutch went into the bedroom and sat on the bed. It was so soft. Then he laid down on it and spread out his arms. It was wide enough that even with both arms out at his sides, they were still on the bed.

He walked outside into the front garden surrounded by stone walls and realised the shrubs he saw when he came in were fruit trees. Some kind of cherries. He picked a couple off one shrub. They were tart, not ripe yet, but delicious to a street urchin.

The raised garden bed near the shrubs was full of some kind of vine full of leaves, spilling over the edge of the bed and trying to root itself into the ground below. Crutch found the base of the vine and felt around in the soft, damp dirt with his fingers.

He could feel something there. Some kind of tuber. He dug, and pulled, and yanked up a sweet potato the size of his fist. Crutch searched around and found some dry leaves and twigs, then pulled up the bottom of his shirt so he could pile them all in.

When he figured he had enough, he took the sweet potato and his kindling inside. He stuck one stick through the sweet potato, then carefully laid out some leaves and twigs. He pulled a match from his pocket. Being around Quicksilver had taught him the wisdom of always carrying matches.

The wisdom of Quicksilver. There's a phrase that doesn't make sense.

He lit himself a nice little fire, got it burning, and fed it with the twigs he'd gathered while he sat there cross legged in the corner of the cottage, holding his sweet potato on a stick over the flames, just high enough that it would cook and not burn.

So this is what it's like to have your own home, thought Crutch. He smiled to himself happily as he smelled the sweet potato cooking and the gentle smoke from his little cooking fire wafted around him. *I could get used to this.*

'What are you doing?' said a voice behind him.

Crutch was so surprised he dropped his sweet potato into his cooking fire. He grabbed it, burning his hands, then looked behind himself to see a woman no older than seventeen with a shocked look on her face standing in the doorway.

It didn't feel right to be sitting there on the floor while a woman stood, so Crutch got to his feet, holding his cane in one hand and his sweet potato on a stick in the other.

'You're him,' said the woman with a hand over her mouth.

Crutch didn't know what to say. The young woman's shock had turned to embarrassment.

'I'm so sorry, your majesty, but you can't cook in here, specially not on the floor like that. You'll set the cottage on fire.'

'I'm sorry,' said Crutch. 'Are you the cottage guard?'

The woman laughed. 'No, I'm Rita, your maid, your majesty.' Rita disappeared outside then came back with a bucket full of water and carefully poured it over Crutch's perfectly built fire.

'How am I gonna cook my sweet potato now?' said Crutch.

'Normally, your majesty, the men staying here leave the food in the garden for the servants to eat. We pick the fruit and leave some on the desk for you.'

'I'm sorry,' said Crutch. 'I didn't know I was taking your food.' He held out the sweet potato on a stick as an apology.

'It's quite alright, your majesty,' said Rita, lowering in a curtsy as she took the sweet potato.

'Could you stop calling me that,' said Crutch. 'I'm not royalty.'

'Sorry, your majesty.'

'Please just call me Crutch.'

'Is it Prince Crutch or Lord Crutch?' said Rita.

'Just Crutch.'

'Doesn't seem right calling you by your first name,' said Rita. 'No one in these cottages has asked me to do that before.'

'Someone has now,' said Crutch, smiling. 'Sorry about messing up the floor.'

'That's alright,' said Rita. 'I'll have to scrub the stone tiles now to get it clean. And wipe the smoke off the walls.'

'Let me help you,' said Crutch.

'You couldn't,' said Rita.

'I insist,' said Crutch. 'I made the mess. The least I can do is help you clean it up.'

CHAPTER 2
WOULD YOU LIKE A PASTRY?

Crutch walked through the towering double doors of the navy office into the foyer, his walking cane clacking on the tiles. He went straight past the six armed navy guards in full dress uniform to a regular working guard he recognised.

'Corporal Markham,' said Crutch. 'Good to see you again.'

'Good to see you, Lieutenant Crutch,' said Corporal Markham, clearly chuffed that Ironbay's double iron cross winner had recognised him.

Crutch expected that. He wanted to find the supply office without letting anyone working there know he had no idea where it was.

'I haven't heard much about you lately,' said Corporal Markham. 'What are you doing these days?'

'As it happens, I start working here today,' said Crutch. 'In the supply office.'

'Putting their best man in charge to prepare for the invasion of Teevilgrad, I'd bet,' said Corporal Markham. 'They'll be lucky to have you.'

'Could you do me a favour and walk me there?' said Crutch.

'Of course, lieutenant. I'd be honoured.'

Corporal Markham led Crutch through the winding corridors until they came to an open door.

'The supply office,' said Corporal Markham.

'Thank you,' said Crutch. 'I'm sure I'll see a lot of you in the future.'

'I'll look forward to it,' said Corporal Markham.

Crutch looked inside. There was a skinny young man behind a desk who stood up as soon as he noticed Crutch was there.

'It's an honour to meet you, Lieutenant Crutch. I'm Private Rennar. They call me Magpie.'

Magpie's body was shaking he was so nervous.

'Interesting name,' said Crutch. 'Is there a reason for it?'

'It's because I'm good at hiding things away, like a magpie. Then finding them again.'

'That sounds like a useful skill here,' said Crutch. He looked at the piles of papers on the desk, the piles of paper on shelves against the walls, and the boxes.'

'What's in the boxes?' said Crutch.

'Papers,' said Magpie.

Of course they'd be filled with more papers. Crutch had no real idea of what he was supposed to do as a supply officer. They told him his job was to make sure the navy ships and the navy barracks were supplied under budget. They didn't tell him with what or what the budget was.

He expected the answer to that question was here among these papers, but he had no idea where to start. They'd promoted him to lieutenant, which made the job harder still. He couldn't just ask someone how to do it. He was supposed to be in charge.

Crutch would have to fake his way through this until he figured things out. Fortunately faking was something he was exceptionally good at.

'Tell me, Magpie, who was the last supply officer here?'

'That would be Lieutenant Reed.'

'And what happened to Lieutenant Reed?'

'He was sitting right at the desk there, and he grabbed his chest and wheezed a bit, then his head dropped to the desk, and he was dead. Just like that.'

'Just like that,' said Crutch. He wondered if this was his future in the navy. Sitting behind a desk until he dropped dead from some kind of seizure.

'Who's been running things since Lieutenant Reed died?' said Crutch.

'That would be me,' said Magpie.

That will make things easier, thought Crutch.

'Good. Tell me what you've been doing,' said Crutch.

'The navy office sends in requisition forms from the ships, the quartermaster, and the other officers at the barracks, and I send out order forms for the supplies they need,' said Magpie. 'I've got a system. Everything comes in on the left side of the desk, then goes around the room clockwise until it goes out the door to fill the order.'

'I see,' said Crutch. 'And why don't you just fill out the order form straight away and send out the order?'

'Lieutenant Reed said you should never do that.'

'Why not?'

'He said if you filled orders too fast, you'd go over budget, and if you go over budget the navy office gets upset, and the office of the secretary of the navy starts sending you letters telling you not to go over budget, and if you keep doing it, they put you in front of the remedial board, and if you keep doing it, they court martial you and throw you in the Ironbay prison, or worse.'

'Worse?' said Crutch.

'They hang you in the city square.'

'So Lieutenant Reed kept from going over budget by slowing down all the orders that came in?'

'Yes,' said Magpie. 'He said you can keep an order in the office for weeks, even months, before the ships or the barracks get upset at you. With the ships, they often sail before they get their order, which means they can't complain at all. And if they sail without an order being filled, then that means they never needed it in the first place, so you can throw that order away.'

'So he kept the budget down by not filling orders at all?'

'Well, it sounds bad when you put it like that,' said Magpie, shuffling papers nervously.

'Show me some of these orders,' said Crutch.

'Here's an order from a ship in the harbour here in Ironbay,' said Magpie.

'Seems simple enough,' said Crutch. 'They want four crates of yams.'

'They're dreaming,' said Magpie. 'If I sent this on to food acquisition, I'd have a couple of their heavies visiting me at night at my place asking me questions.'

'They have people who beat you up if you pass an order on to them?'

'That's what Lieutenant Reed said. He said food orders from ships stop here. He had a special file for them.'

'Where's that?' said Crutch.

Magpie lifted up a small rubbish bin full of paper. Orders by the look of them.

'So you just throw them away?'

'Trust me,' said Magpie. 'Everything runs much smoother that way.'

'Except that the crews on our ships don't get their food.'

'They seem to manage okay,' said Magpie.

'Are there orders you do send out to get filled?'

'Of course,' said Magpie. 'It's not like we're sitting around on our arses all day throwing orders in the bin.'

'So which orders do you fill?'

'Ammunition. We always fill ammunition. There's plenty of metal in Ironbay, and the ships captains get really upset if they run out of ballista bolts.'

'Anything else?' said Crutch.

'Sometimes we fill orders for uniforms if the wind is blowing in the right direction.'

'What does the wind have to do with it?'

'I'm not sure,' said Magpie. 'But Lieutenant Reed always said, if we get a nice north-easterly for a few weeks, then we can fill plenty of orders for uniforms.'

'Let me make sure I've got this right. You never send any food to the navy ships?'

'Never.'

'You just throw those orders straight in the bin?'

'Sometimes we hang on to them for a few days,' said Magpie.

'You fill orders for ammunition?'

'Mostly.'

'And you fill orders for uniforms depending on what direction the wind is blowing?'

'That's amazing,' said Magpie. 'It took me months of training from Lieutenant Reed to get the hang of this job. You've worked it out in one morning!'

Crutch was about to explode into an angry tirade with this idiot paper pusher who seemed to have no idea that there were real navy crews relying on their supplies.

Then she appeared.

'Young Lady Hastings,' said Magpie. 'Wonderful to see you.'

'Nice to see you too,' said Abagail. 'Would you like a pastry?' Abagail carried a hand basket, which she opened to reveal a plate full of delicious looking treats.

'I'd love one,' said Magpie reaching in to take a pastry. 'Thank you, Young Lady Hastings.'

'You're welcome,' said Abagail, smiling with that wonderful crooked face of hers.

'Might be a good time to take a break,' said Crutch. 'Take an hour off, Magpie. Good work today.'

'Thank you, Lieutenant Crutch.'

Once Magpie was gone, Crutch smiled at Abagail. He noticed that she wore the gold necklace with a heart on it Crutch had given her when he got back from Yavenland. It looked stunning, shimmering on the skin of her chest. It was even more stunning that she chose to wear something that came from him.

'You're a sight for sore eyes,' he said. 'How did you get in here?'

'I'm the admiral's daughter,' said Abagail. 'Everyone in the navy office knows who I am. Plus, pastries.'

'There's no one could resist your pastries,' said Crutch. 'I think we could convince Emperor Solokov to call off this whole war for a batch of them if we could get them to Teevilgrad.'

'Let's not talk about the war now,' said Abagail. 'I came to have lunch with you.'

'What a delightful idea,' said Crutch. On the Auld Faithful, there was a morning meal and an evening meal. You didn't get lunch. 'Do all the workers in the navy office stop for lunch?'

'Most of them,' said Abagail. 'I don't know about all of them, but the ones I do know spend more time eating and talking than they do working.'

'That explains a lot,' said Crutch. 'Where would you like to eat?'

'There's a lovely little park with a fountain just a block from here,' said Abagail.

'I know it,' said Crutch, putting his free arm through Abagail's. 'I shall escort you there.'

'Oh Crutch you're such a gentleman.'

'I try,' said Crutch. 'Tell me more about the people you know here in the navy office. After one morning, I've worked out there's a lot of work to do if we want to get these ships supplied.'

'Do you want the nice details or all the details?' said Abagail as they walked through the maze of corridors to the navy office entrance. 'I've spent quite some time in this building, and most of the people here have their guard down around me.'

'Really?' said Crutch. 'You might have some very useful information for me then. Tell me everything, starting with food acquisition.'

'The den of thieves,' said Abagail.

'What?'

'The people inside the navy office call food acquisition the den of thieves. Their only goal seems to be selling food that's supposed to go to ships to fill their own coffers. They know ships captains and quartermasters have their own means of paying for or acquiring food. As long as the food in the navy barracks doesn't run out, they know they can take bribes from merchants and sell food to the black market without any consequences.'

'Does your father know this?'

'Father doesn't talk to the commoners in the navy office like I do. He talks to officers, who mostly spend their time pandering to him and puffing him up. He knows they're pandering to him, but I doubt he knows about the corruption going on.'

Crutch stopped walking for a second, stunned.

'This is crazy. I'll have the lot of the thieves in food acquisition thrown in prison.'

'That wouldn't be a good idea,' said Abagail.

'Why not?'

'They might be called thieves, but food acquisition doesn't keep all that coin for themselves. They pass it on to other departments like the weapons and ammunition department.'

'Why do they do that?'

'Because if they don't, there wouldn't be enough coin to supply navy ships with the ammunition they need or to repair and upgrade their ballistas.'

'Why don't they just ask the navy office for more?' said Crutch.

'No department asks for more,' said Abagail. 'If they go over budget the office of the secretary of the navy sends threatening letters, then there's the remedial board.'

'Magpie told me the same thing,' said Crutch.

'Did he tell you they court martial officers who go over budget and throw them in prison?'

'He did mention it.'

'A supply officer got hanged for it once,' said Abagail.

'That would be a fate I'd like to avoid,' said Crutch.

'Then whatever you do, don't ask for more coin. If you're working in supply, you're expected to find a way to get the job done under budget. Asking for more coin is seen as a failure just as large as going over budget.'

'How did it get this crazy?' said Crutch.

'I can't answer that,' said Abagail. 'It's been this way since I was a little girl, and the navy office was like my own personal playground.'

'So everyone in the navy office is used to you being around?'

'It's like I'm not even there,' said Abagail. 'Would you like a pastry?' She opened a lid on her basket.

'I would,' said Crutch. 'Oh.' All the time Crutch had known Abagail and just now he realised he had seriously underestimated her. She played her game of deception with the navy office staff just like Crutch had played his as a street urchin in the streets of Ironbay.

But she played a much bigger game and went completely undetected. He had to admit to himself that, in her own way, Abagail was much better at this than he was.

'Is there a reason you've spent so many years spying on the navy office?' said Crutch.

'It began as a game I played when I was a little girl,' said Abagail. 'The thrill of knowing things other people didn't know, and people thinking you're just a silly little thing when you have knowledge that could get them hanged.'

'The power of being underestimated,' said Crutch. He knew all about that.

'But as I get older, and after I met you, I'm beginning to understand that I might use this knowledge to make things better for the navy crews. Maybe to help end this war with Estovia.'

'You might,' said Crutch.

'I wasn't sure how to go about it, but I woke up one day, and there you are, the royal navy's new supply officer.'

'Here I am,' said Crutch, smiling. 'So how do we change things for the better?'

'I have a few ideas,' said Abagail as they sat next to the fountain. 'Shall we eat?'

Chapter 3
The Slush Fund

Crutch made his way to the docks. He needed to see the one person he knew who really understood what it was like for a ship's captain to deal with the supply office.

As he got closer to the docks, Crutch could see workers and carts milling around. Many of the ships were being readied for battle.

Soldiers milled around the docks too, officers and non-commissioned officers. Probably making preparations for transporting the men who would invade Teevilgrad. They'd need hammocks to sleep in, upgrades to the galley so they could feed an extra hundred or so men on each ship, and space in the cargo hold for weapons and other gear.

Crutch barely set foot on the Auld Faithful when Boulder greeted him with a huge hug.

'It's so good to see you, Crutch. Are you coming back to be a marine? Please come back and be a marine again. We miss you, Crutch.'

'I miss you too, Boulder, but I'm not back to join the marines. I'm here to see Cedric.'

'That's okay,' said Boulder. 'At least I got to see you.'

Cedric appeared on the deck, and Crutch asked if they could talk in his cabin. Cedric nodded and led the way.

'What can I help you with?' said Cedric once they were inside.

'You've taught me about how to stock a ship and keep supplies up for the crew, but there's something you didn't teach me. Where the coin comes from.'

Cedric smiled. 'It seems the navy finally has a supply officer who's going to do his job.'

'Abagail told me food acquisition at the navy office is called the den of thieves,' said Crutch.

'Really?' said Cedric. 'That doesn't surprise me. No good navy captain relies on the navy office to supply their ship with food. We feel lucky if we can get a few new uniforms for the crew.'

'So how do you pay for food?'

'Three methods. First is the slush fund.'

'The slush fund?'

'The cooks in the galley scrape the fat off their cooking pots and sell it to tallow makers,' said Cedric.

'So it's used to make soap and candles?'

'Yes,' said Cedric. 'You can get a better price for it if you're in a harbour where there's textile manufacturing.'

'Clothes and other fabrics?'

'Yes. They use it as a softener for fabric and to get yarn to run smoothly through their looms. Tallow from sheep brings a premium.'

'There's a whole world I didn't know existed here,' said Crutch. 'So what are the other two methods?'

'Trade. We pay attention to the prices of different food and goods in each port and buy more than we need if we know we can sell it at a good profit in another port we're heading to. When I was beastmaster, at least half the animals we carried were there to be sold. That's why we always had coin to buy fresh animals for the crew to eat.'

'Is that within navy regulations?' said Crutch.

'It's not outside them,' said Cedric. 'Captaining a ship to be self-sufficient is encouraged. How we do that is not detailed in our guidelines.'

'What's the third method?'

'Favours,' said Cedric. 'There's always a rich noble or merchant who wants someone or something transported safely between the territories. We make it happen for them, and in exchange, they give us better prices on the food and goods we buy, or they do us other favours in return.'

'This whole system is just inviting corruption,' said Crutch.

'Not just inviting,' said Cedric.

'Are you telling me navy captains are corrupt?'

'You have to learn to play the game and play it well. If you don't, your crew will starve.'

Crutch's head was spinning. He realised the corruption in the navy supply system couldn't be overcome without a court martial for every captain and every quartermaster in the fleet. Crutch had to rethink his whole approach to the problem.

'Could you teach me how to play the game?' he said.

'Of course,' said Cedric. 'Right now, there's something you can do for me. The Auld Faithful has been in port since we got back from Yavenland, and we were low on food then. Now, we barely have enough to eat. We're living on hard tack and the bare minimum of supplies the quartermaster scrounges from the local markets.

'The crew who can afford it are going to the taverns on the docks to drink to make our watered-down rum and beer last as long as possible. If you could achieve the impossible, we would really appreciate getting some food from the supply office.'

'You write me an order, and I'll get it filled,' said Crutch, having no idea how he was going to do it.

Chapter 4
What's a Toothpick?

Crutch could feel softness all around him. Soft on his back, soft under his head, soft under his legs, soft and light over him. Nothing was swinging. Nothing was rocking.

He opened his eyes, panicked, expecting to be kicked or stabbed. He looked around, and it took him a couple of seconds in the pre-dawn to work out where he was. This was his own room in his own cottage on the navy barracks.

Crutch relaxed. He finally had a roof over his head. His own place where no one would kick him and tell him to move on in the middle of the night. His own place where he could lock the door and not worry about another street urchin, or beggar, or thief stabbing him or robbing him at night for a single copper or a tiny lump of bread.

He sat up. Today he'd start changing the way things were done at the navy supply office, but right now he could just enjoy having his own home.

He got to his feet and walked out into the living room. His living room. He opened the front door and looked out into the small front garden. His front garden. He put a hand in his pocket and found some hard tack there. Crutch always carried enough hard tack to keep him going for a few days. With enough food for three or four days, you'd never go hungry.

Crutch smiled to himself. You never stop being a street urchin.

There was someone at the gate to the garden. She opened the gate, looked up, and saw Crutch.

'Sorry, your majesty. I'm here too early,' said Rita. 'I can come back later when you're at work, your majesty.'

Crutch wondered what the street urchin inside him, who grew up on the streets, would think if he knew one day he'd have his own maid to clean for him. Cleaning. He grew up hiding in the sewers and alleys of Ironbay. The only thing he ever tried to clean was the horse shit off a bit of food that someone had dropped in the street.

'It's okay, Rita,' said Crutch. 'I don't mind.'

'You're very kind, your majesty,' said Rita, dropping her knees in a curtsey.

'Please just call me Crutch. I'm not a king or a prince. Just a navy lieutenant.'

'Yes, your majesty…Crutch.' Rita smiled; her cheeks flushed red. 'Is it okay if I come inside to clean?'

'Of course,' said Crutch, moving aside.

Rita slid past him in the doorway, her dress sliding against him as she went past. She looked into his eyes for a second, her cheeks went red again, and she looked down and moved into the living room.

'I don't think I got all the charcoal off the floor last time I scrubbed,' said Rita, pulling a scrubbing brush from the bucket of water she was carrying. 'If you need anything out of the garden cooked, I can do it for you.'

'Thank you, Rita,' said Crutch. 'That's very kind of you.'

'It's just my job,' said Rita, blushing again.

Crutch would have stayed to help Rita scrub the floor, but he couldn't see any black marks on it. She must have better eyes than him. He figured the best thing he could do was get to the supply office early and get the Auld Faithful's food order filled.

'Okay,' said Crutch. 'I'm going to get food acquisition to supply just one of the orders I have here for the Auld Faithful.'

'And how do you plan on doing that?' said Abagail, sitting in a spare chair in the supply office with papers stacked all around her.

'I'm just going to walk down to their office and tell them to fill the order.'

'And when they refuse?' said Abagail.

'I'll grab whoever's closest and beat the living tar out of him until they all see the error of their ways.'

'So you think beating up someone in food acquisition will get them to deliver food to a navy ship?'

'Won't it?' said Crutch.

'Do you think you're the first person who knows how to fight who's been in their office threatening them?'

'I guess not, since you put it like that.' Crutch realised over the years many ships captains and their crews must have made the trip down to the food acquisition office to set the workers there right.

'If you want to get food acquisition to supply food to ships, you need to find some money for them.'

'We've already discussed why I can't do that.'

'Not quite,' said Abagail. 'We discussed why people working in supply have to go under budget and why asking for more money will get you in trouble and eventually could get you thrown in jail.'

'Seems the same,' said Crutch.

'It's all in the delivery,' said Abagail. 'The king has never had his double iron cross winner and saviour of Ironbay asking to increase the budget for ammunition.'

'You want me to talk to the king?'

'Who else? It's not like you've never talked to him before, and I think he might owe you a favour or two.'

'And tell him what?'

'That the budget for ammunition hasn't changed in over ten years despite the fact we're at war and the navy ships are all going through ballistas as if they were toothpicks.'

'What's a toothpick?' said Crutch.

'It's a little piece of wood that you…never mind about that. What's important here is that you get King Vargus to see that the navy needs more money for ballista bolts.'

'And how will that get food to the ships?'

'Food acquisition moves most of the money it makes through its black market sales to ammunition and weapons. Fund ammunition and weapons and food acquisition can spend money on…'

'Food,' said Crutch. 'I think I just got a headache.'

'It will pass,' said Abagail.

'How will I get the king to see me?' said Crutch.

'I have an idea that might work,' said Abagail. 'But before we talk about that, isn't it time you taught me to fight?'

Chapter 5
You Say The Sweetest Things

Abagail looked at Crutch expectantly, with those wonderful ocean blue eyes and that delightfully crooked face of hers.

'So when do I start learning to kill?' she said. After feeling helpless when the true royals attacked her and her family in the admiral's residence, Abagail had asked Crutch to teach her the art of combat. This would be her first lesson.

'The first step is not getting killed yourself,' said Crutch. 'Or injured. In a fight, being injured is often the first step to being killed. If someone knocks you out, you're dead. If someone immobilises you by taking out your legs, you're probably dead. If someone takes out your arms, you're probably dead too.'

'My goodness,' said Abagail. 'That's a lot of ways to die.'

'There are many, many more ways to die,' said Crutch. 'The most important thing is to be the person who's dealing them out, instead of being the person who's taking them.'

'That sounds promising,' said Abagail.

'When you fight, it's always the attack you don't see coming that kills you. That's as good a place as any to start. What do you have on you?'

'Not much,' said Abagail.

'You can use nearly anything as a weapon,' said Crutch. 'The more unusual and unexpected it is, the more likely you are to catch your opponent by surprise.'

'With an attack they don't see coming?' said Abagail.

'Exactly.'

'I have this belt on my waist.'

'How fast can you get it off?'

'Father says you're a man of honour,' said Abagail as she unclasped the belt, smiling. 'Now I'm starting to wonder.'

Crutch looked at the belt. 'Good for strangling. You can also use it like a whip on someone's eyes to distract them or blind them. That will help you drive home another attack.'

'I'm halfway to being undressed, and that's what you think about,' said Abagail. 'What has being a marine done to you?'

'If you want to be a killer, you need to think like a killer all the time,' said Crutch.

'That's more than a little unsettling, but I think I can get into this mindset,' said Abagail. She pulled the metal clasp off her belt and held it in the palm of her hand. 'So I could use the metal pin in this clasp to stab into someone's eyes or their neck?'

'Or their groin,' said Crutch. Depends where you are at the time.

'It's all so devilishly brutal,' said Abagail.

'What else do you have?'

'You'll love this,' said Abagail, pulling a long hairpin out of her hair, her golden blonde strands falling to her shoulders.

'Nice!' said Crutch looking on in admiration.

'My hair or the hairpin?' said Abagail, fully aware of where he was looking.

'Both,' said Crutch, trying to extricate himself. 'We are talking about killing, though. Do you have a plan for killing someone with your hair.'

'Not yet,' said Abagail.

'So it's the hairpin then,' said Crutch.

'Don't tell me,' said Abagail. 'Let me do it. I could stab this straight into someone's heart or through their eye into their brain. Or I could use it to pin their weapon hand to the wall, then use their own weapon to kill them.'

'You're a natural-born killer,' said Crutch, smiling.

'Oh Crutch, you say the sweetest things to me. Your words are like honey dripping from your mouth.'

Chapter 6
Paper Cuts You?

Crutch sat at his desk, trying to make sense of the piles of papers. He figured he should get a grasp on what they all meant and what each form was supposed to do, even if, the way things stood now, they seemed to do nothing at all.

Magpie was out delivering forms to the different departments. Forms that, for the most part, would be totally ignored.

Crutch was about at the point where he'd like to put a match to the entire office and start fresh when he heard voices in the corridor. Voices he recognised.

'Thank you for your help,' said Sergeant Zander's voice.

'Would've got lost without you,' said Longshot. 'You're a legend.'

Then they were there in the doorway. His marines. He hadn't realised how much he missed being around them every day until they appeared in front of him.

'Hello Crutch,' said Sergeant Zander.

'Hello Crutch,' said Boulder, smiling. All the marines smiled like they were the cats who'd just stolen the milk.

'It's great to see you all,' said Crutch. 'How did you get in?'

'We just told them we're the siege breakers and the heroes of the Kona track, and they led us right here,' said Sergeant Zander, smiling.

'It was like they rolled out a red carpet,' said Longshot.

'You waited until there was no one on the desk and got Corporal Markham to sneak you in, didn't you?' said Crutch.

'Can't keep any secrets from the master of espionage,' said Sergeant Zander.

'I told him you were my friend,' said Boulder, smiling.

'So this is your new job?' said Sergeant Zander, his eyes scanning the papers piled up on desks and shelves around the room.'

'It is,' said Crutch.

'Don't you miss being a marine on the Auld Faithful,' said Sergeant Zander. 'Must be hard not having someone to fight every day.'

'We miss you,' said Boulder.

'I miss you too,' said Crutch. 'But the battles I fight here are just as important as the ones I fought with the marines.'

'Doesn't look like you'd do much fighting here,' said Sergeant Zander. 'Can't be too much risk of injury. Maybe a paper cut.'

'Paper cuts you?' said Boulder, his eyes moving around the room with a whole new level of appreciation.

'I have paperweights like these to keep the papers down,' said Crutch. 'Some days they try to get the best of me, but I'm a royal marine. I adapt and overcome.'

'I can take care of those papers for you,' said Quicksilver, pulling a ball of bluefire out of his pocket. 'I'd love to see this office burn.'

'You brought a ball of bluefire to the navy office?' said Sergeant Zander.

'Maybe,' said Quicksilver defensively. 'You never know when you might need to start a fire.'

'How many times do we have to talk about this,' said Sergeant Zander, snatching the bluefire ball off him. 'Is that the only one?'

'Yes,' said Quicksilver. Sergeant Zander glared at him. 'No.' One by one, Quicksilver pulled another three balls of bluefire from his pockets and reluctantly handed them over to Sergeant Zander.

There was a loud crunch, and splinters flew from Magpie's desk as Boulder smashed a paperweight right through it.

'Boulder, what are you doing?' said Crutch.

'I'm holding down these papers for you,' said Boulder. 'You're my friend.'

Two guards appeared in the doorway.

'We heard something break, lieutenant,' said the first guard. 'Is everything okay.'

Boulder stood over the broken desk with the paperweight in his hand, looking at the guards as if they might be the next thing he had to hold down.

'Everything's fine, private,' said Crutch. 'My friend Boulder here just dropped a paperweight.'

The guard looked at Boulder and Crutch with a level of disbelief.

'He dropped a paperweight, and it broke a desk in half?' said the guard.

'It's a very heavy paperweight,' said Crutch.

'It's holding the papers down,' said Boulder.

Near Boulder, Crutch could see Quicksilver smiling at him. He flashed another ball of bluefire he hadn't surrendered to Sergeant Zander.

'If there's something going on here and you need help, I can call more men, lieutenant,' said the guard.

'I'll be fine,' said Crutch. *As long as Quicksilver doesn't burn down the whole navy office. Right now, that doesn't sound like such a bad idea.*

'Alright,' said the guard. 'But we're just outside if you need us.'

'I really am fine,' said Crutch as they left the room.

'Sorry, Crutch,' said Longshot. 'We didn't mean to get you in trouble.'

'It's not a problem,' said Crutch. 'It's great to see you all.'

'Cedric tells us you're getting the Auld Faithful some food,' said Sergeant Zander. 'We're tired of eating hard tack every meal.'

'I'm working on it,' said Crutch. 'You wouldn't believe how complicated getting a few crates of food is. It's like every sheet of paper in this office and every other department is fighting against me.'

'I'll kill them all for you,' said Boulder.

'No Boulder,' said Crutch. He'd have to be more careful about how he worded things. 'They're not really fighting me. Just making things difficult.'

'I'll give them a good talking to then,' said Boulder.

'Please don't,' said Crutch. 'I know you want to help me, but that won't do any good.'

'Cedric tells us the Auld Faithful is getting more ballistas,' said Sergeant Zander.

'I'll be helping with the test firing,' said Longshot.

'It's always good to master a new weapon,' said Sergeant Zander.

'Can't be long,' said Quicksilver, and the room fell into silence.

No one said what they were thinking. It won't be long until the Auld Faithful and the marines sailed off to the largest, most dangerous battle of their lives. Without Crutch.

'You should come down to the ship one night and eat with us,' said Sergeant Zander. 'Cedric would love to see you.'

'I will,' said Crutch. 'Right after I get some food for you to eat.'

'Can you get us ham?' said Boulder. 'I like ham.'

'I'll try,' said Crutch. 'It's a lot harder than you think.'

'If you can't, it's okay,' said Boulder. 'You're my friend.'

'You're my friend too, Boulder,' said Crutch, as another wave of guilt washed over him, thinking about Boulder and the marines fighting the Estovians in Teevilgrad without him.

'We'd better let Crutch get back to work,' said Sergeant Zander, looking around at the piles of papers stacked high in every nook and cranny of the room. 'Looks like he's got plenty to do.'

'Thank you for coming in,' said Crutch. 'It was great to see you.'

'I can cut down your workload,' said Quicksilver, grinning and flashing his ball of bluefire again. 'Just say the word.'

'No,' said Crutch. 'I really have to deal with these papers the hard way.'

'Sounds like a lot of unnecessary work when the solution is so simple,' said Quicksilver.

'Thank you, but no,' said Crutch.

'See you, Crutch,' said Boulder, looking a little sad that he was leaving his friend behind in this office. 'If you try to cut Crutch again, you'll be sorry,' he said to a stack of papers before he left. 'Crutch is my friend.'

And just like that, they were gone. Crutch wondered how he'd feel when they sailed off to Teevilgrad without him. What it would feel like to be here sitting in an office while his friends were fighting on the docks and streets putting their lives on the line one more time for Ironbay?

They were barely gone when Magpie returned to the office.

'What happened to my desk?' he said.

'Turns out your paperweight is much heavier and much stronger than we imagined,' said Crutch.

'A paperweight broke my desk in half?' said Magpie in disbelief.

'That desk had it coming,' said Crutch. 'You spend way too much time sitting behind it.'

'That is my job,' said Magpie. 'Sitting behind my desk and sorting all these orders.'

'You're wrong there,' said Crutch. 'Let's go for a walk.'

'Okay, Lieutenant Crutch. Where are we going?'

'Down to the docks,' said Crutch. 'There's something I want you to see.'

Chapter 7
Rats & Bugs

As Crutch and Magpie walked down King's Way towards the docks, the road was filled with lines of wagons. Wagons full of weapons driven by soldiers going towards the docks, and lines of empty wagons coming back.

A wagon missed Crutch by a few inches going past.

'Watch where you're walking!' yelled the driver, then the wagon stopped. 'Is that you, Lieutenant Crutch?'

'It is,' said Crutch.

The soldier in the wagon looked back and smiled.

'I fought with you on the Kona track, lieutenant.'

'I remember you,' said Crutch. 'Marbig isn't it?'

'It is.'

'You're a brave man, Marbig. I see they made you a corporal.'

'Wouldn't be alive if it weren't for you. You and Colonel Zander were the best commanders we ever had.'

'Thank you, Corporal Marbig.'

'Are you coming to Teevilgrad?' said Corporal Marbig. 'We could use your help.'

'My fighting days are over,' said Crutch. 'I'm working in the supply office now.'

'You'll be the best supply officer they've ever had,' said Corporal Marbig. 'Pleasure to see you, sir.'

'You too,' said Crutch. 'Good luck in Teevilgrad.'

As they walked on, more soldiers in wagons recognised Crutch and saluted. Two men in the back of a wagon stood at attention and saluted, rocking and bumping from side to side.

'The men sure do respect you,' said Magpie.

Crutch nodded as they came to the docks. As far as they could see in both directions, there were ships taking on weapons, being fitted with ballistas, being readied for war.

'What do you see?' said Crutch.

'What do I see?' said Magpie.

'What do you see?'

'Soldiers and navy men everywhere,' said Magpie. 'They're getting read for war. The invasion of Teevilgrad.'

'Take a long, hard look,' said Crutch. Most of the men you see here won't be coming back. They'll die in Teevilgrad, taking the docks, or getting through the city walls, or getting into Solokov's palace. Or they'll just die in some back alley somewhere with an Estovian blade through the guts.'

Magpie was shocked silent. Seeing thousands of dead men walking will do that to you.

'Come with me,' said Crutch.

Crutch led Magpie to the Auld Faithful.

When they got there, the marines hadn't returned from their expedition into the city of Ironbay and Cedric was elsewhere too. Crutch asked the first mate if he could go below.

'Of course, Lieutenant Crutch,' said the first mate.

Crutch guided Magpie down the ladder to the cargo hold.

'It's nearly empty,' said Magpie.

'These navy ships are being fitted for the Teevilgrad invasion. When they're in port, they don't have any way to get more coin to pay for food. Our navy crews are going hungry.'

'This is terrible,' said Magpie.

'You think our job is pushing papers around on a desk. That's not our job at all. We're responsible for feeding these men and getting them what they need to go to war. And they're going hungry.

'We're sending these men to die on empty bellies. Even murderers and rapists get a final meal before they're hanged.'

'I'm sorry, Lieutenant Crutch,' said Magpie. 'I had no idea.'

'I didn't bring you down here to make you feel bad,' said Crutch. 'I brought you here so you can help me solve this problem.'

'I will,' said Magpie. 'I promise I will.'

They were interrupted by an officer of the army coming down the ladder to the cargo hold.

He got to the bottom and saw Crutch.

'Lieutenant Crutch,' said Captain Travis. 'Great to see you here.'

Captain Travis. He was just a corporal when Crutch fought with him on the Kona track. He was a brave man and an excellent soldier. He'd helped Crutch get the army onside after Lord Rothchester turned them against King Vargus too.

'Good to see you too,' said Crutch. 'How is Tilly and your boy Timothy?'

When he came back from the Kona track, seeing Captain Travis's newborn son helped him understand deep inside that life goes on.

'Timothy is running her ragged now he can walk, but Tilly's in perfect health. How is your Miss Hastings?'

'As lovely as ever,' said Crutch, feeling a warm spot in his stomach just at the thought of Abagail.

'Tell me you're joining us in the invasion of Teevilgrad,' said Captain Travis. 'After the Kona track and the problems with the true royals, I bet General Talbot would be happy to put you in command of the whole invasion force.'

'I'm working in the navy supply office now,' said Crutch. 'I've laid down my sword.'

'Looks to me like you're still carrying it,' said Captain Travis, smiling and looking at Crutch's walking cane.

Crutch laughed. 'I need the cane to walk,' he said. I'm just showing Magpie here why what we do in the supply office is so important,' said Crutch.

'Battles are won or lost on logistics,' said Captain Travis. 'That's something I learned from you. Remember when you made us eat those bugs on the Kona track? That was horrible, but brilliant.'

'I hoped we might get our navy men a little more to eat than bugs,' said Crutch.

'If anyone can knock that supply office into shape, it will be you, Lieutenant Crutch. Wish you were coming with us to Teevilgrad.'

'My fighting days are over,' said Crutch. He was starting to believe that now, but it still made him uneasy thinking about Boulder and the marines fighting in Teevilgrad without him. 'What brings you to the Auld Faithful?'

'General Talbot has assigned us to this ship for the invasion. We're commanded by a Colonel Montague. Lord Montague. He's a noble who seems to have no idea how to get anything done, so I take care of things, like the preparations and loading for war.'

'It's a pleasure to see you,' said Crutch.

'You too,' said Captain Travis. 'You listen to Lieutenant Crutch, Magpie. He's the smartest man I ever met. Me and my mates wouldn't be alive if it wasn't for him.'

'I will,' said Magpie.

'Just don't get caught up a jungle track with him. Unless you like the taste of rat.'

'There are few things in life better than the taste of a freshly cooked rat,' said Crutch. 'Even raw, they're tasty.'

Captain Travis laughed. 'I have to get back to it,' he said. 'I'm sure you have work to do too, Lieutenant. I hope we run into each other again soon.' Captain Travis went back up the ladder.

'You ate rats and bugs on the Kona track?' said Magpie.

'Yes,' said Crutch. 'That's what happens when supply breaks down. It's our job to make sure that never happens in Teevilgrad.'

'Thank you, Lieutenant Crutch,' said Magpie, looking at the ship's near-empty cargo hold. 'I understand now. I really do.'

CHAPTER 8
MY BATTLE

Crutch entered the supply office the next morning and saw Magpie there with his head on the desk, sleeping. It looked like he'd scrounged a couple of empty crates to prop up the middle of the broken desk so he could work on it.

The papers on the desk were piled as high as ever. Spit dribbled out of the side of Magpie's mouth down onto one paper laying on his desk. A candle sat in front of him, long since burned down to wax.

Crutch frowned in annoyance. It seemed his talk on the Auld Faithful the day before hadn't achieved anything.

'Morning Magpie,' he said. 'I see you're hard at it.'

Magpie stirred, then looked up, surprised. He tried to organise his dishevelled hair and wiped the dribble from his face, then from the piece of paper on his desk.

'Sorry, Lieutenant Crutch,' he said. 'I worked through the night. I must have fallen asleep at my desk.'

'Really?' said Crutch. He realised he might have read Magpie wrong.

'I was gonna go home, but then I thought of you and all those soldiers fighting on the Kona Track. Did you get to sleep there?'

'Not much,' said Crutch.

'That's what I thought,' said Magpie. 'Getting this food for the ships is my battle. I thought to myself, 'I can't sleep while our men are going hungry. It's not right.''

Crutch tried not to smile. Maybe his little talk had made a difference.

'So what have you managed to get done?' said Crutch.

'I started thinking to myself, who has food in Ironbay and what are they doing with it? And what do I have to trade to get it off them?'

'That's a nice place to start, said Crutch.

'I made a long list, and by that time it was dark, but I didn't let that stop me. I went down to the mess at the army barracks.'

'What did you find there?' said Crutch.

'The mess sergeant told me he often has food that's close to going off. If he can't cook it in time, he gives it to the pigs. I asked him what he wanted for it, and he told me if I got a wagon and carried it out of his kitchen myself, I could have it free. It would save him sending one of his privates to take one of his wagons to the pig sties on the other side of the barracks.'

'Nice work, Magpie. How many crates did you get?'

'Just four, but the mess sergeant said I could come back any night after he'd finished cooking. He said I should get at least a couple of crates of food every night. Sometimes more like last night.'

'Nice work,' said Crutch. 'It's not much, but it's a start.'

'That's not all of it,' said Magpie. 'I thought, if the army is throwing away food to the pigs, I bet there are restaurants in the city doing the same, so I took the horse and wagon I'd got from the navy supply stables and went door to door to every restaurant I could find.'

'How did that go?'

'Good for the first three or four. I told them I was from the navy supply office collecting food for the navy, and did they have anything they was giving to the pig?. After I showed 'em papers proving who I was and told them I was working with the double iron cross winner, Lieutenant Crutch, they were very generous.'

Crutch had an inkling of where this part of Magpie's story would go.

'Who stopped you doing that?' he said.

'How did you know someone stopped me?' said Magpie.

'I grew up in the same alleys you went down to get the food,' said Crutch.

'Sorry, I forgot you were a street urchin, Lieutenant Crutch. Anyway, I was out by myself in the alley at the back door of one restaurant, and this street urchin put a knife to my throat.'

'A black knife?' said Crutch.

'Yes,' said Magpie, surprised the Crutch knew. 'He wanted to know what I thought I was doing, stealing their food. I told them I was working with you to get food to the navy ships, and he changed his tune right away. Told me to wait, or he and his friends would hunt me down and stick me in the guts with a knife. Then he came back five minutes later with someone who called himself Bram.'

'Leader of the black knives,' said Crutch.

'You know him?' said Magpie.

'He fought on the Kona Track. Saved my life once.'

'I never knew,' said Magpie. 'Once I told Bram that I was working with you and what I was doing, he told me that with a great story like that I should go to the restaurants on the fancy side of the city. They'd be throwing out much better quality food there.'

'So what did Bram want in return for helping you?' said Crutch.

'How did you know he offered to help me?'

'I did mention I know Bram.'

Magpie laughed.

'He told me he'd get his street urchins to help me in exchange for half the food. I told him I'd give him a quarter of the food.'

'How did he convince you to give him half?' said Crutch.

'He told me I'd look awful floating in the harbour, all stabbed full of holes and bloated up, but he could live with it.'

'That sounds like Bram,' said Crutch.

'So I went with the wagon and three of Bram's street urchins to all the fancy restaurants in Ironbay I could find. They close really late, so it was good timing. The street urchins lurked in the shadows while I tried to convince the cooks or the owners to give me the food scraps they were throwing out.'

'That must have been hard,' said Crutch.

'It was. Most of them told me to get lost until I started mentioning your name and telling them I was collecting food for the navy ships. Then a few of them gave me what they had.'

'So did you get a couple of crates?' said Crutch.

'By early this morning, we'd collected two wagons full,' said Magpie. 'I made this list of all the restaurants so we can go back there tonight and do it again.'

Cedric had told Crutch once that when you had a good crew, you didn't need to solve every problem. All you had to do was give a good man some inspiration and direction, and he'd find a way to get things done. He never thought that could work in such a spectacular fashion.

It turned out Magpie was a much better man than Crutch had ever expected.

'That is magnificent,' said Crutch. 'You've done a superlative job, Magpie.'

'Really?' said Magpie. 'That only leaves us one wagon of food. That's nowhere near enough to feed all the navy ships.

'No, but it's enough to feed a few, and every night you can get more restaurants on board. What you've done is brilliant. Come on, get on your feet. We have to go.'

'But I still have forms to fill out here,' said Magpie.

'Forget the bloody forms,' said Crutch. 'We have to deliver that wagon of food to the docks.'

'I was going to get one of the navy office privates to do it,' said Magpie.

'Not on your life,' said Crutch. 'You did all the work getting this food. You're going to see it through to the end and deliver it.'

Chapter 9
More Than A Medal From The King

Sitting at the front of a wagon full of food with Magpie brought back memories of driving the wagon in Teevilgrad for the true compatriots soup kitchen. Then Crutch thought of the true compatriots hall burning and the hanging of the old woman Leena and the harmless street urchin Dima, and his anger for Emperor Solokov boiled in his guts.

'You okay, Lieutenant?' said Magpie.

'I'm fine,' said Crutch, pushing the memories from his mind as best he could. They made their way slowly down King's Way towards the docks. Soldiers and navy sailors they passed stopped, stood at attention, and saluted when they saw Crutch. Crutch saluted right back.

'It's like you're royalty,' said Magpie. 'Having all these soldiers saluting at you.'

'It's you who's royalty today,' said Crutch. 'Bringing a wagon full of food to these navy ships means more to these navy sailors than a medal from the king.'

'Really?' said Magpie.

'Yes,' said Crutch. 'And I would know. I got a medal from the king.'

A huge smile of pride spread across Magpie's face, and his chest raised a few inches. Crutch smiled too as he saluted another group of soldiers they passed.

'Where do you want to take this wagon of food?' said Magpie as they came to the docks.

'Let's start with the Auld Faithful,' said Crutch.

Magpie guided the horse and wagon along the docks at a crawl, giving the navy sailors and dockworkers loading weapons and cargo plenty of time to get out of the way.

When they pulled along side the Auld Faithful, the guard on watch alerted the crew.

'Lieutenant Crutch with a wagon, captain,' he yelled.

Cedric appeared on the deck first, and the marines were right behind him. They walked over the gangplank and onto the docks to greet him. Magpies eyes went wide.

'Are those the siege breakers?' he said.

'They are,' said Crutch as he climbed down from the wagon with Magpie following him.

'Crutch,' said Boulder, smiling and pulling Crutch into a huge hug. 'I missed you. Are you coming back to the marines now?'

'Just bringing you food today,' said Crutch.

'You know you're always welcome if you want to come back to the marines,' said Sergeant Zander. 'It's not the same without you.'

'Thank you, Sarge,' said Crutch. 'Right now, my work at the supply office is more important.'

'You promised us food, and here you are with a wagon full of it,' said Cedric, smiling.

'It was Magpie here who got you the food,' said Crutch. 'He spent all night scrounging the city to get it.'

'Thank you very much,' said Cedric, shaking Magpie's hand. 'Thanks to you, my whole crew can eat something more appealing than hard tack.'

'Good on ya,' said Longshot.

'You're a dead set legend,' said Quicksilver.

The marines took turns shaking his hand and patting him on the back. Magpie beamed happily.

'Magpie here found a way to get you food every day,' said Crutch.

'Really?' said Cedric. 'Your Magpie is full of pleasant surprises.'

'He's a legend alright,' said Longshot.

'This wagon is more than you'll need for one day,' said Crutch. 'I thought perhaps you could share it with another navy ship. Maybe the one moored alongside the Auld Faithful?'

'Wonderful idea,' said Cedric. 'Captain Whitaker will be thrilled.'

'I'll get more tomorrow,' said Magpie. 'I want to feed all the navy ships.'

'If you ever want a change of scenery,' said Cedric, 'I could use you on board the Auld Faithful. You'd make a great quartermaster.'

'You can't have him,' said Crutch. 'I need him at the supply office.'

'I'm sure you do,' said Cedric. 'It was a delight meeting you, Magpie. Splendid work bringing us this food. We're all very grateful. Better get moving. We have food to load.'

Cedric called for crew to help unload the wagon and disappeared onto the next ship on the docks. The Auld Faithful crew swarmed happily over the crates, smiling and laughing as they took it onto the ship.

Cedric reappeared with crew from the next ship along, and in just a few minutes the wagon was empty and Magpie and Crutch were headed back towards the city.

'I can't believe I met the siege breakers,' said Magpie as they pulled away from the docks.

'You didn't just meet the siege breakers,' said Crutch. 'You fed them.'

Chapter 10

Is He Dead?

'I feel like you should be coming in with me,' said Crutch as they approached the palace gates.

'The less people who notice me, the more effective I can be,' said Abagail.

'That makes sense,' said Crutch. Over the last few days, Crutch had been amazed at just how much information Abagail had gathered on the running of the navy office and the machinations that influenced the city of Ironbay. Hiding in plain sight had been incredibly effective.

'You look dashing in your navy dress uniform,' said Abagail. 'Even if it is getting a bit ratty.'

'Thank you,' said Crutch, his voice croaking a little from the nerves he felt looking up at the palace in front of him.

'You'll do wonderfully,' said Abagail. 'It's a good plan.'

Crutch wished he had Abagail's confidence. He'd talked to the king twice before, but the palace and its rooms and the idea of standing in front of the king's counsellors was powerfully intimidating. And this time he would ask for something the king may not want to give.

The palace guard already had the smaller iron door in the palace gates open. 'His majesty is expecting you,' said the guard.

The guard escorted him through a huge open portcullis and down a wide tunnel. Then they were inside the palace, with its high ceilings, polished stone tiles, and elaborate paintings on the wall. They travelled through rooms and corridors filled with wealth Crutch could never have dreamed was possible when he was a street urchin. Just one of those paintings or fancy gold candle fittings on the wall would have fed him for the rest of his life.

Crutch pushed out of his mind what a waste such an ostentatious display of wealth was when there were urchins starving in the sewers. Right now, he had to think like these wealthy nobles so he could find a way to persuade them.

Finally, they came to the chambers for the king's council. The guard left Crutch waiting in front of the large wooden double doors to the chambers, went inside, then returned.

'The king's council will see you now,' he said, holding one of the huge wooden doors open for him.

'Thank you,' said Crutch as he walked through, his walking cane and his shoes clacking on the polished tiles.

The room was huge, dominated by a large circular table with King Vargus at its head. Six men sat in sumptuous leather chairs around the table. Abagail had told Crutch there would be six king's counsellors.

Crutch had been in the war room when the true royals tried to take Ironbay, but Abagail had explained to Crutch that most of the king's counsellors wouldn't necessarily be invited to the war room in a time of crisis. The king's council helped to govern the city, most didn't help to defend it.

The six counsellors looked at Crutch like big cats looking at a piglet that had wandered by accident into their den. Meat for the slaughter.

'This is most unusual,' said King Vargus from his oversized chair. 'I've never had a supply officer ask for an audience.'

'I am most grateful to you for granting it to me your majesty,' said Crutch.

'Difficult to refuse the young man who saved my life twice in one night,' said King Vargus. 'What do you require from your king?'

'It's more what I can do for you, your majesty. We've been at war with Estovia for almost four years now, and the budget for the navy has stayed the same.'

'These are challenging times,' said one of the counsellors, staring at Crutch over his fat gut. 'The navy has to make do like the rest of us.'

Looks like you've been doing just fine, thought Crutch.

'If you've come here to beg for money, you've come to the wrong place,' said another counsellor. 'We have none to spare.'

'Of course,' said Crutch. 'I've not come to ask for money, your majesty,' said Crutch. 'Not directly. I have a proposal that should increase your revenue and give the navy the supplies it needs so desperately.'

'Sounds intriguing. Please continue,' said King Vargus.

'Right now there's a shortage of textiles in Ironbay, your majesty.'

'The young man is right there. It's hard to find a rag in Ironbay that some seamstress hasn't seconded for use in sewing a handkerchief or a scarf. There are crocodiles running naked down King's Way, searching for a slip of fabric to cover themselves.'

The counsellors laughed.

'The closest territory is Saldoria, with its plantations of kapok trees and its looms for making cloth,' said Crutch. 'But merchant ships have trouble making the journey unless there's a north-easterly wind blowing. Merchant ships coming from the north don't like changing their voyage because the area has known pirates, and sometimes Estovian ships have been known to pass that way.'

'We're familiar with the trade routes of the Ironborn territories, young man. Please get to the point,' said another counsellor. 'We don't have all day.'

'My proposal, your majesty, is that you enact a royal decree that navy ships heading home from the north change their route and pick up cloth on the way back to Ironbay. At present, your kingdom is already buying cloth at full price for uniforms. You'll be able to get it at the cheapest price possible from the looms in Saldoria. And you can sell on all the extra cloth to seamstresses and merchants here in Ironbay.'

'Won't my navy captains be a little put out being ordered to pick up bolts of cloth from Saldoria?' said King Vargus.

'My proposal, your majesty, is that you split the profits with the navy ships bringing in the cloth. One fifth goes straight to the ship, one third to the navy office to supply ammunition, ballistas, and war supplies to the navy ships, and the rest goes to your treasury.'

'I, for one, hate the idea,' said one counsellor.

The counsellors laughed.

'Won't be able to charge inflated prices for your cloth,' said another counsellor.

They would be making fun of Lord Counsel Chudwell. Abagail told Crutch Lord Counsel Chudwell had the most to lose in this arrangement. Apparently, when they sat around doing needlework, the ladies talked quite a lot about why fabric wasn't getting to Ironbay and who controlled the import and the sale of cloth.

'If I might continue, your majesty?' said Crutch.

'Please do,' said King Vargus.

'The kingdom is not skilled in the sale of cloth. I propose that the company of Chudwell Mercantile be awarded the tender to sell all the excess bolts of cloth our navy ships bring to Ironbay. Perhaps for payment of one tenth of the revenue raised from those sales.'

'Splendid idea!' said the Lord Counsel Chudwell.

The counsellors laughed again.

'Barely even started singing, and you've already changed your tune.'

'I know a great idea when I see it,' said Lord Counsel Chudwell.

'Especially if it fills your purse.'

'It seems our iron cross winner is also somewhat of a diplomat,' said King Vargus. 'What does our Lord Counsel for the armed forces think of the idea?'

The table turned to look at an old, wrinkled man slumped back in his chair with his eyes closed. That would be Lord Counsel Hollingsworth, once the highly respected General Hollingsworth.

Abagail told Crutch that Lord Counsel Hollingworth's days as a general were well behind him. By the look of him, it wouldn't be long before all of his days were well behind him.

'Is he snoring?' said one lord counsel.

The lord counsel next to Lord Counsel Hollingsworth nudged him in the ribs. From Abagail's descriptions, Crutch guessed that was Lord Counsel Highmount. 'Wakey, wakey,' he said.

'What's that?' said Lord Counsel Hollingsworth, his eyes blinking as he adjusted to the light.

'What do you think of Lieutenant Crutch's idea?' said King Vargus.

'Which idea is that?'

'To bring in bolts of cloth on our navy ships and sell them at a profit.'

'Will it go over budget?' said Lord Counsel Hollingsworth.

'No,' said Lord Counsel Chudwell. 'In fact, it should make our kingdom a handy profit.

'Listen closely to me, Lieutenant Crush,' said Lord Counsel Hollingsworth, seemingly oblivious to what Lord Counsel Chudwell told him. 'You can do what you want, but if you go one copper piece over budget, I'll have the sergeant at arms hang you from the gallows in the city square as an example to everyone.' He banged his fist on the wooden table to drive home each word. 'Not-one-copper-piece-over-budget. Do you hear me?'

'I do, Lord Counsel,' said Crutch. At least he knew now why the navy hadn't seen an increase in their funding for years.

'Let that be a lesson to you,' said Lord Counsel Hollingsworth, who then slumped back in his chair, exhausted from the effort. His eyes closed, and his mouth hung open.

'Is he dead?' said Lord Counsel Chudwell.

'I believe he's snoring,' said Lord Counsel Highmount.

'Well, that's a relief.'

'Easy for you to say. You don't have to sit next to him.'

'I believe you have your answer,' said King Vargus. 'Do what you want, but don't go over budget. Think you can manage that?'

'I can, your majesty,' said Crutch.

'You look like you could use a new uniform yourself,' said King Vargus. 'Thank you for bringing this to us. First original idea I've seen in years.'

'Yes, marvellous stuff,' said Lord Counsel Chudwell.

The other lord counsellors laughed.

'Marvellous for you.'

'And your purse.'

'You may leave,' said King Vargus. 'I believe you have some work to do. Have the decree written up, and I'll sign it.'

'Yes, your majesty,' said Crutch. 'Thank you, your majesty.'

As he walked from the room, Crutch could hear King Vargus speaking.

'Take note of this,' he said. 'Lieutenant Crutch brought us the kind of idea I expect all of you to bring to this table. I've a mind to toss one of you and have the lieutenant join our counsel.'

'Never!'

'A commoner on the king's counsel. Preposterous!'

'He doesn't have the breeding for it.'

King Vargus smiled at their uproar. It was obvious to Crutch this was a game he played to rile them up.

'And yet he comes here with an original, well-thought-out plan,' King Vargus said. 'Perhaps you rabble could inspire me with your superior, high-born intellects in future…'

Chapter 11
No Cheating In A Fight

Crutch got to the navy office early in the morning before Magpie was there. Magpie would be snatching a couple of hours sleep before he drove his wagon full of food to the docks.

Crutch found Magpie's list of restaurants, found a blank piece of paper, a quill, and some ink. He wrote quickly. He wanted to get this done before the private came in.

Within half an hour, he had a small pile of letters written.

'Just in time,' said Crutch as Magpie walked into the office.

'Am I late, Lieutenant Crutch?' said Magpie.

'No, I'm early,' said Crutch. 'And you don't have to worry about getting here in the morning. I know you're out getting food all night. You can sleep in if you want.'

'I couldn't,' said Magpie. 'Not while there's navy men going hungry.'

'Here's something to give to those restaurants who gave you food,' said Crutch. 'That should keep them happy.'

Magpie looked at the pieces of paper Crutch gave him and smiled.

'This is wonderful! A thank you note from double iron cross winner Lieutenant Crutch from the supply office. They'll be thrilled.'

'I thought I should put some of the paper in this office to good use for a change,' said Crutch. 'I added in a request letter from me with the official navy office stamp on it you can show to any of the restaurants who haven't given you anything yet.'

'This is brilliant,' said Magpie. 'Thank you so much, Lieutenant Crutch.'

'Thank *you*,' said Crutch. 'You've been doing magnificent work here. I've asked the admiral to promote you to sergeant, and he's already approved it.'

'No. You can't be serious?'

'I'm very serious,' said Crutch. 'I have your stripes right here. Could you stand at attention, please, Sergeant Rennar?'

Magpie stood erect and puffed his chest out, a huge smile on his face. Crutch took great delight in attaching the stripes to the shoulders of his shirt.

'Not the best job, but you can get Miss Hastings to make that look a little neater when she comes in today,' said Crutch. 'Congratulations, sergeant.'

'Thank you, lieutenant. This is the greatest thing that's ever happened to me. I can't wait to tell my mum.'

'Why don't you go tell her now?' said Crutch. 'I'm guessing she's barely seen you for quite some time. It might be nice for her to know why.'

'I couldn't,' said Magpie. 'I still have more forms to fill in.'

'I'll take care of it,' said Crutch. 'You deserve a few hours off.'

'Thank you, Lieutenant Crutch. Thank you for everything.'

Seconds after Magpie left, Abagail came into the office. This was as good a time as any for Crutch to fulfil his promise to her.

'Shall we train?' he said.

'Here in the supply office?' said Abagail. 'Shouldn't we do it out in the open somewhere, where we won't run into things and there's grass if we fall down?'

'When you fight, you won't be in some pleasant place with soft grass. You'll be pushed into a corridor or in the corner of a room, using whatever's there to keep you alive. And trying not to let the obstacles get you killed.'

'That makes sense,' said Abagail.

'I'll keep this simple. We'll pretend this wooden paper creaser I'm holding is a dagger. If my dagger gets you anywhere important before you can kill me with whatever you have and whatever you can find, then you're dead. If you kill me first, you live.'

'It's all so splendidly brutal,' said Abagail.

'It's more fun than the real thing.'

'In what way?'

'In a real fight, you're slipping around in blood and body parts,' said Crutch. 'And you get covered in it.'

'That's really horrid,' said Abagail. 'Did you start this way, with wooden daggers?'

'I started on the deck of the Auld Faithful in unarmed combat training. Sergeant Zander paired me off with Boulder.'

'Boulder? He's a giant. At least he's gentle.'

'In combat, he's a highly trained killer,' said Crutch. 'And that includes hand to hand combat.'

'So he took it easy on you?'

'No, Sergeant Zander wouldn't allow that. You train like you fight.'

'My goodness. What happened?'

'Boulder smashed me to the deck over and over until I was unconscious.'

'So Sergeant Zander put you with someone your own size after that?' said Abagail.

'No. The next day, he paired me with Boulder again.'

'Did he knock you unconscious again?'

'No. I knocked Boulder's feet out from under him with my walking cane, then smashed him in the throat and the head until he collapsed to the deck.'

'My goodness. Was he alright?'

'He survived,' said Crutch. 'Shall we begin?'

Within the first twenty seconds, Crutch had stabbed Abagail with his fake wooden dagger at least half a dozen times.

'Dead,' he said each time he stabbed her. 'Dead, dead, dead again. So dead.'

Abagail frowned in frustration.

'You're too fast. I can't get to you before you stab me.'

'Correct,' said Crutch. 'What are your other options? Don't tell me. Just do them.'

This time, as Abagail came towards Crutch, she picked up a heavy ledger from the desk and thumped it down onto his dagger arm. The wooden paper creaser clattered on the floor, and Crutch let out a howl.

'I'm so sorry,' said Abagail. 'Did I hurt you?'

'Dead again,' said Crutch, putting a large wooden peg he had hidden in his belt to her chest.

'Well, that's not fair,' said Abagail.

'You don't fight to win awards or display your honour. You fight to kill your opponent before he can kill you.'

'So cheating is fine?' said Abagail.

'There's no cheating in a fight,' said Crutch. 'You go full on doing everything you can, and you don't stop for anything or anyone. Hesitation will get you killed.'

'So you're saying if you scream like a nancy boy, I should just keep on beating into you?'

'Yes. That's exactly what you should do. Keep fighting until your opponent is dead. There's no injuring them and hoping they stop.'

'And no rules?' said Abagail.

'No rules. If you can do something, anything, to injure or kill your opponent, you do it. Don't waste a second thinking about it. Just do it.

'Okay,' said Abagail. 'Are you sure?'

'I'm sure.'

Abagail backed off to the other side of the room, then moved towards Crutch slowly. She picked up a paper weight from the desk. It was made of solid rock. Crutch really didn't want that getting him in the head, or the knees, or any of his soft parts. He watched Abagail as she came, passing the chair now.

Abagail drew back her arm, ready to throw the paperweight, and with her other hand she grabbed the top of the chair and swung it round so it hit Crutch's wooden paper creaser. It shot out of his grasp and fell on the other side of the room. But he was ready with his wooden peg. Abagail smacked that out of his hand by swinging the chair back the other way, hitting his arm hard.

Before he could get out of the way, she brought down the paperweight on his head, gently but hard enough that he knew he was beaten.

'I believe you're dead,' she said, smiling.

'I believe I am,' said Crutch. 'Nice work.'

'I have a good teacher,' said Abagail, moving in closer.

'You're a good student,' said Crutch, mostly because he couldn't think of anything else to say with her so close to him.

Abagail pulled Crutch's head in with her hand and kissed him on the lips. He closed his eyes and took in the sweetness of her, the taste of her lips, the smell of her perfume, the warmth of her body next to his.

'Dead again,' said Abagail.

When Crutch opened his eyes Abagail had a smile on her face and her hair pin at the side of his neck.

'That is so devious,' said Crutch, smiling back. 'I love it.'

Chapter 12
A Foul Gift
That Keeps On Giving

The increase in revenue to the supply office came just in time. The orders for full ballistas and ballista bolts tripled. There were orders for swords, spears, axes, and arrows too.

When Crutch saw the order for six ballistas for the Auld Faithful, along with six hundred ballista bolts, the reality of what was coming hit him hard.

'Seems we're invading Estovia soon,' said Crutch.

'When do you think it will be?' said Magpie.

'I couldn't say for certain,' said Crutch. 'From the size of these orders, it looks like they're building up to a full fleet attack. Have you heard anything from the army?'

'My cousin is a sergeant in the regulars,' said Magpie. 'They've been recruiting, training, and doing marching drills for weeks.'

'That would explain why I can't sleep past five o'clock in the morning,' said Crutch. The navy barracks were right next door to the army barracks, and the noise from thousands of soldiers mustering before dawn was impossible to sleep through.

'Will be good to stick it to Igor,' said Magpie.

It would be good, thought Crutch. He remembered looking eye-to-eye at Emperor Igor Solokov in the People's Plaza in Teevilgrad. Back then, he knew the war with Estovia would never be over until Solokov was dead. Nothing he'd seen since had changed his mind.

Then he thought about all the good people he'd met in Teevilgrad when he ran the soup kitchen there. People who didn't want any part of Solokov's war. People who would die in their thousands when the Ironborn fleet and its army invaded.

The true compatriots might hate Igor Solokov, but they loved Estovia, and they'd fight to protect their country from an invasion.

'I bet they'd love to have their iron cross winner with them when they storm Teevilgrad. Will you be rejoining the marines?' said Magpie. '

'I'll be right here with you, making sure our ships get what they need,' said Crutch. 'Wars are won and lost on logistics, and that makes you and me the most important men in the navy.'

'Really?' said Magpie.

'No doubt about it.'

An uneasiness fell over Crutch when he thought about the Auld Faithful going to Teevilgrad without him. He imagined Boulder and Sergeant Zander landing on the docks and fighting in the streets of the city without him. He thought of Quicksilver and Longshot in a desperate struggle to survive, fighting Estovians defending their homeland.

And he thought of Cedric standing at the helm, brave, steadfast. Cedric, who'd fought the pirate Wyld Dog in a duel to save Crutch from being whipped. If it wasn't for Crutch, Cedric would still be a beastmaster, relatively safe in the hold of the ship.

Somehow it didn't seem right that they would all sail to war while he was safe in Ironbay.

Magpie left early to start on his food pick-ups. That left Crutch alone in the office until Abagail came in. Her eyes were red, and her body trembled.

'What's wrong?' said Crutch.

'It's mother. She says now I'm coming of age, I need to be promised to a young lord, someone from the nobility.'

'But she knows you're with me,' said Crutch.

'Mother says it's unseemly for a young lady to be wed to a commoner, and especially unseemly to be wed to a commoner who grew up in the sewers.'

'Did you mention that commoner saved your life and hers?'

'I told her that, but she doesn't care. She wants to marry me off to a noble.'

'What does your father say?' said Crutch.

'He says he's not happy about it, but he won't interfere.'

'So what are you going to do?'

'I don't know,' said Abagail. 'If mother won't let me be with you, I don't want to be with anyone.'

Crutch was silent. With all the time they'd spent together since he started working in the navy office, Abagail had started to find her way into every part of his life. She was there when he worked; they had lunch together, they trained together. And at night they'd go on walks together.

Now he found it impossible to imagine living without her.

What could they do?

They couldn't run away. With the war, there was nowhere safe to run to. He was too well known to hide anywhere in Ironbay.

'Say something,' said Abagail.

'I don't know what to say,' said Crutch. 'I love you.' He'd never said it before, and now was one hell of a time to say it. But it was all he could think of. 'I love you so much it hurts.'

'I love you too,' said Abagail. Tears ran from her eyes. 'I can't be with anyone else. I just can't.'

Crutch stood and put his arms around her as she sobbed. For a few seconds, he felt like crying too, but then something stronger boiled up inside him.

Anger. He was angry at Lady Hastings for forcing this on Abagail. He was angry at the world for making him a street urchin, forced to eke out a living on the streets and in the sewers instead of growing up with a roof over his head. It seemed that was a foul gift that just kept on giving, piling its shit over him when he least expected it, like a flush of sewerage.

He was angry at the world and its stupid rules that made no sense. Why would Abagail be better off with some prissed-up young lord who didn't give a damn about her? Why did Lady Hastings want to torture her? Could knowing which fork to use or how to hold it really make that big of a difference?

Abagail's sobbing stopped.

'Are you still allowed to see me?' said Crutch.

'I've always spent a lot of time here in the navy office,' said Abagail. 'Mother doesn't know what I do when I come here, and she's never tried to stop me.'

'And lunches?'

'She doesn't want me seen in public with a commoner. It's unseemly now I'm coming of age.'

Crutch wondered if Lady Hastings considered how unseemly it would have been to have her throat cut by a solider when the true royals launched their coup. Right now, he wished he hadn't protected her. What was it the soldiers had said? *The only good noble is a dead noble.*

'So we eat lunch here in the office?' said Crutch.

'We can do that,' said Abagail. 'Mother doesn't spend any time in the kitchen. She doesn't know what I bring here.'

'Let's hope your mother has a change of heart. Until then, we'll stay out of sight.'

'So you'll still see me?' said Abagail. 'Even if we can't wed?'

'Of course,' said Crutch. But inside, his anger boiled and that feeling that he'd lived with his whole life came back. That whenever something good happened, sooner or later it would turn to shit.

'Thank you,' said Abagail, her face wet with tears. 'I'm sorry.'

'It's not your fault,' said Crutch.

It's just the way life is when you're a street urchin. If you stay still too long, someone will come along and kick you in the guts.

Chapter 13
I Like Abagail

Crutch arranged to meet Cedric in front of the restaurant. This was only the second time he'd been to one of these fancy establishments that nobles frequented, and he didn't want to embarrass Cedric, so he made sure to wear his best navy dress suit. Rita had cleaned it and pressed it for him, especially.

When the restaurant came into view, he smiled. Cedric had brought Boulder with him.

'Crutch,' said Boulder when he got close. Boulder took him into a huge hug.

'Boulder was missing you, so I brought him along,' said Cedric.

'I was missing you,' said Boulder, smiling happily.

'Shall we go inside?' said Cedric.

They met the concierge at the front of the restaurant.

'Table for Lord Cedric Beaumont,' said Cedric in his deep, booming voice.

'Of course,' said the concierge. 'Welcome, Lord Beaumont. Right this way.'

They walked past tables with nobles dining and sipping wine to a table in the corner. Crutch sat with his back to the wall. Cedric and Boulder had their backs to the window. Old habits as a street urchin never die, thought Crutch. With his back to the wall, Crutch could see someone who meant him mischief way before they got to him.

Outside in the street, Crutch could see the wealthy people of Ironbay, the nobles, the rich merchants, and the children of rich merchants walking by.

'Your waiter will be along shortly,' said the concierge.

'This is very kind of you,' said Crutch.

'You got food for me and the crew of the Auld Faithful; it seems only fair I should get some food for you,' said Cedric.

'You brought us soup,' said Boulder, smiling and looking handsome in his best navy dress uniform.

The last time Boulder was in a fancy establishment, he was dressed in a suit Sergeant Zander bought for him that was way too tight and pretending to be Lord Boulderdash. The navy dress uniform was a much more sophisticated look.

The waiter arrived carrying a small basket of tiny bread rolls.

'Some bread for you,' he said as he placed the basket on the table in front of Crutch. 'Can I get you some drinks?'

Crutch looked at the bread rolls. They looked delicious. He might work in the navy office now and get fed twice a day in the mess hall of the navy barracks, but the street urchin still ran deep in him. He knocked one of the candlesticks off the table.

'Sorry, so clumsy of me,' said Crutch as the waiter kneeled down to the floor to retrieve the candlestick and the candle. Cedric watched the waiter too, as Crutch stuffed as many bread rolls as he could fit into his pockets.

Boulder watched and laughed as he did it. There were just two bread rolls left after Crutch had filled his pockets. Boulder stuffed both into his mouth, smiling the whole time.

When the waiter got up and returned the candle and the candlestick to the table, the bread basket was empty. Boulder sat there with his cheeks bulging, grinning at Crutch, who tried not to laugh.

'I'll have your best wine,' said Cedric. 'Would you men like some rum? Maybe some honeysap premium?'

Crutch remembered what happened the last time he drank honeysap premium rum in Honeysap Grove. Burning down this restaurant or half of Ironbay didn't seem like a good idea.

'Just some lolly water for me,' said Crutch. 'You can get some honeysap premium for Boulder here, though.' Boulder nodded in agreement, his cheeks still bulging with the bread rolls.

'And if you could bring some bread,' said Cedric. 'That basket seems a little short.'

The waiter looked at the bread basket, confused. 'Of course, Lord Beaumont,' he said leaving with the empty basket.

Boulder laughed, and the two bread rolls sprayed onto the table.

'What are you two up to?' said Cedric.

'Nothing,' said Boulder, stuffing the bread rolls back into his mouth and chewing furiously.

'Nothing at all,' said Crutch checking his newly acquired bread rolls were safely in his bulging pockets.

Cedric smiled and shook his head. 'So tell me how you're finding your work in the supply office?' he said.

'It's challenging,' said Crutch. 'Getting anything done is painfully slow.'

'You must tell me how you managed to get food to us. I already had Magpie explain how he got the first wagons of food but supplying all the ships. That hasn't happened in at least a decade.'

'It was complicated,' said Crutch. 'I had to convince the king to let the navy import bolts of cloth for part of the profits. Then we used the money to pay for ammunition. That meant the people working in food acquisition could use their revenue to buy food for the navy ships instead of selling the food on the black market to fund buying ammunition.'

'Wait. Food acquisition paid for our ammunition?'

'Yes. Ballista bolts, arrows, and the like,' said Crutch.

'This whole explanation is giving me a headache. The navy office is lucky they have you in the supply office,' said Cedric.

'Not just me,' said Crutch. 'Abagail was the one who explained the machinations of the supply office to me.'

'Abagail?' said Cedric. 'Well, that young lady is full of surprises isn't she?'

'I like Abagail,' said Boulder.

Speak of the devil, and she'll appear, thought Crutch. Looking out the window, he could see Abagail with a pudgy young man holding her hand as they walked.

'You've got a good woman there,' said Cedric. 'You want to hold on to her as tight as you can.'

'Abagail's not my girlfriend any more,' said Crutch as Abagail and the young lord stopped. The young lord pulled her into his arms. From where he sat, it looked like Abagail had a smile on her face.

'Well, that's a surprise,' said Cedric. 'You both seemed so close.'

'I'm not the kind of man Abagail needs,' said Crutch.

The young lord's face was inches from Abagail. Crutch imagined what that face would look like after he'd punched it a few times. A cracked lip and a broken nose would be a huge improvement as far as Crutch was concerned.

'You're about as fine a young man as any young woman could hope for,' said Cedric. 'If she doesn't see that, then you're better off without her.'

The young lord leaned in and kissed Abagail. Crutch pictured him lying dead in a pool of blood right there in the street. Abagail might not like it, but she'd get over it, just like she did the dead Estovians at her birthday party.

'Stop talking about Abagail!' said Crutch.

'My apologies,' said Cedric. 'Matters of the heart are most challenging when you're young. It will all be behind you soon enough.'

'I like Abagail,' said Boulder.

Chapter 14
Accidents Happen

Crutch had tried sleeping late in his soft bed, but it just felt strange. After all his years in the marines getting up to train an hour before dawn, he would wake up at that time, with his body itching to hit something.

So this morning he got up and went into the living room and munched on one of the bread rolls he'd pilfered the night before. He practiced swinging his wooden cane around his head, fighting an imaginary attacker. He moved fast, balancing and moving with his good leg while he swung the cane around and stabbed forward with it.

After years of training, it was second nature to stay on his feet. His weak leg was barely a hindrance.

First Crutch imagined he was fighting an Estovian swordsman, parrying and dodging his sword, moving to get him to commit his body, then stabbing at him.

Then he imagined he was fighting Young Lord Chudwell. He saw that slimly stuck-up, turd's face, and the anger churned in his guts. He imagined killing him slowly, stabbing him in his foot, then his leg, then a couple of thrusts into his guts, but not anywhere that would kill him.

In his mind, he saw Chudwell screaming and begging for mercy, but Crutch was a marine. There'd be no mercy. He saw Chudwell bleed as he stabbed over and over, into his arm, into his shoulder, always delaying the killing blow.

Then he smiled as he drew back his cane with the blade out and thrust it straight into Young Lord Chudwell's head, right between the eyes.

'Your majesty,' said Rita. 'The couch!'

Crutch came out of his killing trance and looked in front of him. He'd slashed and torn the cushions of the couch to pieces.

'I'm sorry,' said Crutch, retracting the blade in his walking cane. 'I didn't know you were here.'

'Corporal Turner will kill me,' said Rita.

'I did the slashing,' said Crutch, looking at the wreckage of the couch cushions. 'It should be me who gets in trouble for it.'

'Maybe I can sew up the cushions so no one knows,' said Rita, moving to the couch and looking closer at the damage. She picked up one of the cushions and bits of its torn fabric and the filling fell to pieces onto the floor.

'I'm really sorry,' said Crutch. 'I don't want you to get in trouble.'

Rita was right next to him. 'These things happen sometimes,' she said, looking into his eyes. 'I'm sure it was an accident.' She touched his chest with the fingertips of her hand.

'You're being too kind,' said Crutch. 'I have coin. I can pay for repairs.'

'Let's see if I can fix it myself first,' said Rita, running her hand down from his chest to his arm and squeezing his hand. 'I'm good with a needle and thread. And other things.'

'You'd have to be a magician to fix that,' said Crutch, looking at the tatters of the couch cushions.

'You'd be amazed what I can do, your majesty,' said Rita, still squeezing his hand.

'Please don't call me your majesty,' said Crutch. 'I'm just an ordinary person like you. Can you call me Crutch?'

'I can call you anything you like,' said Rita, voice low and soft, her eyes locked on his, her body close to his, her hand still squeezing.

'Thank you,' said Crutch, gently pulling his hand away. 'I should get to work. Thank you for your help with the couch. If you need any coin, just let me know.'

'I will,' said Rita, sounding disappointed for some reason.

As he left his cottage, Crutch noticed something. For the first time since Abagail told him she would be promised to a young lord, he wasn't fuming with anger.

Chapter 15

Your New Boyfriend

Crutch's anger returned with force when Abagail arrived in the supply office.

'Good morning, Crutch,' she said, the smile on that wonderfully crooked face now making his guts churn. Why was life trying to torture him?

'I saw you last night with your new *boyfriend*,' said Crutch.

'Were you following me?' said Abagail.

'No. I was in a restaurant with Cedric and Boulder when you happened to walk by,' said Crutch. 'You both looked very friendly.' Crutch didn't tell her he saw them holding hands and kissing. Or that he felt like sticking a blade through the young lord's eye to see if it would make him more attractive.

'Oh, Crutch. You musn't get angry. I don't want to have anything to do with young lords like Jerry Chudwell.'

'You seemed to be having quite a lot to do with him,' said Crutch.

'Mother says, since I won't fraternise with young lords like a young lady should, that she will choose young lords for me to see.'

Crutch fumed. 'And how was Jerry Chudwell?'

'He was an absolutely horrid, fat pig,' said Abagail. 'Mother says I should be grateful that any young lord shows an interest in me, with my crooked face.'

As much as it gave Crutch some satisfaction that Lady Hastings choice of suitors was so awful, he hated to see Abagail unhappy. Mostly. But even though he hated seeing her unhappy, he was glad she was unhappy too. His brain ran in circles, and his guts churned with a vile mix of hate, anger, and confusion that he struggled to control.

'So will you see him again?' said Crutch.

'I'd rather go for a swim in the sewers,' said Abagail.

'You can cool off that way,' said Crutch. 'But I don't recommend it.'

Abagail looked at Crutch for a second, and a smile broke on her lips. Then she started giggling. Crutch couldn't help himself. As churned up as he was inside, he broke into a laugh too.

'You could always make me laugh,' said Abagail. 'Remember that first time at my birthday party when you stuffed a huge slice of cake in your mouth and swallowed it without even chewing?'

'I was hungry,' said Crutch defensively.

Abagail looked at his hurt expression and laughed again. She put her hand on his. The touch sent tingles up his fingers to his spine. He longed to take her in his arms, to hold her, to kiss her. But he could never do that again.

Even feeling her hand on his was an excruciating torture. He pulled his hand away like he'd been burned. Abagail looked down as he pulled his hand away, then looked up into his eyes, hurt.

'Mother made me see Jerry the first time, and she says I have to see him again. I don't have any say in it.'

'You looked happy enough together,' said Crutch.

'I was being polite as a young lady is supposed to,' said Abagail. 'Jerry tried to…he tried to…'

'He tried to what?' said Crutch.

'I'll tell you, but only if you promise me you won't hurt him.'

'Tell me what he did, then I'll tell you if I'll hurt him,' said Crutch.

'Then I won't tell you.'

'For pity's sake,' said Crutch. 'Fine. I promise I won't hurt your precious little Lord Chudwell. Is that what you want?'

'Do you mean it?'

'I just gave you my word.'

'He tried to take liberties with me,' said Abagail, visibly upset when she spoke about it.

'What kind of liberties?' said Crutch.

'He tried to touch me…in places…places a young lady shouldn't be touched.'

'Did you stab him with your hairpin or strangle him with your belt?'

'I wanted to, but a young lady doesn't do those things to a young lord who's courting her.'

'Then I'll do it for you,' said Crutch.

'No, you won't,' said Abagail. 'You gave me your word.'

She was right. Abagail knew Crutch wouldn't break a promise he'd made to her.

'I promised I wouldn't hurt him,' said Crutch. 'I never promised I wouldn't have words with him.'

'You can't talk to him about it,' said Abagail. 'I'd be mortified.'

Crutch looked at the pained expression on Abagail's face. There was nothing he could say that would remove that pain. But he could at least do something about the source of the pain.

'I'll be discreet,' he said.

Abagail spent the next ten minutes trying to convince Crutch not to talk to Young Lord Chudwell. Eventually Crutch agreed with everything she said, knowing that he and the slimy young lord would be having a conversation he wouldn't ever forget. Crutch's only thoughts now were how to do it in a way that kept Abagail's reputation as a young lady intact.

Chapter 16
The Heroics Come Easier

When the invitation came to dine at Lord Counsel Chudwell's residence, Crutch wasn't surprised. The lord's wealth had exploded since navy ships started bringing in bolts of fabric. He got a cut on every sale, so it was entirely predictable that he'd want to show his appreciation.

The lord had extended his gratitude to any assistants in the supply office, but Lady Hastings wouldn't allow Abagail to dine with a commoner like Crutch, even if it was in the home of the boy who courted her and a lord counsel.

The stupidity made Crutch's blood boil.

So he stood at the entrance of Lord Counsel Chudwell's mansion in his best navy dress uniform, with Magpie at his side. Magpie wore a suit that looked like it was hand-sewn and patched together in the candlelight by his mother or his aunt.

'Mum spent all night sewing me up this suit,' said Magpie. 'Does it look good?'

Magpie looked chuffed to be wearing it, and Crutch wasn't about to take away his happiness. If Lord Counsel Chudwell and his sleazy son Jerry didn't like Magpie's suit, he'd get Magpie to take it off and personally stick it up their fat arses.

'You look magnificent,' said Crutch, ignoring the collar that was significantly higher on one side and the bottom of the jacket, with the left side hanging a good four inches lower than the right.

Crutch went to lift the knocker on the large wooden mansion door, but before his hand reached it, the door opened. A servant inside looked at Crutch, then looked Magpie up and down like he was assessing a pile of cat shit deposited on the doorstep.

'Can I help you?' the servant said.

'I am Lieutenant Crutch, and this is my most valued assistant, Corporal Rennar. We have an invitation to dine from Lord Counsel Chudwell.'

'Of course,' said the servant. 'Do come in.'

He guided them both through an entrance lobby and into a large dining room with a long dining table covered in food.

'Colonel Crutch and his assistant, Corporal Rennar,' announced the servant as they entered the dining room.

'Lieutenant Crutch,' said Lord Counsel Chudwell, rising to his feet and waddling over to greet them. 'It's a delight to see you. I'm so glad you could come.' The lord looked at Magpie and frowned.

'Thank you for the invitation,' said Crutch. Amazing what making a fat lord even richer than he already was would do for his attitude towards you. 'This is Corporal Rennar. He and Young Lady Abagail Hastings were both responsible for coming up with the idea of getting the navy ships to bring in fabric from Saldoria.'

'Really?' said Lord Counsel Chudwell, clearly reconsidering his assessment of Magpie now that he knew he was a source of revenue. 'It seems Ironbay owes you a debt of gratitude.'

'The supply office couldn't run without Magpie here,' said Crutch. 'He is exceptional at finding solutions to the endless stream of problems that arise.' Magpie smiled proudly and puffed his chest out.

'Indeed. Did you mention Young Lady Abagail Hastings? My son has been courting her. I had no idea she worked in the supply office.'

'Right beside us,' said Crutch. 'The entire endeavour of importing fabric from Saldoria was her idea.'

'Well, it seems Young Lady Hastings has more talents beyond her good looks,' said Lord Counsel Chudwell. 'Did you hear that, Jerry? Your Young Lady Hastings is quite the mastermind at the supply office.'

Young Lord Chudwell had moved in behind his father to greet Crutch.

'She's very bright,' said Young Lord Chudwell with a smarmy grin.

You'll see how bright she is the next time you try to grope her and she sticks a hairpin through your eye.

'Young Lady Hastings isn't here with you?' said Lord Counsel Chudwell.

'She couldn't make it tonight,' said Crutch. *Because fat, stuck up nobles like you think it's unseemly to be seen with a commoner like me. But it's just fine for her to go out in public with your gropey pig of a son.*

'Wow!' said Magpie. 'What is that painting?'

Magpie stared up at a painting on the wall on the other side of the room. It pictured a noble with a sword leading Ironborn troops in some kind of battle against a monster made of dark shadows and an army of shadow wraiths. Storm clouds swirled around the monster as it raised its hands and called down lightning from the sky.'

'That's my grandfather, the great General Chudwell, leading the charge against the Scourge,' said Lord Counsel Chudwell.

'The Scourge?' said Magpie. 'I thought the Scourge was just a fairy tale.'

'Oh no,' said Lord Counsel Chudwell. 'It was very real. A formidable beast with powerful magic that threatened to conquer the Ironborn territories when we were weak after the war with the Voldheim.'

'And your grandfather led the Ironborn army?' said Magpie.

'Of course. Nobles make much better commanders,' said Lord Chudwell. 'Come. Let's take a closer look at the painting. I'll tell you the whole story.'

Crutch snorted his disbelief. The Chudwell's were so pathetic they made their ancestor the hero in a fairy tale. If Crutch had to, he'd bet Young Lord Chudwell's grandfather had never done anything more dangerous than pricking his finger with a sewing needle.

Lord Chudwell led Magpie away to give him a closer look at the painting, leaving Crutch and Jerry Chudwell alone together.

'Young Lord Chudwell,' said Crutch.

'Corporal Crutch. I'll be telling everyone I met the double iron cross winner. That's something the other young nobles will be jealous about.'

'I wish the feeling was mutual,' said Crutch. 'And it's Lieutenant Crutch now.'

'Sorry,' said Young Lord Chudwell with a fake smile that made Crutch want to punch him hard enough to remove it from his face. 'So what was it like breaking the siege of Ironbay?'

'Mostly involved a lot of killing,' said Crutch. 'I was on the boom of an enemy ship when an Estovian tried to stab me with a dagger. I pushed the blade of my walking cane through his chest.'

Crutch lifted his walking cane and released the blade inches from Young Lord Chudwell's face. Chudwell flinched as Crutch smiled. 'The Estovian sailor fell off the boom and dropped to the deck, where his neck snapped. I threw oil on another Estovian who tried to get to me and set him alight. I could smell his flesh burning as he fell to the deck screaming.'

'That sounds dreadful,' said Young Lord Chudwell.

'It was over quite quickly,' said Crutch. 'The Kona Track was much worse. There I had to use a dagger to cut clean through the throat of an Estovian scout who tried to get away and warn his compatriots.'

'Oh my,' said Young Lord Chudwell.

'Thousands more Estovians came down the track after us. I lost count of how many I had to cut or stab with my cane, their guts spilling out on the mud.' Crutch held the blade up to Young Lord Chudwell's face. 'See how sharp that is. Left a lot of Estovian blood on the track. Guts, eyes, cut throats. This blade did it all.'

'Well, that really is awful,' said Young Lord Chudwell, his eyes wide with fear. 'Not what I expected at all.'

Crutch wondered if there was some way he could just end Young Lord Chudwell's life right now and get away with it. Promise to Abagail or not, he really wanted to hurt someone, to kill someone. The fury in him boiled so hot it was like his head was ready to explode.

He took a long, deep breath, calmed himself, and spoke.

'I believe we have a mutual acquaintance.'

'Really?' said Young Lord Chudwell.

'Yes. Young Lady Hastings. Abagail Hastings.'

'Of course,' said Young Lord Chudwell. 'Father said you work with her in the supply office.'

'Not just work with her. Abagail and I have been close friends for several years,' said Crutch. 'Since she was twelve.'

'Well, that's delightful,' said Young Lord Chudwell.

'Yes, it is. Young Lady Hastings is quite forthright with me. We've been friends so long, she tells me everything.' Crutch stared straight into Young Lord Chudwell's eyes. A fierce, killing look full of menace. 'Everything.'

The young lord's hands and his lips began to tremble.

'It was a foolish mistake. I didn't mean to…'

'Didn't mean to what?'

'I got carried away with the moment. I'm so sorry. Please. I'm so sorry.' Tears started running down his cheeks and snot out of his nose.

'For pity's sake, get a hold of yourself,' said Crutch, looking around to see if Lord Counsel Chudwell was watching. 'This is embarrassing.'

'I won't do it again,' said Young Lord Chudwell. 'Please don't kill me.'

'Next time you see Young Lady Hastings, I expect you to afford her all the dignity and respect she deserves as a young lady,' said Crutch.

'I will,' said Young Lord Chudwell. 'I promise I will.'

'I sincerely hope you do,' said Crutch. 'Remember, Young Lady Hastings tells me everything, and I keep the blade in my walking cane sharp and ready to cut.'

'Never again, I promise,' said Young Lord Chudwell.

'Clean yourself up and stop snivelling,' said Crutch, seeing Magpie and Lord Counsel Chudwell coming back to them. 'Try to act like a man.'

'So back then it was my grandfather who saved Ironbay and its territories from a threat even greater than the Estovians,' said Lord Counsel Chudwell as he returned with Magpie after looking at what Crutch was fairly certain was a painting of a fairy tale. 'A hero for every age, eh, Lieutenant Crutch?'

Crutch faked a smile. 'Indeed,' he said.

'Of course, when you're born of noble blood, you're made of sterner stuff than a commoner,' said Lord Counsel Chudwell. 'The heroics come easier. Isn't that right, son?'

'Yes, father,' said Young Lord Chudwell, his face down as he wiped away the last of the tears from his eyes.

'Shall we eat?' said Lord Counsel Chudwell, leading them all towards a dining room with a large, long wooden table.

'I'd love to eat,' said Magpie, beaming. 'I'm starving.'

Crutch sat opposite Young Lord Chudwell at the dining table and glared at him for the rest of the evening. Young Turd Chudwell tried desperately to avoid Crutch's hostile glare, but Crutch was relentless. Every time Young Lord Turd looked up, Crutch's eyes were fixed right on his.

Crutch entertained himself with fantasies of throwing his steak knife across the table into the Young Lord Turd's chest and stabbing him in the eye with the dessert fork. He dreamed of a world where he could dispatch the Young Lord Turd at the table, and it would pass barely rating a mention.

'Lieutenant Crutch, it seems you've stabbed my son in the eye repeatedly with your dessert fork, then cut his throat open with your spoon,' he imagined Lord Counsel Chudwell saying. *'I didn't even think it was possible to kill someone with a dessert spoon. So creative. Oh well, he wasn't much of a son. No great loss. Would anyone care for pastries?'*

Magpie enjoyed an animated conversation with Lord Counsel Chudwell. The lord took great delight in sharing all the fictional military exploits of his ancestors, and Magpie sucked up all the stories like they were actual accounts of warfare. At least Magpie was having a good time.

If the supply office wasn't making Lord Counsel Chudwell rich, Crutch knew that the lord would treat Magpie like he was a dog turd stuck on his fancy crocodile leather shoes. But it was good to see Magpie happy, dining like he was a noble in the comical suit his mother hand sewed for him.

As the evening came to an end, Crutch and Magpie made their exit.

'Thank you for your hospitality,' said Crutch as they left.

'Thank you for your help in the supply office,' said Lord Counsel Chudwell. 'A little dinner was the least I could do to show my appreciation.'

He's right about that, thought Crutch.

'If you like, I could send Young Lord Chudwell to lend you a hand there.' said Lord Counsel Chudwell. 'He's quite skilled at office work.'

'I don't know,' said Young Lord Chudwell, trying to avoid Crutch's glare.

'Surely you'd like to spend more time with Young Lady Hastings,' said Lord Counsel Chudwell. 'Especially if you're going to wed.'

Young Lord Chudwell trembled as Crutch raised his walking cane. At the thought of Young Lord Turd marrying Abagail, it was all Crutch could do to stop himself from releasing the blade and ending the little shit right there in the foyer of the mansion.

'It's not good to change a formula that's working,' said Young Lord Chudwell. 'You taught me that.'

'Such wisdom at a young age,' said Lord Counsel Chudwell. 'Your grandfather would be proud of you.'

'Indeed,' said Crutch, tapping the Young Lord Turd on the chest with the handle of his walking cane. 'Let's hope that wisdom lasts.' The young lord flinched with every touch of the cane. 'Thank you again for a delightful evening.'

Then Crutch and Magpie left. As they went, Crutch could hear Lord Counsel Chudwell behind them.

'That went well, don't you think? Commoners might be inferior and uncivilised, but that doesn't mean we can't show them some of our high born hospitality on occasion. You seemed overawed by Lieutenant Crutch. Remember, war hero or not, he's still a commoner. Every Chudwell is braver and better with a sword. It comes down to breeding, you see…'

Chapter 17
It's Not My Fault

They were already doing their fight training in the office, so Abagail and Crutch continued on as normal. But now Crutch found it hard to hold down his anger. He wanted to hit someone, anyone.

When he was angry, fighting brought out the animal in him, and he had never been angrier. When he was a street urchin, he didn't have enough energy to stay angry for long. He'd be exhausted and desperately searching for a way to get his next scrap of food.

Now he was eating two or three meals a day, he had anger to burn.

'When your opponent has a sword, your biggest danger is getting cut,' said Crutch. 'When you're cut, you start bleeding, and you can lose your strength or pass out from the loss of blood.'

'That sounds horrid,' said Abagail, with that sweet, crooked face. Just looking at that face used to fill Crutch with joy. Now it filled him with pain.

'Even a small cut from a sword can be enough to lose the fight for you once you start bleeding. So rule number one is keep the blade of the sword away from you.'

'How do you do that?' said Abagail.

'Soldiers use shields and their weapons,' said Crutch. 'But in a fight, you may not be lucky enough to have either, so you improvise with anything you're carrying or anything in your reach.'

'Like this paperweight?' said Abagail, lifting the heavy rock paperweight off the desk.

'That's better than nothing,' said Crutch. 'But it's small and leaves your hands exposed.'

Abagail picked up a chair and held it in front of her.

'What about this?'

'Much better,' said Crutch. 'It's heavy and hard to swing around, but it will save your life if you keep it between you and the swordsman. It also takes less skill to use than something lighter.'

'This broom?' said Abagail.

Crutch smiled. 'Nice choice. But you have to learn how to use it.' Crutch raised his walking cane. 'Just imagine this cane is a sword.'

'I've seen it when the blade is out,' said Abagail. 'I don't have to imagine.'

'Good,' said Crutch. 'Never let the sword inside your guard.'

'Okay,' said Abagail. She held the broom with the handle out.

Crutch moved forward, slid his walking cane along the handle of the broom, slipped around it, and held the cane to her chest.

'Dead,' said Crutch. 'Don't let the sword inside your guard.'

Abagail frowned and squared up again, the broom out, ready to defend herself. For an instant, Crutch could see those lips on Jerry Chudwell's, and anger churned in his guts.

Crutch pushed forward again. Abagail was quicker this time, moving to make it harder for Crutch to get his cane around the broom. But not hard enough. He moved right, then left, then slid his cane around when Abagail overcorrected trying to keep it out.

'Better. Still dead,' said Crutch, levelling the cane at her breast. He imagined Jerry Chudwell pushed up against her breast, and his anger rose even more, like a beast with teeth eating its way out of his guts and chewing him up alive.

Abagail held the broom up again, ready for another round. She was improving, knocking off his feints, keeping her distance in the cramped space of the office.

This time, he got behind her defence, prodding her in the buttocks with his cane. He imagined Jerry Chudwell's hand on Abagail's buttocks, and he felt like his chest would explode.

'Remember, your opponent will adapt too,' he said. 'Be ready for anything.'

'You don't have to raise your voice,' said Abagail. 'You're only two feet away from me.'

'A loud voice will be the least of your problems when someone comes at you with a sword,' said Crutch. 'Get your guard up.'

Abagail's bottom lip quivered slightly, but she held up her broom, ready to go again. Crutch pushed forward again, hitting the broom over and over in a blinding fit of rage, until finally he hit it hard enough to knock it clean out of her hands.

She looked down at the broom on the floor of the office, then up at Crutch, her face a picture of sorrow.

'It's not my fault,' she said, a tear running down her cheek.

Crutch stopped, her sorrow and her tears draining his anger, turning it to guilt.

'I know it's not your fault,' he said. 'I'm sorry. So sorry. I wouldn't ever hit you.'

Crutch couldn't go on like this. Seeing Abagail every day was a special kind of torture. It was agonising. He loved her so much it hurt, and it hurt even more because he knew they couldn't be together.

'Does it hurt you too?' said Crutch.

'So bad I want to die,' said Abagail.

Chapter 18
Forty Barrels Of Hard Tack

Abagail's plan of having the navy ships bring in bolts of fabric was going so well Crutch never even thought about the possibility of something going very wrong.

Only a few days after he'd dined with Lord Counsel Chudwell, Abagail was in the office when he got there looking upset. Nothing new about that. These days, she always looked upset, but it hurt Crutch to see it.

'Did you hear the news?' she said.

Just looking at her caused him physical pain now. She was so close to him, but she might as well be a thousand miles away.

'What news?' said Crutch.

'The Estovians burned the kapok plantations and the mills at Saldoria.'

'What?'

'It's horrid,' said Abagail. 'Everyone in the navy office is talking about it. I feel so guilty that what we did led to this.'

'It's not your fault,' said Crutch.

His mind spun. To burn down an entire plantation means the Estovians must have been able to land at least twenty or thirty men on Saldoria without being challenged. And it meant something even worse.

'There must be a spy in the palace,' said Crutch.

'My goodness,' said Abagail. 'You're right.'

Crutch thought of all the innocent people in Saldoria. All they did was grow the special variety of soft kapok unique to the island

and spin and weave it into fabric. The Estovians must have found out through one spy or another that Ironbay funded their ammunition by selling bolts of cloth so Solokov got men onto the island and burned it down.

The way the funding chain went was so convoluted that the spy had to be someone who had contact with a lord counsel. It seemed impossible they could have worked it out without inside knowledge.

When would the senseless killing of innocents end? Crutch felt his anger build. Anger at Lady Hastings for trying to promise Abagail to a young lord. Angry that Lady Hastings didn't think he was good enough, despite the fact that she'd be dead if it wasn't for him.

Crutch was angry that all the work they put in at the navy office just burned to the ground. He remembered Teevilgrad and how Solokov had crushed the true compatriots there, hanging innocent women and children, and he seethed at that all over again.

Magpie came into the office carrying a ledger.

'Lieutenant Crutch…'

'What!' yelled Crutch.

Abagail looked at Crutch in shock, hand over her mouth. Seeing her shock forced him to regain his composure.

'I'm sorry, Magpie. What is it?' he said.

'I just got an order from the Auld Faithful,' said Magpie. 'Forty barrels of hard tack and hundreds of ballista bolts and arrows. They must be shipping out any time now. I thought you'd want to know.'

'I did want to know,' said Crutch. 'Thank you, Magpie. I'll have to leave you both here.'

'Where are you going?' said Abagail.

'I'm off to see Cedric.'

When Crutch got to the Auld Faithful and told Cedric he wanted to speak with him, Cedric ushered him into the captain's cabin.

'I heard you were shipping out to Estovia,' said Crutch.

'That would be the worst kept secret in Ironbay,' said Cedric. 'The Auld Faithful is carrying the lead group of soldiers for the first landing.'

'I'd like to come with you,' said Crutch. Crutch didn't say what he felt, that he wanted to kill someone. Anyone.

'Are you sure?' said Cedric. 'I have to admit I liked the idea of you safe in Ironbay.'

'I doubt I'm safe here. Since they burned the kapok mills in Saldoria, I expect I've become a target.'

'So you think you'll be safer on a warship heading into Estovian territory?'

'I don't care about being safe,' said Crutch. 'I want this war to be over. And if that means I have to kill that bastard Igor Solokov myself, then I'll do it.' Crutch's anger boiled now. He wanted to rip someone's throat out badly.

'I've never seen this in you before, Crutch. Are you okay?'

'Never been better,' said Crutch, lying. 'I can't stand the thought of you and the marines going into battle while I sit at home.'

'I understand that. We'd be lucky to have you, and of course you can come back to the Auld Faithful.'

'Thank you,' said Crutch.

'But you can't be a corporal.'

Crutch hadn't thought of that. 'Why not?'

'That embarrassing little masquerade has gone on long enough. I can't have a corporal on my ship ordering everyone around like you do. Also, we'll be carrying troops with us. You need to stay a lieutenant and officially take on the responsibilities of the rank.'

'I don't order people around,' said Crutch.

'Really?' said Cedric. 'When you rescued Admiral Hastings and General Talbot from the true royals, who made the decisions?'

'I did,' said Crutch. 'Why?'

'They're both capable men. They lead the Ironborn army and the navy. But they never would have gotten themselves and their families safely to the palace without you giving the orders.'

'What are you trying to tell me, Cedric?'

'Leadership is taken, not given. You didn't have any problem ordering around a general and an admiral because it was the smartest thing to do at the time. Very few men in the navy would be brave enough to order their superiors around. One way or another, you do it all the time. You even do it with me.'

'I do?'

'With me, you appeal to my emotions, or my logic, but yes, you do it with me.'

'I'm sorry,' said Crutch.

'Don't be sorry for being a leader. People trust you and respect you; you care about them, and you do everything you can to keep them safe while you're completing a mission. You can't pretend to be a corporal any more. It's time for you to take the rank that matches your leadership skills.'

'If I'm a lieutenant, does that mean I'll be Sergeant Zander's superior officer?'

'The army would have made Sergeant Zander a permanent colonel in the army by now, but he won't accept the post. I don't know why not.

'The simple answer is yes. The way I see it, you've been commanding the marines since Sergeant Zander was injured in Papageenar. You're a lieutenant, and you'll stay a lieutenant when you return to the Auld Faithful. At least until you become a captain.'

'Thank you, Cedric,' said Crutch. 'That's quite the compliment.'

'The whole of Ironbay owes you a huge debt,' said Cedric. 'A promotion was way overdue.'

'I've never told you this, Cedric, but you're the closest thing I've ever had to a father. Everything I have is because you gave me a chance.'

'Now who's giving the compliments,' said Cedric, visibly moved. His normally deep voice sounded choked up as he said, 'If you were my son, I'd be very proud of the young man you've become.'

Chapter 19

You Always Find A Way

As soon as rejoining the Auld Faithful became official Crutch and Sergeant Zander were summoned to the army office.

'General Talbot would like to speak with both of you,' said Cedric, reading the single piece of paper a messenger had delivered.

'Any idea what this is about?' said Sergeant Zander.

'No. It just says to report to the army office for an appointment with General Talbot. No details.'

Crutch and Sergeant Zander walked there. As they got outside the huge wooden doors of the front entrance, Sergeant Zander smiled.

'Last time we went in the back way coming from the jail,' he said.

'I remember,' said Crutch. 'Then the general sent us to lead the first reserve on the Kona Track.'

'You didn't have to remind me of that,' said Sergeant Zander.

'You started it.'

'I guess I did.'

They made their way to the front desk. The officer behind the desk looked up and raised his eyebrows.

'Lieutenant Crutch and Sergeant Zander here to see General Talbot,' said Crutch, handing over the message Cedric had given them.

'Heroes of the Kona Track,' said the officer. 'It's an honour to meet you.'

'Thank you,' said Crutch.

'General Talbot is expecting you,' said the officer. He motioned to a guard who stood at the side of the desk. 'Corporal Ludbrick will escort you to his office.'

They followed Corporal Ludbrick up three flights of stairs, with Crutch's cane clacking on the stairs as he went up. Then they walked down a long corridor and stopped outside two large wooden doors.

'Been here before,' said Sergeant Zander as the corporal knocked.

'Who is it?' yelled a voice from inside. Crutch immediately recognised it as General Talbot.

'Lieutenant Crutch and Sergeant Zander here to see you, general,' yelled Corporal Ludbrick.

'Excellent,' yelled back the general. 'Let them right in.'

Corporal Ludbrick opened the door and motioned them through. They entered a large, wood-floored room with half a dozen armed guards. General Talbot sat at a long wooden desk they recognised from the last time they were here.

'A pleasure to see you both,' said General Talbot as they approached. 'I hear you're joining the invasion of Teevilgrad.'

'We are,' said Crutch.

'I'll cut to the chase,' said General Talbot. 'I need strong leaders like you in the invasion force. I'd like to make you both colonels.'

'Acting colonels?' said Sergeant Zander.

'Acting, permanent, whatever position you'd like,' said General Talbot. 'My best officers and sergeants are the handful of men you trained who made it back alive from Papageenar. Finest damn soldiers I've ever had.'

'Where would we be assigned?' said Sergeant Zander.

'I planned on placing the soldiers for the first invasion on the Auld Faithful under the command of Lieutenant Crutch. And you would be in charge of getting through the city wall, Sergeant Zander. You'll both be colonels, of course.'

'Can I speak freely, general?' said Sergeant Zander.

'You're the best damn commander I've ever seen in the field. You and Crutch. You can say whatever you like.'

'It's a mistake,' said Sergeant Zander.

'A mistake?' said General Talbot. 'Why do you say that?'

'Too many cooks,' said Sergeant Zander. 'When we land on the docks at Teevilgrad and when we take the city walls, we need one man in charge. One man making the decisions. With thousands of soldiers, it will be total chaos at it is. We don't need two colonels giving orders, making the confusion worse.'

General Talbot looked at Sergeant Zander and at Crutch for a few long seconds, then nodded his head.

'You're right,' said General Talbot. 'Just confirms that you should be in charge, Sergeant Zander. Or should I say Colonel Zander?'

Crutch felt relieved. He wanted to do some serious killing more than anything. He itched for it deep down in a place most men tried to pretend didn't exist. But he didn't want the responsibility of leading a regiment of soldiers. Not after the Kona Track.

'That's not what I had in mind,' said Sergeant Zander.

'You're full of surprises,' said General Talbot. 'What do you suggest?'

'I was with Crutch in Teevilgrad, and there's no one who understands the Estovians better than he does. He got us in there and got us out alive with Solokov's glowstone. I didn't think it was possible, but somehow he did it.'

'I heard the rumours, but I had no idea Lieutenant Crutch took the lead,' said General Talbot.

'He didn't just take the lead,' said Sergeant Zander. 'He nearly brought down Emperor Solokov single-handed. The brilliance of it still boggles my mind. There's only one man who should be in charge of the invasion of Teevilgrad, and that man is Lieutenant Crutch.'

'What?' said Crutch.

'You're the perfect choice,' said Sergeant Zander. 'You're the only choice if we want to have a chance of killing Solokov. You nearly did it last time with just us marines. This time you'll have an army with you to finish the job.'

'That's the kind of talk I love to hear,' said General Talbot. 'What do you say, Lieutenant Crutch? Would you like to lead our invasion force and rip Emperor Solokov's guts out?'

Crutch thought about all the people he'd like to kill in this stinking world full of nobles and tyrants. He thought of the soup kitchen burning in Teevilgrad, of young Dima, and that brave old lady Leena hanging on nooses in the People's Plaza.

He thought of Andreas the musician, using his last few words to stand defiant. He thought of Anton and Yelena and all the Estovians in Teevilgrad who starved while Solokov sat fat and happy, feasting in his palace.

'I'll rip his guts out and feed them to his fat face,' said Crutch.

'You've got some fire in your belly,' said General Talbot. 'Congratulations on your promotion. I'll make all the arrangements, Colonel Crutch.'

'Can I make one more suggestion, general,' said Sergeant Zander.

'Of course.'

'Colonel Crutch will be so critical for us if this invasion is going to succeed, we need to keep him alive.'

'What did you have in mind?' said General Talbot.

'I would like my unit of marines to be assigned to him as bodyguards.'

'With you leading his bodyguards, he'll be the safest man in Teevilgrad,' said General Talbot.

'No one's safe when two armies are trying to kill each other,' said Sergeant Zander. 'But we'll do our best or die trying.'

'I know you will,' said General Talbot. 'Sergeant Zander, I commend you on your selflessness. It's quite breathtaking. I've never seen anything like it in all my time as a general.'

'Just doing my duty,' said Sergeant Zander.

'I'll be doing my duty right along with you,' said General Talbot. 'Along with Young Lord Talbot.'

'You're coming with us?' said Crutch.

'Indeed, I am. An invasion this size needs support from someone who understands all the complex operations of the Ironborn armed forces. Myself and Young Lord Talbot will be with the troops who land after you get a foothold on the docks at Teevilgrad.'

'Do you think Young Lord Talbot is ready for this?' said Crutch.

'You saw what he can do with a sword,' said General Talbot. 'He's become quite the officer, thanks in no small part to the training you and your marines gave him when he was with you on the Auld Faithful.'

'He's still so young,' said Crutch.

'He's about the same age as you when you took command on the Kona Track,' said General Talbot. 'I admit I have my anxieties, but the boy was born to be a soldier, and I won't deny him his destiny.'

'I'm sure you know what's best,' said Crutch.

'I doubt that,' said General Talbot. 'But I've made my decision, and I'll stick with it.'

After exchanging pleasantries, Crutch and Sergeant Zander left the general to the enormous task of coordinating the invasion of Teevilgrad. As they walked back to the Auld Faithful Crutch was still somewhat in shock.

'You really think I can lead the landing in Teevilgrad?' said Crutch.

'I know you can,' said Sergeant Zander.

'But I've never led more than a hundred soldiers,' said Crutch.

'The number doesn't matter,' said Sergeant Zander. 'You have a head for it and the most important talent of all for a commander.'

'What's that?' said Crutch.

'It doesn't matter how bad shit gets or how hopelessly outnumbered you are; you always find a way.'

Chapter 20
Abagail Is Lucky To Have You

Crutch waited at his cottage for Rita the maid to arrive before leaving for the navy office. He was looking out his front door when he saw her unlock the gate and come walking down the path through the garden.

When she saw that he was watching her, Rita smiled, a red blush on her cheeks.

'Good morning, Crutch,' she said, walking into the doorway with her bucket, so close to him her dress brushed up against him.

'Good morning, Rita. I have news for you.'

Rita smiled and looked into his eyes. 'Is it something I'll like?'

'I don't think it's something anyone likes, but it has to be done,' said Crutch. 'I'm leaving with the navy fleet for Estovia.'

Rita looked at Crutch with worry on her face. 'You're leading the troops in the invasion?'

'Some of them,' said Crutch.

Rita put her hand on Crutch's arm. 'You're so strong,' she said. 'And brave.'

'Just doing my duty,' said Crutch.

'Promise me you'll make it back alive,' said Rita. 'And don't get hurt.'

'Battles are unpredictable,' said Crutch. 'I can't promise anything.'

'I'll miss you when you're gone,' said Rita. 'And I'll worry about you, fighting in the war.'

'You should have less cleaning to do,' said Crutch. 'Less cushions to repair. Less charcoal to scrub off the floor.'

Rita laughed. 'Oh, Crutch. You're so funny.' She hugged him, her face inches from his. 'Come back to me,' she said.

Her lips were so close, her eyes closed as if she was waiting for something. Crutch wasn't quite sure what. He pushed her away gently.

'I hope this doesn't mean you'll be out of work when I'm gone,' said Crutch.

Rita looked at Crutch, disappointed about something again.

'I'll tend to the gardens and stop the cottages from getting dusty,' she said. 'There's always plenty of work to do.'

'Thank you for looking after my cottage,' said Crutch.

'That's my job,' said Rita, turning her back on Crutch and heading into the living room to clean.

Crutch stood outside the admiral's office behind two navy guards in full dress, standing on each side of the large wooden doors. He could hear the admiral talking inside.

Seeing the admiral was something he wasn't looking forward to, but there was something he had to do before he left with the fleet for Teevilgrad.

'This is most irregular,' said the admiral's voice from inside. 'Send him in then.'

The door opened, and the head of the admiral's assistant popped through.

'The admiral will see you now, Lieutenant Crutch.'

Crutch walked through the doors to see Admiral Hastings sitting behind his large desk made of polished wood.

'I'm curious as to how you got all the way to my office, Lieutenant Crutch?' said the admiral. 'Or is it Colonel Crutch now?'

'I'm sure you were informed that General Talbot made me colonel for the invasion, admiral,' said Crutch. 'There are some advantages to being a double iron cross winner. The guards assume you have a right to be places where you don't.'

'I suppose I shouldn't complain. It seems you've been using those iron crosses of yours to great effect in the supply office,' said the admiral. 'I am grateful.'

'Thank you, admiral. I'm sorry it didn't work out so well for Saldoria.'

'The enemy will always be looking for ways to scuttle out plans. It can't be helped.'

'That's kind of you to say, admiral, but I still feel guilty,' said Crutch.

'The responsibility of command weighs heavy on us all,' said the admiral. 'If this is about Abagail, you should know I have absolutely nothing to do with that.'

'Really admiral?' said Crutch.

'I have told Lady Hastings repeatedly that you're a man of honour, and Abagail is lucky to have you.'

That caught Crutch by surprise. He'd assumed that the admiral was behind the plan to promise Abagail to someone from the nobility.

'So you don't care that I'm a commoner?'

'I have to be honest with you, Crutch; when you first came along I was shocked that Abagail would want to spend time with a boy who came up from the streets. But when I got to know you, I understood why. Abagail is an exceptional judge of character.'

'And yet she's to be promised to someone of noble birth.'

'Not my doing, I assure you. Lady Hastings is determined that Abagail should be cared for in the manner she's accustomed to and is seen with young men who won't compromise her reputation.'

'I would never…'

'I know now that you'd never do anything to hurt Abagail or her reputation, but there it is, unfortunately. Lady Hastings usually gets her way, and in affairs involving her daughter, I'm afraid I just don't have any authority at all, despite being admiral of his majesty's navy.'

'I understand, admiral,' said Crutch.

'I honestly hope you do,' said the admiral. 'Will that be all?'

'Truth be told, admiral, as much as I appreciate your explanation, I actually came here to talk about my replacement as supply officer,' said Crutch.

'That's something you can talk to your superior officer about,' said the admiral.

'Of course, admiral, but in this case there's a request I need to make directly to you.'

The first thing he always noticed about Abagail was her wonderful crooked face and her ocean blue eyes. But the next thing he noticed when he came into the supply office was that her neck was bare. She wasn't wearing the gold necklace Crutch had brought her as a gift from Yavenland.

'Is it true?' said Abagail.

'Yes, it is,' said Crutch.

'When do you leave for Teevilgrad?' said Abagail. Seeing her so close to him with those blue eyes so sad was a torture now. He wanted so bad just to take her in his arms, but he couldn't do that. Not ever again.

'In the next day or two.'

'Will you be a marine again?' said Abagail.

'General Talbot has made me an acting colonel. I'll be leading the first force onto the docks in Teevilgrad.' *And I'll finally get to kill someone.*

Abagail put her hand over her mouth in shock.

'Do you always have to be a hero?' she said.

'Solokov has to die,' said Crutch. 'It's time to end this war, and I have to do my part.'

'But you're doing your part here, in the supply office.'

'It's not the same,' said Crutch.

'It's just that I'll miss you. And I'll worry about you every second you're gone.'

Crutch was silent. He couldn't tell her that he was already missing her. That knowing he couldn't be with her was like someone ripped his heart out and was stomping on it, over and over, every time he saw her. That he woke with his guts on fire, like someone had kicked him, and every time he thought of her, it just got worse. That the only way he could survive was to get as far away from her as he could, so he wouldn't have to live through the torture of seeing her.

'Say something,' said Abagail, her bottom lip trembling.

'I'm going,' said Crutch. 'I might come back alive; I might not. Either way, you should move on.'

'Don't say that,' said Abagail.

'Find someone who makes you happy,' said Crutch. 'That's all I want. For you to be happy.'

'You're the only one who ever made me happy,' said Abagail, the first tears welling up in her eyes.

Crutch wished he knew what to say, but there was nothing he could say to make this better. He wished he could hug her and hold her, but he couldn't do that either. He turned and left her sitting there in the supply office, crying, alone.

Chapter 21
Black Tide

The marines and Cedric gathered in the galley the night before the fleet was scheduled to ship out for Teevilgrad.

'You're the highest-ranking officer on this ship now,' said Sergeant Zander.

'That's not true. On a ship, the ship's captain is the highest authority. Isn't that right, Cedric?'

'Yes, colonel,' said Cedric, smiling. 'Whatever you say, colonel.'

'Don't start that,' said Crutch.

'Sorry, colonel,' said Cedric, his smile even wider.

'We're all happy to have you back with us,' said Longshot. 'The Auld Faithful's not the same without you.'

'That's the truth,' said Quicksilver. 'I'm a grown man, but I'm not ashamed to say I missed you.'

'We all missed you,' said Cedric.

'Missed you,' said Boulder, grinning happily.

'And when it comes to who's in command,' said Cedric. 'We'll all be proud to follow your orders any time. You've proven yourself time and time again.'

'That's the truth,' said Sergeant Zander.

'Saved all our lives more times than I can count,' said Longshot.

'What I don't understand is why General Talbot didn't promote you, sergeant?' said Cedric.

'He tried,' said Sergeant Zander. 'I turned the promotion down. I told the army that when we invade Teevilgrad with Colonel Crutch leading the invading force, he'll need a squad of bodyguards to keep him alive.'

'I'm glad to hear that,' said Cedric. 'You'll need all the protection you can get. We load the troops onto the Auld Faithful tomorrow.'

In the pre-dawn, the docks were full of soldiers marching in an ordered fashion. Around a hundred and fifty men marched to each warship on the docks. The sight was breathtaking in its scope. Thousands of men in uniform, standing at attention with officers shouting orders.

Crutch recognised many of the men he'd fought with on the Kona track, now officers themselves.

'The Royal Expeditionary Army,' said Cedric. 'Ironbay's finest come to do their duty.'

Crutch was impatient. He itched to do some fighting and some killing. The anger burning in his guts churned away at him, and he wanted to hit someone. He figured he'd get more than enough chances to do that once they got to Teevilgrad, but he really didn't want to wait that long.

The men in front of the Auld Faithful were led by what looked like an overblown parody of an officer. Some idiot noble some other idiot noble had given command to.

The idiot raised his ceremonial sword and waved it around like he knew what he was doing, and shouted out orders that his troops clearly didn't understand. Behind him Captain Travis relayed real orders to the Ironborn soldiers.

'Nice to see Captain Travis in charge,' said Sergeant Zander.

'Who is that idiot with the sword?' said Crutch.

'That must be Lord Hargreave,' said Sergeant Zander. 'Captain Travis mentioned him.'

'Mentioned him to me too,' said Crutch, anger boiling in his guts as he stared at the pompous noble there on the docks, waving his sword around like he was a schoolboy about to play a game of soldiers. 'Could you get these men on board, Sergeant Zander?'

'Will do, Colonel Crutch.'

It took the better part of an hour for all the ships to load their troops and the last of their supplies and weapons. They were highly efficient, but the sheer size of the operation ate up time, and the early morning sun broke through the clouds by the time they were fully loaded.

The ships left the docks with the Auld Faithful in the lead, the first mate at the helm. Crutch stood at the stern with Cedric and watched ship after ship make sail and join the fleet, moving in formation.

'There must be thirty ships following us,' said Crutch. With every ship in full sail punching through the waves, the sight was breathtaking.

'Thirty two,' said Cedric.

'This must bring back memories for you as a fleet commander,' said Crutch.

'It does,' said Cedric. 'Some good, some not so good.'

'I'm sorry,' said Crutch as he remembered that Cedric had lost his entire fleet when he was betrayed at the siege of Crestona.

'It's the nature of war,' said Cedric. 'A glorious, magnificent fleet of ships sporting the finest equipment Ironbay can manufacture and the finest young men she can train. But when it comes down to it, our single purpose is to kill.'

Did Cedric sense it in him somehow? Did he know that right now Crutch wanted to lash out, to kill, more than anything else?

'When I was just a young lieutenant,' said Cedric, 'our ship visited the tiny territory of Exaldia. Every three or four years, a black tide would wash in on Exaldia, poisoning everything that lived in the ocean. Fish, crabs, seaweed.'

'What was in the water?' said Crutch.

'The people didn't know. They just knew it was death carried in on the ocean. The black tide left thousands of poisoned fish dead or dying on the shore, bringing untold suffering for the sea life and the people of Exaldia who relied on the fish to survive.'

'That's terrible,' said Crutch. 'But I don't get the connection.'

'The older I become, the more I see it. The Ironborn navy, the Royal Expeditionary Army...' Cedric pointed at the warships following the Auld Faithful, full of soldiers, bristling with ballistas. 'We are the black tide.'

Chapter 22
A Flaming Serviette

Captain Travis sat with Crutch and the marines in the galley for the morning meal.

At the next table, Lord Hargreave sat alone, being tended to by his valet. In front of him, his table was set with an ornate tablecloth, knives, and forks of three different varieties laid in precise rows.

'What is he doing?' said Crutch.

'He thinks it's beneath him to sit with commoners,' said Captain Travis. 'He eats alone, with his valet waiting on him.'

'Maybe you should give that a try now you're a colonel,' said Longshot. 'You could make Quicksilver your valet.'

'That'd work well if you wanted every meal burned to char,' said Sergeant Zander.

'And the table,' said Longshot.

'And the kitchen,' said Sergeant Zander.

'That's not fair,' said Quicksilver. 'I'd make a great valet.'

'I can't see it working out,' said Sergeant Zander. 'Cookie barred you from the kitchen years ago.'

'That fire spreading to the cutting table wasn't my fault,' said Quicksilver.

'Yes, we heard,' said Sergeant Zander. 'It was the kitchen hand's fault for interrupting you while you were pouring oil and tar into the fireplace.'

'That's right,' said Quicksilver.

Lord Hargreave's valet carefully placed a plate full of ham perfectly centred between the knives and forks. The lord picked up a fork and a knife from the outside and began eating. After his first mouthful, the valet passed him a cloth serviette, and he patted his lips.

'Is the ham to your satisfaction?' said the valet.

'It's cold and clammy, but I suppose these are the sacrifices we are forced to make in the service of our king.'

'Think you could do that, Quicksilver?' said Sergeant Zander. 'Carry around a plate of ham and hand Crutch a serviette so he can pat his lips?'

'Maybe a flaming serviette,' said Longshot. The marines laughed. 'I could see Crutch now. 'Where is my serviette, Quicksilver?' 'There you are, sir.' 'Why are my eyebrows on fire, Quicksilver?' 'That would be the flaming serviette, sir.''

'Laugh it up, guys,' said Quicksilver as the marines burst into laughter again. Quicksilver's eyes went glassy, like he was picturing something in his mind. 'A flaming serviette is a pretty good idea though.'

'Setting Lord Hargreave on fire seems like a good idea right now,' said Captain Travis.

'What do you mean?' said Crutch.

'He's never been in battle; never got blood on his sword, but he acts like he knows everything,' said Captain Travis. 'It's a joke. He doesn't even know how to use a sword properly.'

'Who made him a colonel?' said Crutch.

'That would be King Vargus,' said Captain Travis. 'I heard his father has been a close personal friend of the king for decades. I can't begin to tell you how happy I am that you're leading the invasion, Colonel Crutch. But if Hargreave is with us giving orders, he'll get a lot of good men killed.

'I'll take care of it,' said Crutch.

Later, Crutch found Colonel Hargreave, Lord bloody Hargreave, strutting around on the deck of the Auld Faithful like he owned it with his valet in tow.

'Colonel Crutch,' said Lord Hargreave. 'It's an honour to share the command with you. Can't wait to get in amongst it and show those Estovians who the best fighters are.'

'Yes, I'm sure we'll have a splendid time killing every living thing in Teevilgrad,' said Crutch. 'I wonder if you'd like to help me prepare the men?'

'Of course,' said Lord Hargreave. 'What did you have in mind?'

'Perhaps a little duel on deck between you and myself,' said Crutch. 'You can show off your skills with a blade, and we can give the troops some tips.'

'That sounds like a cracking idea,' said Lord Hargreave. When shall we do it?'

'There's no time like the present,' said Crutch. 'Sergeant Zander, have the men assemble here on deck. Me and Lord Hargreave are having a duel.'

'Will do, Colonel Crutch,' said Sergeant Zander, smiling.

It took just a few minutes for the troops to get to the deck, pushing in together all the way to the rails. Sergeant Zander made them leave a nice, big circle Crutch and Lord Hargreave could fight in.

'Shall we use practice swords?' said Lord Hargreave.

'You can use your real sword,' said Crutch. 'I'll just use my walking cane.'

'Are you sure?' said Lord Hargreave.

'Quite sure,' said Crutch. 'And don't go easy on me. If you can hit me, you should do it.'

'You're just a cripple. That seems quite dangerous.'

'We're going to battle, Lord Hargreave. I've heard that can be quite dangerous too. May as well get used to it.'

'Very well. But I did try to warn you.'

Crutch smiled. He would enjoy fighting this pompous prick. He nodded at Sergeant Zander.

'A duel,' yelled Sergeant Zander. 'Between Lord Hargreave and Colonel Crutch. Colonel Crutch will use his walking cane. Lord Hargreave will use his sword.'

'That doesn't seem fair,' said one of the soldiers.

'How's he gonna defend hisself with a walking cane?' said another soldier.

'No quarter will be given,' yelled Sergeant Zander.

'Lord Hargreave will kill him.'

'If the lord doesn't fall over on his arse swinging his fancy sword.'

Lord Hargreave squared with Crutch, holding his sword out like a fencer. He came towards Crutch, prodding and thrusting ahead of him as he advanced.

To Crutch, who had fought and trained with real swordsmen, this felt like fighting a child with a toy sword. He didn't even bother to raise his walking cane, anticipating every move and hobbling around to avoid the sword.

'There's one thing you need to understand about battle,' yelled Crutch as Lord Hargreave stabbed at him. 'Your enemy doesn't care if you have a fancy title or a fancy sword.'

Lord Hargreave moved faster, stabbed, and swung more frantically, getting frustrated as Crutch hobbled around casually, avoiding every attack.

'We're going to Teevilgrad, the heart of Estovia,' yelled Crutch, shaking his head as Lord Hargreave launched another stabbing flurry. He even managed to look like a pompous prick when he fought, with his chest puffed out and his nose held high.

'Every Estovian there will have just one purpose,' yelled Crutch. 'To kill you before you can kill them.'

Crutch stepped aside as Lord Hargreave lunged forward, swung back his walking cane, and smacked the lord hard on his back as he went past. It felt good to strike a blow on a lord, like he was striking a blow against all the nobility who thought he wasn't good enough for a young lady like Abagail.

Not good enough just because he had to grow up in streets and the sewers of Ironbay while these prissy, pomped-up nobles were waited on hand and foot by maids and servants.

Lord Hargreave turned and snarled at Crutch. 'Stand and fight like a man,' he said.

Crutch stood stock still, like a statue, and let Lord Hargreave advance straight toward him. Lord Hargreave came forward fast, thrusting and stabbing the way a six-year-old boy playing soldiers would. Crutch dodged the sword, pushed it aside with his arm, made one step forward with his good leg, and elbowed Lord Hargreave in the face.

'The Estovians will use every dirty trick they can think of to put you in the ground,' yelled Crutch. 'There are no rules in combat.'

Lord Hargreave took a handkerchief from his pocket and wiped blood from his nose. He put the handkerchief back in his pocket, then swung wildly at Crutch, a swing that could have taken Crutch's head off if he hadn't dodged it so easily by stepping aside and ducking at the last second.

Crutch used the momentum of the swing and smacked Lord Hargreave on the back of his sword hand with his walking cane. Lord Hargreave's sword dropped from the noble's hand and slid across the deck.

'Maybe get your valet out here to help you swing your sword,' said Crutch. Crutch looked over at Lord Hargreave's valet. Did he just smirk? Even his own valet couldn't stand the pomped-up prick.

Lord Hargreave moved to try to pick up his sword, but Crutch moved in front of him.

'When you lose your weapon,' yelled Crutch, 'and you will lose your weapon, you use daggers, fists, your teeth, whatever you can find at hand to tear your enemy to pieces. Make him wish you were still using your sword.'

Crutch casually tossed his walking cane to Longshot, who caught it with one hand. Then Crutch grinned and beckoned for Lord Hargreave to come at him. Lord Hargreave put up his fists like he was in a boxing match and came at Crutch.

'I'll take that smirk off your face, you filthy commoner,' he said.

Lord Hargreave was a fairly decent boxer. Crutch ducked and dodged, and one of his fists grazed Crutch's chin. But Crutch had trained at this range against daggers. Being grazed by a dagger could kill you. Being grazed by a punch was much more forgiving.

As Crutch dodged, Lord Hargreave got frustrated, trying to punch harder and quicker, but he couldn't land a solid punch. The soldiers began to laugh.

'Why won't you fight me, you filthy coward?' said Lord Hargreave.

'If you insist,' said Crutch. He grabbed one of Lord Hargreave's arms as it came towards him to balance himself, and kicked the lord in the crotch with his good leg. Crutch brought his leg back to the ground, then punched Lord Hargreave in the face with everything he had.

The lord fell to the deck on his back, and Crutch was on him in an instant, thinking of every noble who'd cursed at him or let him starve when he was a street urchin. Every noble who looked at him like he was a dog turd left on the street when he was begging for a measly copper coin.

He thought of Young Lord Chudwell with his hands on Abagail, hands that had no place being there. Crutch vented his rage in an uncontrolled fury until he felt a hand on his back.

'It's up to you, Colonel Crutch,' said Sergeant Zander. 'But you might want to stop there.'

Crutch looked at Lord Hargreave lying on the deck, his face bloody, a couple of teeth knocked out on his shirt. Crutch retrieved his walking cane from Longshot and got to his feet.

'Listen up,' yelled Sergeant Zander. 'Colonel Crutch was taking it easy on Lord Hargreave. How do we know he was taking it easy?'

'Because he's still alive,' said Longshot.

'Still alive,' said Boulder, smiling.

'This is not a game,' yelled Sergeant Zander. 'The only way you'll stay alive in Teevilgrad is by killing the Estovians before they can kill you. Tomorrow we start your real training.'

Chapter 23
Throw Him Overboard

Once he'd regained consciousness, Lord Hargreave found Crutch on the deck.

'This is an outrage,' said the pompous prick. As he spoke, Crutch could see the gaps in his teeth. Knocking a couple of them out didn't improve his appearance, but it sure did feel good to give him a permanent reminder of what commoners could do.

'The only outrage,' said Crutch, 'is that someone made you a colonel when you can't fight for shit.'

'That kind of language is unbefitting for an officer,' said Lord Hargreave. 'This is what happens when they give commoners a commission. Swearing and brawling.'

'Getting your arse handed to you in a duel is not brawling,' said Crutch. 'And you're only complaining because you made yourself look like an idiot.'

'How dare you speak to me like that?'

'I can speak to you any way I want to. This is not a game of soldiers, Hargreave. In a few days, we'll be leading these men into battle. I want to get as many of them back alive as I can. And right now their biggest danger is if you're there on the docks of Teevilgrad giving them orders.'

'How dare you? I am a colonel and a lord. I will not be spoken to like a common servant.'

'A common servant deserves more respect than you do. At least they work for a living.'

'I won't stand for this,' said Lord Hargreave. 'I shall report you.'

'Go right ahead,' said Crutch. 'Perhaps you could put in a report with General Talbot. He's just a couple of ships behind us. I'm sure Captain Beaumont would be happy to bring his ship alongside. You're both nobles after all.'

Cedric had moved within earshot and smiled when he heard that.

'Happy to do it, Lord Hargreave,' said Cedric.

'If you could,' said Lord Hargreave. 'Then you'll have your come uppance, Colonel Crutch. You foul commoner.'

Lord Hargreave waited at the rail, his chest puffed out, as Cedric sent up the signal flags to arrange the boarding. The marines gathered around Crutch waiting too.

'This should be fun,' said Sergeant Zander as General Talbot's ship came alongside.

Lord Hargreave stepped across, nose high, while the crew of both ships pulled on grappling hooks to keep the ships close. The general waited for him on the deck. Crutch and the marines couldn't quite make out what was being said, but Lord Hargreave said something while the general listened.

Then General Talbot started shouting. Crutch's favourite part of the exchange was when General Talbot backhanded Lord Hargreave in the face so hard the lord fell to the deck. After a good two or three minutes of dressing down, Lord Hargreave retreated back to the Auld Faithful.

General Talbot came to the rail of his ship fuming.

'Colonel Crutch,' he yelled.

'Yes, general,' said Crutch as Lord Hargreave pushed past him, rubbing a new bruise on his mouth.

'If Lord Hargreave gives you any more trouble, throw him overboard. I don't have the time or the patience for this nonsense.'

'Yes general. Will do general,' said Crutch.

'Carry on,' said General Talbot. 'I'm counting on you and your marines to get these soldiers ready before we arrive.'

'We'll do our best,' said Crutch.

'I know you will,' said the general.

Chapter 24
Tomorrow We Won't Be So Gentle

Crutch and the marines gathered together in the galley to talk about the invasion of Teevilgrad and how they'd prepare the men.

'The first thing we need to do is take out the ballistas on the docks,' said Sergeant Zander. 'Then the rest of the troops can land without taking enemy fire.'

'I remember they had ballistas on the docks, but I don't remember how many,' said Crutch.

'There were twelve,' said Sergeant Zander. 'And I can tell you exactly where they were.'

'How do you remember them so well?' said Crutch.

'While the street urchins loaded the wagon with food and you were busy making deals with the ship captains, I was just sitting there. Hours of looking up at those ballistas and working out how we'd take them out.'

'Nice one, Sarge,' said Longshot.

'You never stop being a marine,' said Quicksilver.

'It's not gonna be easy,' said Sergeant Zander. 'But I have a few ideas.'

'Are we gonna burn 'em,' said Quicksilver.

'No,' said Sergeant Zander. 'We need those ballistas to defend the docks from Estovian warships.'

'Oh, come on, Sarge. Let me burn 'em. It'll be much quicker.'

'Sergeant Zander is right,' said Crutch. 'We have to control the port so we can keep getting supplies, and the last thing we need is the Estovians taking back the docks when we're in the city. Then we'd be stranded without supply of weapons or food.'

'So we train the men on how to take the ballistas,' said Sergeant Zander. 'That's the first step. I've been going over something in my head, but we'll need the ship's carpenter and some of the soldiers to help.'

Crutch asked for permission from Cedric to build something on the forecastle of the Auld Faithful.

'Anything that helps you get more of these boys back alive from Teevilgrad, I'm okay with,' said Cedric.

'Thank you, Cedric,' said Crutch.

'Wait,' said Cedric. 'This doesn't involve Quicksilver teaching the soldiers how to burn things does it?'

'No Cedric. No burning.'

'Well, that's a relief. Carry on then.'

The ship's carpenter started building it as soon as they told him what they needed. He had as many soldiers as he could use ready to help him, and the building went fast. Before they slept for the night, it was finished.

Sergeant Zander rang the ship's bell an hour before dawn and kept ringing it while the rest of the marines went below, ordering the soldiers up on deck. Once they were assembled, Crutch addressed them.

'Every day we train an hour before dawn,' he said. 'Why do we train an hour before dawn marines?'

'Because that's the best time for killing,' said the marines in unison.

'The best time for killing is an hour before dawn when your enemy is still sleeping and you have the cover of darkness,' said Crutch. 'You get good at what you train, and you get good at what you train against.

'When we invade Teevilgrad, the first thing we have to do is land on the docks and disable their ballistas. And we have to do it while we're under enemy fire. So that's what we'll be training.'

Crutch pointed to the wooden tower the ship's carpenter had built on the forecastle with the help of the soldiers. Boulder, Longshot, Quicksilver, and Damen had climbed to the top.

'That tower is the enemy ballista,' said Crutch. 'I know there's not a real ballista at the top of that tower, which is fortunate for you. But Boulder will be simulating a ballista firing on you.'

Boulder grinned, holding up a thick wooden pole.

'You'll break into groups of twelve, and you will attack the ballista one group at a time and disable it. Arrow fire will not work against these ballistas. They have shields. We can't use fire. We need the ballistas undamaged so we can use them ourselves to defend the docks. Use your heads and come up with your own solutions starting now.'

'You heard the colonel,' yelled Sergeant Zander. 'First group of twelve, attack that ballista now!'

A group of twelve soldiers assembled hastily, talking to each other.

'What are you waiting for?' yelled Sergeant Zander. 'The Estovians are firing on you. You don't have time for a chinwag. Take that ballista!'

Up on the tower, Longshot took aim at the soldier leading group. Longshot had arrow shafts with the metal heads removed. He'd told Crutch they wouldn't fly worth shit, but over the short distance on the ship, it wouldn't matter. He let his first arrow fly, and it hit the soldier in the chest.

'Haven't even started moving, and one of you is dead already!' yelled Sergeant Zander kicking the soldier's legs out from under him. 'Get up that tower and stop that ballista from firing now!'

The soldiers ran across the deck towards the tower. Boulder threw the first pole so hard it knocked the solder at the front of the line off his feet. Crutch walked along behind the soldiers. He looked at the soldier who'd been knocked off his feet, lying there trying to regain his breath.

'That looks like it hurt, soldier. Let me help you get up.' He smacked the soldier on his leg with his cane, then prodded him in the guts, then hit him around the side of the head. Crutch was enjoying hitting someone. Anyone.

Sergeant Zander saw Crutch laying into the soldier lying on the deck and yelled, 'The battlefield is not your hammock or your warm, comfy bed. If you lie down on the battlefield, you die. If you're knocked down, get back up.'

The soldier got back to his feet just in time for Boulder to throw a pole straight into his guts and knock him back off his feet again. As he lay on his back, wheezing, Crutch hit him over and over with his walking cane.

'Stop-lying-down-in-battle,' he said, smacking the soldier with his cane as he said each word.

The soldier dragged himself to his feet, unsteady on his feet as Crutch hit him, then half ran, half staggered towards the tower on the forecastle, with Crutch hitting him on the arse with his cane for good measure.

The first group of soldiers climbed the tower, weapons slung. As they got to the top, Damen and Quicksilver swung with wooden swords, hitting them hard. Soldier after soldier fell back four yards down to the deck. After the entire first squad of soldiers had fallen at least once, Sergeant Zander started yelling again.

'You'll have to do better than that,' he yelled. 'In Teevilgrad, you'll be fighting trained killers and you'll be making that trip to the ground minus your heads or your arms. You sorry lot can go to the back of the line. Next squad up.'

Squad after squad of soldiers attacked the tower. Crutch took great delight in hitting as many of the soldiers as he could with his cane any time they did anything that might get them killed in battle. It felt good to be striking out.

It became obvious to Crutch that these soldiers had been drilled by the army so they'd take orders and run into battle, but none of them had been taught to think. They all just ran headlong towards the tower and climbed up, expecting that somehow what hadn't worked for the last five squads would somehow miraculously work for them.

When it came to real combat, they were idiots. And if they didn't change, come the invasion of Teevilgrad they'd be dead idiots.

When every squad had taken their turn at attacking the tower Crutch addressed all the soldiers.

'Congratulations,' he said. 'Every one of you is dead.'

'Dead,' said Boulder from up on the tower, grinning. At least someone was enjoying this.

'You're a sorry bunch of idiots,' said Crutch.

'Idiots,' said Boulder.

'If you fight like soldiers, you'll die like soldiers. Your job is to find a way to stay alive while you kill the enemy. Tomorrow we do this again, and we'll keep doing it every day until you sorry lot learn how to be killers. Do you have anything to say, Sergeant Zander.'

'I do,' said Sergeant Zander. 'I'll be going into battle with you lot in Teevilgrad. Right now, the way you fight, you'd all get me killed. I don't know what it's like to be dead, but by all reports, I'm fairly certain I wouldn't enjoy it. You all need to use your brains.'

'Use your brains,' said Boulder from up in the tower.

'Dying is nature's way of telling you to fight smarter,' said Sergeant Zander. 'Innovate and adapt.'

'You have one job from now until tomorrow morning,' said Crutch. 'Find better ways of attacking this tower. Today, we took it easy on you. Tomorrow, we won't be so gentle. Dismissed.'

Chapter 25
Nice Try Still Dead

After the training, Crutch and the marines gathered together in the galley eating their morning meal.

'Do you think we should give them some tips?' said Damen.

'Telling them what to do won't work,' said Crutch. 'That's the problem with them. They've been trained to follow orders, but no one has taught them how to solve problems themselves.'

'Colonel Crutch is right,' said Sergeant Zander. 'They have to work it out themselves. The best thing we can do is make it harder for them.'

'Good work today on the tower men,' said Crutch. 'Especially you, Boulder.'

'Thank you, Crutch,' said Boulder, smiling. 'I like throwing poles.'

'Damen, it looked like you were taking it easy on them,' said Crutch.

'I didn't want to injure anyone,' said Damen.

'We're preparing them to fight in battle,' said Crutch. 'They need to feel the fear of getting hurt or killed. And they need to fight against men who mean it. You're using a wooden sword. How much damage could you do?'

'You're telling me you want me to fight as hard as I can? Without quarter?'

'Exactly,' said Crutch.

Damen smiled. 'Okay,' he said.

The next day, an hour before dawn, they started again. The first squad of soldiers tried using shields to stop the wooden poles Boulder threw.

The problem was Boulder threw from high enough that they had to hold their shields up high, which took quite some strength. And Boulder threw hard enough that holding the shield to hold back one of his throws while standing and moving forward was beyond the strength of most men.

One squad tried kneeling so they could prop the shields on the deck and cower behind them. That didn't work. Boulder was able to throw at them from above as soon as they got close to the tower.

To make it even more difficult, when they got closer, Damen came down from the tower and engaged them. They had to choose between trying to fight a master swordsman kneeling or standing and having Boulder's poles smacking into them.

Damen was merciless whenever he got anywhere near a soldier, creating openings and swinging hard with his wooden sword. The soldiers who fought him limped away or had to be dragged away.

'Don't expect your enemy to die for you,' yelled Crutch. 'Expect them to innovate and adapt too. The only way you stay alive is by anticipating their next move or by adapting to their next move fast.'

Another squad tried forming a shield cocoon with shields over their heads. They didn't have the strength to hold the shields up when one of Boulder's throws hit them.

'You'll have to do better than that,' yelled Crutch. Crutch knew variations of using shields was not going to be enough to disable the ballistas in Teevilgrad. Squad after squad threw themselves against the tower with Boulder throwing poles, Longshot shooting arrows with the arrow heads removed, Quicksilver dropping rocks on them, and Damen hitting anyone in range with his wooden sword. Not a single squad got a man to the top of the tower. Most never got on the tower.

Crutch imagined what the carnage would be like when the Estovians used real weapons in Teevilgrad. He began to wonder if anyone would come up with an original solution when Captain Travis and his squad took a turn.

Captain Travis had been a corporal on the Kona track with the first reserve. This might be interesting. When the squad formed up with a shield wall, Crutch was disappointed. But when one of the men started swinging a sling around his head behind the shield wall, his interest perked up. What where they planning on doing?

The soldiers moved forward fast to get the slingman in range and waited until immediately after Boulder had thrown one of his poles at them, the force knocking one soldier back two feet. The other soldiers opened up a gap in the shield wall, and the slingman let loose with a perfect shot that hit Boulder in the face.

'Shit,' said Boulder, wiping his eyes.

The next throw was at Longshot, another perfect shot that hit him in the face.

'That's disgusting,' said Longshot, wiping his eyes too.

Crutch could smell it. That familiar smell from the cargo hold where he worked with Cedric years ago. Pig shit. They were throwing pig shit. Nice!

But they still had to deal with Quicksilver dropping rocks on them and Damen hacking at them with his wooden sword. For the first time since they started this training, Crutch was eager to see what devious plan Captain Travis and his squad had devised.

When Damen came down the tower to meet the squad, six men with shields and spears peeled off and surrounded him, keeping their distance. The other men got to the wall and spread out, throwing grappling hooks up to the top. Six grappling hooks all coming from different directions.

Crutch worked out Captain Travis's strategy now. He'd correctly surmised there was no way up that tower to the ballista without losing some soldiers, so his plan was to attack from as many directions as possible and overwhelm the defenders. This might not even work with just one squad, but with two or three, getting control of the ballista was inevitable.

Boulder threw poles at the soldiers surrounding Damen. Surrounding him meant some had their backs exposed to the tower. That was something Captain Travis would need to work out a solution to.

Damen hacked and prodded his way through the spearmen, but not fast enough, and an ordinary Estovian soldier would be dead trying to fight six spearmen with shields at the same time. Even three or four Estovian soldiers would struggle.

Longshot fired his wooden arrows at every soldier he could, and Quicksilver pulled off grappling hooks and dropped rocks on them, but they couldn't defend every part of the tower with six men coming up. Three made it to the top of the tower and drew their practice swords.

On the deck, Damen was down to the last two spearmen. They wouldn't last long, but distracting Damen gave Captain Travis's soldiers the chance they needed to get up the tower.

Quicksilver engaged one soldier in swordplay, while Boulder used a pole to swing and knock the other two off the tower. Crutch smiled when he realised the last soldier on the tower was Captain Travis. Damen belted the last spearman on the deck with his wooden sword. He could let Boulder, Quicksilver and Longshot belt the hell out of Captain Travis but their tiwi bird friend from the Kona track didn't need a lesson like the other soldiers did.

'That's enough. Nice try,' yelled Crutch. 'Still dead, but nice try. With more soldiers, that would've worked. Unlike the rest of you sorry lot, who seem determined to meet your deaths at Teevilgrad. Innovate and adapt. This is not a game. If you don't overcome the ballistas in Teevilgrad, every one of you will be dead.'

'You heard the colonel,' yelled Sergeant Zander. 'Innovate or die. Next squad.'

Chapter 26
Force Of Numbers

Later in the galley, eating their evening meal, Captain Travis sat with the marines.

'The pig shit was a nice touch,' said Crutch.

'Thank you, colonel,' said Captain Travis. 'I really thought through this one, and I can't see a way of taking those ballistas without losing soldiers.'

'I don't think there is one,' said Crutch. 'We'll be the first Ironborn on the docks, and that means many of our men will be the first to die.'

'Then we have to win,' said Captain Travis. 'I can't let my men die for nothing.'

'You've got all the soldiers thinking now at least,' said Sergeant Zander. 'Now they can see if they use their imaginations, they can come up with something that gives them a chance.'

'Taking the ballistas and the docks is just the first step,' said Crutch. 'After that, we have to get through the city wall or the city gates.'

'Fire,' said Quicksilver.

'Yes, that might do it,' said Crutch. 'But we have to expect they'll be prepared for us with soldiers on the wall. Getting the fire where we need it could be a challenge.'

'Also, we need a path wide enough that thousands of our soldiers can travel through it without getting killed,' said Sergeant Zander. 'Fire might clear a path, but getting through it safely might not be so easy.'

'I say we just set the whole city on fire and watch it burn,' said Quicksilver.

'If we thought that would work, we'd do it,' said Crutch. 'The problem is, Emperor Solokov will be somewhere safe, waiting us out with his best troops. This war won't end until Igor is dead.'

'Get me close enough, and I'll set him on fire too,' said Quicksilver.

They all laughed.

'Getting through the city to the palace will be a bitch,' said Sergeant Zander. 'Solokov will make sure he's got troops and probably civilians to make that journey as unpleasant as possible.'

'You're right,' said Crutch. 'Solokov will be hoping the people in Teevilgrad will make us fight for every inch.'

'Hoping?' said Captain Travis.

'We spent quite a bit of time in Teevilgrad,' said Crutch. 'Most of the Estovians there don't think too highly of their emperor.'

'They'll still fight to stop Ironborn troops taking over their city, though,' said Sergeant Zander.

'Unless we can convince them it's Solokov we want, not Teevilgrad,' said Crutch.

'That's not gonna be easy when we start killing their soldiers and landing thousands of troops on their docks,' said Captain Travis.

'No, it's not,' said Crutch. 'It might be worth a shot, though.' Crutch didn't mention that he had brought face paint with him and clothing to disguise himself as Crujge, the old Estovian merchant. He brought Estovian clothes for Boulder too. Hope is never enough. You need to plan.

'Do you think General Talbot will let us sneak into Teevilgrad in disguise?' said Sergeant Zander.

'I think the general would let us do almost anything if it would save lives,' said Crutch. 'I'm just not sure we could pull it off.'

'It's a nice dream, though,' said Sergeant Zander. 'Imagine if we could get the true compatriots to rise up against Solokov and help us take the palace.

'The true compatriots?' said Captain Travis.

'They're a group of Estovians who want an end to Solokov's rule and to war with Ironbay. Led by Anton Ivenko, if he's still alive.

They're good people, and many of them are soldiers, or komitav, their secret police. They can fight.'

'I'm trying to work out how you got so familiar with the people of Teevilgrad?' said Captain Travis.

'We lived there,' said Sergeant Zander.

'It's amazing what a good disguise can do,' said Crutch.

'I'm a pumpkin,' said Boulder, grinning.

'Boulder went into Teevilgrad disguised as a pumpkin?' said Captain Travis.

'Kind of,' said Crutch.

'It's nice to dream about it,' said Sergeant Zander, 'but I think the reality is, we'll have to take Teevilgrad head-on and overwhelm them with force of numbers. The true compatriots still love their country and their city. I can't see them coming to our side.'

'Seems a shame to send good men in to die, though,' said Captain Travis. 'A lot of these soldiers are just boys.'

'Just like the Kona track,' said Crutch, talking about it but trying to push down the memories of bloodshed there. 'On that topic, how is your boy, and your wife, Tilly, Captain Travis?'

Chapter 27
Fire Is Always The Answer

As the fleet got close to Teevilgrad, the lookout spotted a ship near the horizon.

'Estovian ship,' yelled the lookout. A deckhand rang the ship's bell, bringing Crutch and the marines onto deck.

'Head for that ship,' said Cedric from the bridge.

They chased the ship, but it turned tail as soon as they saw it.

'They know we're coming now,' said Sergeant Zander.

'They've most likely known for weeks,' said Cedric. 'Spies in Ironbay would have warned them about our fleet build up.'

'Funding the true royals and burning Saldoria were all strategies designed to slow us down,' said Crutch. 'They've been expecting an invasion for months, probably since we left with parts of Teevilgrad burning.'

Crutch knew he was right. What he didn't anticipate was the scale of the preparations. When Teevilgrad finally came into view, the harbour was guarded by every ship the Estovians could muster.

There were at least a dozen warships. They'd mounted ballistas on merchant ships. Through an eyeglass, Crutch could see longboats near the docks of Teevilgrad with ballistas. On the roofs of buildings just behind the docks, they'd mounted more ballistas.

'Looks like they're not giving up easily,' said Crutch, handing the eyeglass to Sergeant Zander.

'Invading was always gonna be a bloodbath,' said Sergeant Zander.

'There's another problem,' said Cedric. 'I hoped we'd meet their warships out in the harbour. That way, we could break their line and stop them from defending their docks.'

'But now they're all anchored at the docks, ballistas pointing straight at us,' said Crutch.

'Yes,' said Cedric. 'They've expected an invasion, and they're using their ships as an extra line of fixed defences to stop us.'

'So we have to disable the ballistas on the ships before we can even get to the ballistas on the docks,' said Crutch.

'And having those warships anchored at the docks means we can't dock easily ourselves. We have to anchor against one of their ships.'

'That means we have to run our men across one of their ships to get to the docks,' said Sergeant Zander. 'And if I was an Estovian, I'd have my best men waiting in the hold away from the fire of arrows and ballista bolts.'

'And come out as soon as we try to run across,' said Crutch.

'Exactly,' said Sergeant Zander.

'I say we should just burn the lot of 'em,' said Quicksilver.

'Just let me at them,' said Damen. 'I'll cut every one of them to pieces.'

'I admire your enthusiasm,' said Crutch, 'but a ballista bolt will kill you just as dead as anyone else. And even you won't survive being surrounded by a hundred Estovian soldiers.'

'I'd like to give it a try,' said Damen.

'You will not,' said Cedric. 'That's a direct order from your ship's captain.'

'We need a plan,' said Sergeant Zander.

'Our fleet commander won't bother trying to starve out the city,' said Cedric. 'After your adventure into Teevilgrad we know that Solokov is perfectly happy to let his people starve.'

'Fire is the answer,' said Quicksilver.

'How will fire help us take control of the docks and land all our troops?' said Crutch.

'In my experience, it doesn't matter what the question is; fire is always the answer,' said Quicksilver. 'I have sacks full of bluefire with me.'

'We can't risk setting the docks on fire,' said Sergeant Zander. 'If they're destroyed, we'd have to get our troops to shore on longboats. That would be carnage. They'd pick us off with their bowmen and their ballistas while we're in the water.'

'Can't we burn them just a little bit?' said Quicksilver, disappointed.

'No. Not even a little bit,' said Sergeant Zander.

'So they'll have their soldiers waiting in the holds of the warships?' said Crutch.

'Enough to make using them as a way to the docks a bloodbath.'

'How deep do you think the water around the docks is?' said Crutch.

'Shallow,' said Sergeant Zander. 'Deep enough for a warship at low tide, but not much more than that.'

'Cedric, could you send up the signal flags?' said Crutch. 'Let General Talbot know we need to talk to him.'

'Will do, colonel,' said Cedric.

Chapter 28
Fire Is Still The Answer

The Auld Faithful was on the far left side of the fleet. Their plan started on the far right.

Two longboats with sails raised set out from the Ironborn ships there, heading straight for the docks. Ship's bells rang from the Estovian ships on the docks, and men swarmed the decks manning the ballistas.

As soon as the longboats were in range, the ballistas on the ships rained bolts down on them. The longboats kept moving towards the docks, and the closest burst into flame. Blue flame.

'Nice work, Quicksilver,' said Crutch as the marines held on to the climbing ropes of the Auld Faithful, their bodies submerged in water up to their necks.

The second longboat burst into flames too.

'Nothing I love more than a nice fire in the evening,' said Quicksilver, smiling.

The fire from the ballistas on the Estovian ships intensified. They aimed for the sails and the masts of the longboats. One ballista scored a direct hit on a longboat mast. It shattered the mast in two in a shower of splinters that immediately caught fire. The sail fell into the hull of the longboat and caught fire too.

With one longboat disabled, the gunners on the ships directed their ballista fire at the longboat still sailing. In a terrifying hail of ballista bolts, the longboat's sail and rigging were ripped to shreds, falling into the hull in pieces and bursting into flames.

The Ironborn ships launched two more longboats from the right side of the fleet. They sailed towards the docks, the gunners on the Estovian ships waiting for them to get in range.

'How long do you think it will take them to work out there are no sailors on those longboats and this is a distraction?' said Longshot.

'We have another dozen of those longboats set to launch,' said Crutch. 'That will keep the Estovians occupied for a while. But we have a lot of swimming to do. Let's go.'

The marines split into three groups, two men each. Boulder was with Crutch. Each of them targeted one Estovian ship. As they got closer, Crutch and Boulder dove underwater until they were at the hull of the Estovian ship at the docks. From right in next to the hull, the Estovian crew wouldn't be able to see them from the deck.

Or at least, they wouldn't be able to see them unless they looked for them. On the other side of the harbour, more longboats sailed towards the docks; more were shredded by the Estovian ballistas. Crutch could hear the ballistas on the ship above them firing.

Cedric had taken Crutch aside before he went over the railing of the Auld Faithful.

'You're a colonel now,' said Cedric. 'You should be ordering your men to do this, not doing it yourself.'

'If this goes bad, I don't want the blood of good men on my hands,' said Crutch.

Crutch was lying. He just wanted the chance to kill somebody, and right now he was so angry he didn't care if he died.

Boulder and Crutch went along the hull, attaching blue fire balls just below the water with Quicksilver's sticky black goo. Crutch had remembered when they were chased from Yavenland that bluefire burned underwater.

He hoped it would burn hot enough to go through the hulls of these Estovian ships. Quicksilver told Crutch it would, but Quicksilver would say anything to get a chance to set things on fire.

Quicksilver had set the timers to go four minutes after they were placed, which should mean Crutch and the marines would be almost back to the Auld Faithful before they went off. Crutch and Boulder surfaced close to the hull, hopefully still concealed from the crew above. If the crew on another ship looked over, they could be in trouble.

Crutch heard voices from right above him, but he couldn't make out what they were saying. Had someone seen them? Had they seen marines under the hulls of the other Estovian ships? He didn't know, but with the bluefire balls placed, it was time to go.

He signalled to Boulder to dive under and head back to the Auld Faithful. Crutch took a couple of deep breaths, then went as deep under the water as he could. He swam till his lungs burned, then he swam some more. The further he could get away from the Estovian ship before surfacing, the better the chances of getting away unseen.

Finally, he came up, took a breath, then dived under again and swum as hard as his arms and legs would push him through the water.

When he was forced to come up the next time, he could hear shouting on the Estovian ships. He looked to his left and saw Quicksilver surface and a ballista bolt whizzing through the air right at him. Quicksilver dove under with the ballista bolt splashing in the water where he went down. Crutch didn't know if the Estovians had hit him, but he knew if he hung around to find out, he'd be next.

He dove under again, and a ballista bolt splashed in the water by his head, grazing his cheek as it went past. He dove deeper and swam as hard as he could. His lungs burned, his arms and legs burned, but he kept swimming.

He swum until he was about to pass out from the lack of air, then he came up to the surface of the water. He could see the Auld Faithful in front of him, just a hundred yards away. But if he was a hundred yards away, that meant he was still in range of the Estovian ballistas.

Getting to the Auld Faithful was his salvation. Where he was now was certain death. He saw Boulder surface thirty yards in front of him and look back. Crutch waved him to go on to the Auld Faithful.

'Keep going!' he yelled, and Boulder submerged just before a ballista bolt splashed near his legs. Crutch dove under again as ballista bolts splashed in the water around him.

Somehow he kept going, forcing his legs and arms to move when they were on fire with the pain. He had to hold his breath and stay underwater when every fibre in his being wanted him to surface and gulp in air.

He swam until he couldn't take it any longer and surfaced. Fifty yards to the Auld Faithful. A ballista bolt splashed just behind him. Was he out of range? He didn't wait to find out. He dove under the water and swam again, exhausted but scared enough to keep going.

When he came up, he was just ten yards from the Auld Faithful, and Boulder was there waiting for him.

'Are you okay, Crutch?' said Boulder. 'You're bleeding.'

'It's just a tiny cut,' said Crutch, feeling his face. 'Did they get you?'

'No,' said Boulder.

'Nice night for a swim,' said Sergeant Zander from behind them. Behind him were Damen, Longshot, and Quicksilver.

'Are you okay, Quicksilver?' said Crutch. 'I saw a ballista bolt fired at you.'

'Got a cut on my leg,' said Quicksilver as they all swam to the climbing ropes on the side of the hull. 'Let's get on board so we can see the fun.'

The Auld Faithful crew and the soldiers cheered the marines as they climbed back on board. As Crutch got to the deck and looked back to the docks, he could see why. Below the water line of all three ships was a blue glow, and smoke was pouring out of their hatches. The bluefire was working.

'Isn't it beautiful?' said Quicksilver, smiling.

'It sure is,' said Sergeant Zander.

All three ships started sinking into the water. Estovian soldiers swarmed onto the deck to escape.

'Can you get our ballistas in range?' said Crutch to Cedric.

'I can colonel,' said Cedric.

'Do it,' said Crutch. 'We don't want any of those Estovians alive when we start taking the docks.

Cedric moved the Auld Faithful closer, while Crutch waved to the Ironborn ships nearby to follow their lead.

'Fire as soon as you're in range!' yelled Crutch to the men manning the ballistas.

The first ballista bolts rained down on the sinking Estovian ships, creating carnage on the decks. A handful of brave Estovians tried to stay and man the ballistas on the sinking ships.

'Take out those ballistas,' yelled Crutch when the first ballista bolt was fired on the Auld Faithful.

One Estovian on a ballista was skewered on a ballista bolt and flung all the way to the docks when a shot from the Auld Faithful hit him. More ballista bolts hit the Estovian soldiers on the deck, now wading through water up to their knees as they tried to flee. The Auld Faithful and the other Ironborn ships that could get in range rained ballista bolts down on them. Some hit, some stuck in the deck, the mast, or went short into the hull.

'Pick your targets,' yelled Sergeant Zander. 'Make every shot count. Every Estovian we kill now is one less we have to fight when we land.'

The first Estovians off the ship started making it to the docks, out of the range of their ballistas. Dozens of them, running for their lives, dripping with water and blood from wading across a deck underwater, filled with corpses of their compatriots.

Longshot was up in the rigging, firing arrows. Only Longshot could fire an arrow at that distance. Every ten or fifteen seconds, another arrow would sail across and bury itself into an unfortunate Estovian. From above him, Crutch could hear Longshot yell.

'That one's for Zanithburg, you Estovian bastards. That's for Quicksilver's ear. That's for Benn.'

Sergeant Zander came to Crutch.

'If we're gonna invade, we need to do it sooner rather than later,' he said. 'We don't want to give them time to regroup and add more hazards or bring more soldiers to the docks.'

'We'll go as soon as they clear the ships of Estovians,' said Crutch. Cedric, who stood close enough to hear, nodded his head.

'Soldiers, prepare to land!' yelled Crutch. 'Cedric, could you raise the flag? Let the other ships know the time has come.'

'Yes colonel,' said Cedric, and relayed the orders.

Chapter 29
If You Stop You Die

A buzz went through the soldiers as they checked their shields, their helmets, and their weapons. Captain Travis went from man to man, talking to them.

'When you get on the docks, don't stop for anything,' he said. 'Keep going forward and get to those ballistas. You won't be able to see. Just keep going away from the water.'

Crutch looked down the line of ships. The sight of so many ships, bristling with soldiers and weapons, was breathtaking.

The Auld Faithful and five more ships full of soldiers would land first. They'd have to dock alongside the three half-sunk Estovian ships, run across their half-submerged decks, then over the docks, and climb up to the ballistas on top of the buildings. With Estovian ballistas and bowmen firing on them every inch of the way.

But they did have plans to make the invasion of the docks a little less deadly. Every Ironborn soldier they saved was one more to help get through the city walls and into Emperor Solokov's palace.

The Auld Faithful was the first ship to get within range of the Estovian ballistas on the docks. Bolts started hitting the hull and the deck of the ship, and the gunners on the Auld Faithful returned fire the best they could.

Crutch saw one Ironborn soldier take a ballista bolt through the chest, just thirty feet from where he stood. The man flung backwards and toppled three soldiers behind him. He lay there on the deck of the Auld Faithful as the soldiers got out from under him. He was already dead.

Better that way, thought Crutch. If he was still alive, he'd be groaning in pain and he'd die anyway. It was a mercy that it was over in an instant for him.

Quicksilver and Longshot crouched low behind shieldmen near the bow of the Auld Faithful, waiting to get in range with a slingshot.

Crutch waited until they were close enough that they couldn't miss, then yelled, 'Slings away.'

Quicksilver handed Longshot a ball of shitfire. Longshot put it into his sling, stood, and let it loose, landing a perfect shot on the half-sunk Estovian ship at the docks. Other slingman on the Auld Faithful and the five other Ironborn ships sailing for the docks started hurling shitfire too, and in a few seconds, brown smoke billowed from the half-sunk ships and the docks.

Initially, Cedric had been angry with Quicksilver that he'd hidden a good portion of the glowstone they'd stolen from the vault in Teevilgrad right on the Auld Faithful. They'd had it with them, sailing all the way to Yavenland and back, through the wild storms and the wild weather.

Cedric told him it was a miracle they were alive. But he'd relented a little when they realised just how useful the glowstone could be if they used it to make shitfire so they could fill the docks with brown smoke.

The biggest problem now with so many balls of shitfire thrown on the docks was they couldn't see where they were headed. Cedric told them any sailor worth his salt could make a heading and turn at the right time when they saw the top of the ship's mast at the docks.

The Estovian gunners were obviously using the top of the mast of the Auld Faithful to aim because ballista bolts kept raining down on her. But it was obvious they fired blind. None of the bolts hit the crew on the deck.

Crutch saw the mast of the half-sunk ship. This would be a tight squeeze, having to share space next to the Estovian ship with another Ironborn ship.

'Prepare to board,' yelled Crutch as Cedric swung the Auld Faithful around in a perfect arc. Crutch could hear the hull of the Auld Faithful kissing the hull of the sunken Estovian ship.

The other Ironborn ship didn't come in so clean. It scraped along the bow of the Auld Faithful's hull, then slammed into the submerged hull of the Estovian ship. Crutch could hear Cedric cursing under his breath.

The crew of the Auld Faithful threw their grappling hooks onto any part of the Estovian ship they could. The rails of the Estovian ship were about three feet lower than those of the Auld Faithful. Their soldiers would have to jump or climb down. The crew had climbing ropes ready for them.

'Get your arses onto that ship, then onto the docks,' yelled Crutch.

'You heard the Colonel,' yelled Captain Travis. 'Go, go go!'

'If you stop, you die,' yelled Sergeant Zander from next to Crutch. 'Get your arses moving and keep 'em moving. Don't stop for anything.'

The smoke was thick here, and it stank. It stung Crutch's eyes and made it hard to see, but he could make out the crew in the Ironborn ship next to them pulling around the ship with grappling hooks to get it alongside the sunken Estovian ship. He saw one crew member on that ship take a ballista bolt to the head. The bolt exploded his head into a spray that flew across the ship and onto the soldiers behind him. The rest of his body flopped to the deck, the rope from the grappling hook slipping from his hand and pulled over the railing.

Crutch blocked out any thoughts of compassion, any thoughts that the crewman was even a person. He went to that cold place inside him where there was only anger and hate. The time for killing had finally come. He'd waited the entire voyage from Ironbay for this, and now the time was here. His hands shook in a combination of fear and anticipation.

He'd read that despite the bloodshed, the horrors, and the death, retired soldiers missed the battle, and now he understood why. You're never so alive as when you're so close to death.

'Come back alive,' said Cedric.

Crutch looked at the worry on Cedric's face and nodded. But this was not the time for worry or second thoughts. It was time to throw your life over the side of the ship, like tossing a set of dice, and hope the fates fell your way.

Right behind him Boulder stood, carrying a huge shield. Boulder would be Crutch's shieldman for this invasion, putting himself in front of anyone or anything that tried to do Crutch harm.

On Crutch's other side was Damen, carrying a shield and a sword. Cedric had insisted Damen carry a shield, which was strange. Cedric had never given any input into how the marines fought before. But Damen was one of the marines, and Cedric was his captain, so he didn't argue about it.

The soldiers went over the rail and down the climbing ropes in rows. Ballista bolts and arrows came in at random. Steady, relentless, and deadly when they hit.

From the deck, Crutch saw one man shot through the back by a ballista bolt and pinned to the hull of the Auld Faithful. He hung there groaning until another soldier cut the bolt away, and he fell to the railing of the Estovian ship, snapping his back. His dead body hung with his legs crushed between the two ships, and his upper body submerged in the water.

When the soldiers stepped onto the deck of the Estovian ship, they sank almost to their waists in sea water that washed with the waves. The first lines of soldiers waded through the water fast, making it to the other railing. From that side, ballista bolts sailed over their heads.

If they stopped where they were, the soldiers coming behind would be trapped with ballista bolts and arrows raining on them. It was already a bloodbath, but stopping would make it a bloodbath that never ended. The only way to stop the arrows and the ballista bolts was to get across the docks and kill the Estovians firing at them.

'Keep moving!' yelled Crutch. 'Get onto those docks and up to those ballistas.'

'You heard the colonel,' yelled Captain Travis. 'Get your arses up onto the docks.

By standing on the ship's rail, the soldiers could then step up to the docks. The first soldier who stepped up took an arrow to the face and fell straight back down, landing on his back on the soldiers below him, covering them with his blood.

'Get onto the docks now!' yelled Sergeant Zander. 'The only way we stop those arrows is to kill the Estovians firing them!'

'Get up there and kill some Estovians,' yelled Captain Travis.

The soldiers roared and climbed. Brave men. Most of them about to die. Crutch knew those who died didn't matter. It was the soldiers who lived to kill Estovians who mattered. This was war at its most brutal and bloody. A battle of attrition, bringing an overwhelming force to bear on a well-entrenched and armed enemy.

Chapter 30
Nature's Way Of Telling You To Run Faster

An entire line of a dozen soldiers climbed to the docks at once, with more climbing up behind. About half of the first line made it three yards and were cut down in a hail of arrows and ballista bolts. Blood spilled over the docks and ran down onto the men still climbing.

Further down, Crutch could hear the soldiers on the ship next to them climbing and yelling, getting to the docks. And he could hear the arrows and the ballista bolts, hear bodies thumping onto the timber planks of the docks. More men dying. Would they have enough to get the job done?

Crutch and the marines moved close to the railing of the Auld Faithful, staying low with shields up. Soon it would be their turn to climb down, cross the Estovian ship, and get onto those docks, into that cauldron of blood and death.

The marines were the last line of the offence. If they failed, the entire invasion would have failed. They'd also be dead.

Crutch watched the last line of soldiers in front of them climb over the rail. The shooting of ballista bolts and arrows had slowed in here near the ship's railing. Soldiers must be getting closer to the buildings on the other side of the docks the Estovian ballistas were mounted on. They'd be making better targets for the Estovians.

The fog of brown smoke made it hard to see. It also stank and clawed at the back of Crutch's throat, making him feel like gagging.

It was hard to complain, though. Right now, that brown smoke was the only thing keeping them from being shot.

Crutch and the marines climbed over the rail of the Auld Faithful. Boulder was right next to Crutch, shield on his back, as he clambered down the side of the hull on the climbing ropes.

They got to the rail of the Estovian ship and stepped on and into the water on its deck. Crutch sank to his waist and realised the water was red with the blood of Ironborn soldiers. He was coating his body with the blood of his men.

They waded as fast as they could through the water. Boulder had his shield up in front of Crutch. Crutch had to peer around the side to see in front of him. Crutch was just thinking that being a colonel was a pain in the arse when a volley of arrows bounced off the metal shield. One of the soldiers in front of him took an arrow to the arm and to the chest and fell into the water.

Damen sheathed his sword and dragged the soldier up by the shirt. When the body came up lifeless, he dropped him back in the water and drew his sword again. They stepped up to the rail on the other side of the ship, then onto the docks, and into hell.

Crutch slipped on the blood as soon as he put a foot on the docks. Boulder caught him before he could fall. Through the brown fog of the shitfire, Crutch could see bodies everywhere. Men cut down by ballista bolts or arrows before they'd barely walked five yards.

Longshot counted under his breath as he moved forward. He stopped, Quicksilver handed him a ball of shitfire, and he set it loose, throwing it towards an Estovian ballista Crutch couldn't see. Then Quicksilver handed him another ball, and he swung his sling around his head and threw that one too.

'That should get both the ballistas closest to us,' he said. 'They'll be firing completely blind until we get to them.

'And rip their heads off,' said Damen.

Crutch could hear yelling ahead of them. That was a good sign. Someone was alive, alive and making a fight of it, hopefully.

As they moved, they saw more soldiers, some stunned from the shock of battle or unsure what to do. One soldier lay in front of them, shaking with fear. Lie there more than a couple of minutes, and he'd be a pin cushion for every arrow and ballista bolt that hit this part of the docks.

'Get on your feet!' yelled Sergeant Zander, pulling the soldier up by the back of his shirt. A soldier right next to both of them took an arrow to the throat and toppled onto the wooden planks of the dock.

'Arrows are nature's way of telling you to run faster,' yelled Sergeant Zander. 'Run!'

Crutch and the marines picked up the pace too. Crutch powered along with his walking cane and his good leg, Boulder at his side, keeping that shield up. This fifty yards was the killing zone, the easiest place for the ballistas and the bowmen to fire blindly and hit someone.

Crutch could hear arrows bouncing off Boulder's shield, then they stopped. In front of him was a building with ropes hanging from up above. The soldiers must have thrown grappling hooks to secure these.

'Up the ropes,' said Crutch to Boulder, who grabbed one rope while Crutch grabbed the rope next to him.

Crutch climbed the rope with both hands, his dagger in his teeth, and his walking cane in his belt. When he was halfway up, an Estovian soldier toppled past him, missing him by inches. After him came an Ironborn soldier. He glanced down and saw both their bodies smashed on the planks of the docks below him.

He kept climbing. He could hear voices from the roof of the building, yelling, fighting, screaming. Up there, men were fighting and dying. Hopefully, more Estovians were dying than Ironborn.

He got near the top of the rope and was about to throw his hand over the side of the roof when an Estovian appeared with an axe. The Estovian looked at Crutch, and looked at the rope he climbed, and swung down to cut the rope.

Normally, that would be the smart move if you're defending a roof. Cut the rope, and the enemy soldier falls to his death anyway, and you've destroyed one path the enemy has of getting to you. But in this case, it was the wrong move.

The Estovian looked down in surprise to see that Crutch had buried his dagger in the Estovian's foot and now used it to pull himself onto the roof.

The Estovian swung his axe again, but Crutch was too quick. He grabbed the Estovian's other ankle, pulled the dagger out of his foot, and drove it into his groin hard. The Estovian toppled over the edge of the roof, dragging Crutch over with him.

Chapter 31
Crazy Bastard Is My Middle Name

As he started to fall, Crutch pulled his dagger out of the Estovian's groin and rammed it into the wooden beam on the top of the roof. The Estovian fell off the roof but grabbed Crutch's weak leg as he went.

Another bad choice.

Crutch knew he could only hold the weight of both of them for a few seconds. He looked down at the Estovian clinging to his leg and bleeding from his groin. Crutch took aim and kicked him hard in the face with his good leg.

The first kick wasn't enough. The Estovian clung on tighter, drawing blood from Crutch where his nails dug into Crutch's ankle.

Crutch pulled his good leg back and kicked. Harder this time, using all the force he could muster. He landed a heavy blow with his heel to the Estovian's jaw. It was enough to stun him, and the Estovian fell, dropping to the planks of the docks below, joining the pile of dead and broken bodies there.

Crutch pulled himself up onto the roof. He barely got to his feet and drew his walking cane from his belt when another Estovian soldier came at him out of the brown smoke, swinging at him with a sword.

Crutch stepped to the side, then forward, turned as the Estovian passed, then pushed him as hard as he could. The Estovian turned back towards Crutch, then realised his mistake as he slipped off the side of the roof. He grabbed the beam Crutch was just on, his sword dropping to the docks below.

Crutch released the blade on his cane and drove it straight into the Estovian's face. This was no time for sentiment or mercy. The Estovian lost his grip on the beam, and he fell.

Crutch turned and tried to look through the brown smoke. Where were his men? Where was the ballista?

Boulder appeared out of the haze.

'Are you alright, Crutch?' he said. 'I couldn't find you in the smoke.'

'I'm fine, Boulder. Let's get the Estovians off this roof and take this ballista.'

'Okay, Crutch,' said Boulder, and put the shield in front of him, making it even harder to see.

Crutch recognised one voice out of the smoke, yelling orders. Captain Travis. He moved towards the voice, trying not to slip on the blood on the roof. As he did, a strong wind blew away the brown smoke.

The scene around him was carnage. He saw at least a dozen Ironborn men lying dead on the roof, cut with swords, punctured with spears, or poked through with arrows. The Estovian ballista was ahead of him, surrounded by ten Estovians wielding shields and spears. Inside the semi-circle were bowmen, shooting arrows between the heads of their compatriots.

Captain Travis commanded half a dozen of his own men who had shields and axes, swords, or spears. Not enough men to break the shield wall the Estovians had around the ballista. Every few seconds, the ballista fired off another bolt. It aimed to the left now, towards the Ironborn men who had landed in the ship next to the Auld Faithful.

As the brown smoke from the shitfire cleared, Crutch could see the carnage down there. Maybe thirty or forty Ironborn soldiers left, desperately slipping and running through the blood and guts of the fallen, trying to make it to the building next to them, to the ballista that kept firing at them. Two ballistas aimed at them, along with at least a half-dozen bowmen.

All of the soldiers from the Auld Faithful were dead or on the roof, fighting for their lives. Crutch needed an idea, and he needed it fast. They were outnumbered. If they took this ballista, they could turn it on the Estovians on the next roof. Then maybe those soldiers down there had a chance. If they couldn't take all three ballistas at this end of the docks, the invasion was over, and they'd all die.

Longshot and Damen appeared next to Crutch. Then Sergeant Zander and Quicksilver.

'We need to get control of that ballista now,' said Crutch.

'We can't go through that shield wall,' said Sergeant Zander.

'We go through the one place there are no shieldmen,' said Crutch.

'Right in front of the ballista,' said Sergeant Zander. 'You are one crazy bastard, colonel.'

'Crazy bastard is my middle name,' said Crutch.

Crutch and the marines moved fast, heading for the ballista. They couldn't give the Estovians a chance to realise what they were doing and adapt. Crutch heard at least half a dozen arrows bounce off Boulder's shield as they went.

To get to the front of the ballista and avoid the spearmen in the Estovian shield wall, they would have to stand right in front of it where the Estovian gunner could fire on them and tear them to pieces.

Crutch heard a massive clang as a bolt from the ballista hit Boulder's shield. It hit at an angle, and Boulder used his strength to deflect it, but the force at this range was so huge that Boulder went flying back. Back and over the edge of the roof.

Crutch didn't have time to look or worry about Boulder. He went forward, used his cane and his good leg, and jumped onto the ballista. A spearman to his left thrust at him with a spear that would have found his leg. But Damen had jumped with him and smashed the spear aside with his shield, then ran the Estovian through with his sword.

Crutch thrust the blade of his cane straight through the ballista gunner's face, moved forward, and jumped into the middle of the Estovians. Sergeant Zander was right behind him, sword out, slashing and thrusting.

Being attacked from inside their semi-circle of men threw the Estovians into chaos. From outside of them, Captain Travis and his men pressed their advantage, and the Estovian shield wall fell into disarray.

Crutch, Damen, and Sergeant Zander caught the first three Estovians by surprise, attacking them from behind. As the others turned to see what was happening, Captain Travis and his men took out another three from the front.

With only six men left and Ironborn on both sides of them, the Estovians did what any good Estovian would do. They fought valiantly to the death. Emperor Solokov would never forgive a soldier who failed to do his duty. It was fight to the death now or be tortured, then hanged by Solokov's thugs later.

It was brutal, unnecessary killing at its worst. Crutch took out two Estovians by stabbing them in the back with his cane when they were busy trying to defend themselves against Captain Travis's men. The rest fell quickly, and the roof was clear of live Estovians, but this part of the battle was far from over.

'I can't hold on much longer,' said a voice from over the edge of the roof. Boulder!

Crutch and Sergeant Zander ran to the roof's edge and looked over. There was Boulder clinging on, his arms trembling with fatigue. Damen came to the edge and helped Sergeant Zander pull him up.

'I knew you'd save me,' said Boulder, smiling.

'Good work, Boulder,' said Crutch, then turned back to the men around the ballista. 'Man that ballista and fire on the Estovians on the next roof,' yelled Crutch.

There were still around twenty Ironborn troops trying to make it to the next building, with arrows and ballista bolts raining around them and into them. When the Ironborn gunner opened up from their roof, the Estovian shieldmen tried to protect their gunner. The first bolt went straight through a shield, into the Estovian holding it, and flew him straight off the other side of the building.

'Longshot,' said Crutch. 'Shoot at their gunner. Boulder, are you up to throwing a spear?'

'Yes, Crutch,' said Boulder.

'Pick up the spears lying on the roof here and take out some of those Estovian shieldmen,' said Crutch.

'Okay.'

Boulder picked up a spear and took out a shieldman with his first throw. A brutal, spinning throw that went into the leg of a shieldman who had his shield up high, trying to keep arrows away from the gunner on the ballista behind him.

As he fell, Longshot used the gap he left to fire an arrow into the head of the gunner on the ballista. The Estovian shields closed again, and another Estovian took over, firing the ballista. This gunner was smart enough to see the immediate threat and turned his ballista towards their roof. Their bowmen did the same.

'Shields!' yelled Crutch.

But shields wouldn't stop a ballista bolt. The first Estovian bolt went straight through the shield of one of Captain Travis's men and knocked him back off the roof. Crutch could hear the sickening thud as he hit the planks of the docks below them.

The ballista aimed straight at Crutch, loaded and ready to fire, when Longshot put an arrow straight through the gunner's face.

Distracting the Estovians on the next roof had worked. Ironborn men had climbed up the other side and now came on to the roof of the building next to them and attacked the shield men from behind the ballista.

Boulder and Longshot wreaked havoc on the shieldmen, who had to decide between protecting themselves from the arrows and spears or from the Ironborn troops now on the roof behind them. They put up a good fight, but the end was inevitable.

'Get a ladder across so we can get to that building,' yelled Crutch. Captain Travis and one of his men found the Estovian's ladder used for getting up to the roof and laid it down to make a bridge to the next building so they could run to the second ballista. Crutch was the first to go across, crawling fast on his hands and knees clinging to the sides of the ladder.

Once he got to the second ballista, Crutch looked over to the third building and the third ballista. It was slaughter for the Ironborn troops there. The two ships that landed further up the docks to take that ballista must have come under heavy fire from the Estovian ships further along. The sails of the Ironborn ships were ripped to shreds, and the decks of the two ships were littered with Ironborn soldiers and blood.

Before General Talbot sent in more ships filled with soldiers, their first invasion had to secure the first three Estovian ballistas on the docks. That would prevent the Estovians firing freely on the Ironborn troops as they landed. Right now, the troops who were tasked to capture that third ballista hadn't even made it past the first twenty yards of the docks.

The handful of them still alive cowered in whatever cover they could find on the half-sunk Estovian ship.

'Get a gunner on that ballista,' yelled Crutch. 'Aim for the next ballista. We need to give our men a chance.'

The third ballista was still fully manned with at least a dozen Estovian shieldmen, bowmen, and swordsmen. And they could fire at Crutch and his men without worrying about hitting their compatriots.

The first ballista bolt came in and missed Crutch by inches, burying itself in the roof to his right. An Ironborn gunner got to the ballista on Crutch's left and was immediately shot through the head with an Estovian ballista bolt. Arrows rained down from the Estovian bowmen. Boulder was at Crutch's side with his shield, and deflected two arrows coming straight at him.

Crutch needed to do something, or they'd all die right here on this roof. It was obvious the Estovians wouldn't let them take that third ballista and with another ballista behind it, taking it would mean putting the forty men he had left in the way of yet another barrage of ballista fire.

CHAPTER 32
DOES A CROCODILE SHIT IN THE WATER?

He needed to get that third ballista clear so General Talbot could land the rest of the army and overwhelm the Estovians on the docks with numbers. But he didn't have the men to do it.

'Quicksilver,' yelled Crutch. 'Did you bring any bluefire with you?'

'Does a crocodile shit in the water?' said Quicksilver, coming to Crutch's side looking way too happy for someone in deadly combat.

'How do you feel about setting those Estovians on fire?' said Crutch.

'I feel really good about it,' said Quicksilver. 'I can set the whole docks on fire if you want.'

'Get Longshot to throw some bluefire onto those shieldmen and that ballista. We want them to burn, but we don't want a fire so big we can't put it out.'

'Yes, colonel,' said Quicksilver with a maniacal grin. 'We'll burn 'em real good.'

'A fire we can put out,' said Crutch.

'You know you're taking all the fun out of this,' said Quicksilver, handing a ball of bluefire to Longshot, who had his sling out and was ready to use it.

General Talbot wanted all the ballistas intact so they could use them to defend the docks from an Estovian counterattack or an attack from sea, but Crutch couldn't see any other way to take that third ballista.

Longshot landed the first ball of bluefire right on top of the ballista. The bluefire went off immediately, setting the ballista and its gunner alight. Longshot landed the next ball of bluefire at the feet of three Estovian shieldmen who tried to run but were too slow. The bluefire set them alight too.

'Captain Travis, I want you to get ladders over to that building. We need to take out the rest of those Estovians and get that fire out.'

'Yes, colonel,' said Captain Travis, then barked out the orders to his men.

This was far from over. Once they got onto the next building Estovian ballistas would fire on them from the next building and from the Estovian ship at the docks. Crutch looked behind them and saw the Auld Faithful pull out of the docks, with three more Ironborn warships coming in formation from the fleet.

The Auld Faithful moving would make room at the docks for ships full of soldiers, landing and unloading one at a time. The Auld Faithful and the three Ironborn ships headed for the next Estovian ship at the docks. They fired as soon as they were in range, with the Estovians firing back.

With the Estovian ship completely occupied taking fire from four Ironborn ships, it would be unable to fire on the building Crutch's men needed to take. Captain Travis's men threw ladders over the gap between the buildings. The Estovians still alive fired on them with arrows, but most of those were deflected with shields.

One Ironborn soldier took an arrow to his shoulder as he crawled across a ladder. He clutched the arrow with one hand, then toppled off the ladder, dropping to the docks below with a sickening thud.

'Don't crawl!' yelled Captain Travis. 'Run across those ladders with your shields up.'

Behind them, Crutch could see the first Ironborn ship full of men docking. Soldiers poured out of the ship, General Talbot among them, yelling orders.

Most of Captain Travis's men were over, fighting what was left of the Estovians next to their burning ballista. Half of their men burning left them in disarray. Ironborn soldiers cut them down or pushed them off the roof one by one.

General Talbot was already near the walls of the building below Crutch.

'Good work, Colonel Crutch,' he yelled from below.

'Thank you, general. We need some buckets, sir. Had to use fire to take that last ballista.'

'Buckets!' yelled General Talbot.

'After we take this fourth ballista, we can let the ships take out the ballistas on the buildings one at a time now they can sail in formation,' yelled Crutch. 'Then you can take your men in and clean up any Estovians still alive.'

'That's why I made you colonel,' yelled General Talbot. 'You're always thinking.' General Talbot turned to a squad forming up behind him. 'Who wants to take that fourth ballista?' he yelled.

'My men are ready,' said a young officer. Crutch recognized the voice. Young Lord Talbot.

'Then do what you trained to do,' yelled General Talbot.

'Look at that,' said Longshot as Young Lord Talbot's men sprinted at full speed in perfect formation with their shields up.

'I've never seen that done before,' said Sergeant Zander. 'He must have trained the hell out of them to get them up to that speed.'

'Longshot, start firing on that fourth ballista,' said Crutch. 'Boulder, start throwing spears at any of those Estovian soldiers who think about firing on Young Lord Talbot's men. Captain Travis, get your men to fire on the Estovians on the fourth ballista. Spears, arrows, rocks, whatever they've got. Let's give 'em something to think about.'

'Yes, colonel,' said Captain Travis.

Young Lord Talbot's men reached the building the fourth ballista was on in less than thirty seconds. The sheer speed meant the Estovians barely had time to shoot at them. Young Lord Talbot's men re-slung their shields over their heads so their hands were free.

'They made some kind of special harness so they can climb with their hands free while their shields protect them,' said Damen.

'Clever,' said Sergeant Zander. 'Why didn't we think of that.'

As their shield men climbed up the building, Young Lord Talbot and two other men crept along the wall. The only way they could be seen by the Estovians at the top of the building was if they leaned well over the edge to look down.

No soldier would expose himself to enemy fire like that.

Young Lord Talbot and the other two soldiers with him crept to the opposite side of the building his squad had climbed then they started climbing themselves.

'How did they get so fast?' said Damen.

It was like they ran up the side of the building; they were so quick.

'That's what good training does,' said Sergeant Zander.

As the main squad climbed over the edge of the building, re-slung their shields, and engaged the Estovians, Young Lord Talbot and his two men were already coming over the other side of the building. The Estovians didn't even know they were there.

Young Lord Talbot and his two men cut down three Estovians from behind with their swords. Then his two men picked up their shields and spears, and all three of them drove straight for the ballista where its gunner was still pointed in the other direction.

Before the two shieldmen near the rear of the ballista could even turn, Young Lord Talbot's men ran them through with spears. Young Lord Talbot stepped between them and thrust his sword into the gunner's back.

One of Young Lord Talbot's men dropped his shield and manned the ballista, firing the first bolt into the Estovians in front of the ballista. He took out two of the Estovians with his first shot.

Young Lord Talbot and his other man attacked the Estovians who were left from behind the ballista, while the rest of his squad attacked them from the front.

Being attacked from the front and the rear, the Estovians fell fast, and as soon as they were down Young Lord Talbot ordered them to form a shield wall and to start firing at the ballista on the next tower. There was no pause to celebrate their victory; not a second wasted.

This was highly trained, efficient killing at its best. Or its worst, depending on how you looked at it.

'I've never seen anything like it,' said Damen.

'That's our boy,' said Sergeant Zander, brimming with pride.

'You trained him?' said Damen.

'Taught him how to fight,' said Sergeant Zander.

'We all did,' said Longshot.

'And how to climb,' said Quicksilver.

'And how to break off fingers,' said Boulder, grinning.

From the ground, General Talbot ordered a squad to take the next ballista. They seemed so slow compared to Young Lord Talbot's squad, but their speed didn't turn out to be an issue.

'They've broken,' said Sergeant Zander.

He was right. The Estovians on the next tower ran to their ladder, threw it down, and started climbing. Some didn't wait for the ladder. They went straight over the edge and climbed down without it.

Crutch looked further along the docks to the other buildings with ballistas. The Estovians were leaving those too. But they were doing it in an orderly fashion. There was no panic, no fear.

'Not broken,' said Crutch. 'Someone has ordered them to retreat.'

Sergeant Zander looked up to the other ballistas and immediately saw what Crutch had seen.

'You're right,' he said.

'If they're retreating, they'll have something planned for us that's much worse than those ballistas,' said Crutch.

'Right again, colonel,' said Sergeant Zander.

The Ironborn soldiers on the docks below them cheered as the Estovians made their orderly retreat. Crutch and the marines stood and watched in silence. They all knew the real fight for Teevilgrad had barely begun.

Chapter 33
The Next Man Will Be Hanged

Crutch and the marines came down from the building the ballista was on and joined General Talbot and the troops on the docks. The troops formed up with shieldmen at the front and marched for the city gates.

'Do you have any idea what the Estovians have waiting for us at the gates?' said General Talbot.

'None,' said Crutch. 'But whatever it is, I know we won't like it.'

When they got within sight of the city gates, they stopped and stood for a long moment.

'I didn't expect that,' said General Talbot. 'What are they up to?'

The city gates were wide open. Beyond them, Crutch could see civilians evacuating their homes, fleeing deeper into the city towards the palace.

'I don't like this,' said Sergeant Zander. 'Why would they leave their walls unmanned?'

'Only one way to find out,' said Crutch. 'Marines, who'd like to do a little reconnaissance.'

'I'm with you, colonel,' said Longshot.

'Me too,' said Boulder.

'I go wherever you go,' said Sergeant Zander.

'Do we get to burn something?' said Quicksilver.

'Not yet,' said Crutch.

'I'll still go with you,' said Quicksilver, disappointed. 'But a mission's not the same unless I get to set something on fire.'

General Talbot laughed.

'I don't know how you get this rabble to fight,' he said. 'You and your marines don't have to be the first into the city. We have plenty of well trained men who can do the job.'

'But we know Teevilgrad,' said Crutch. 'We lived here undercover for weeks.'

'Can I send some soldiers with you?' said General Talbot.

'This will be much quicker if we go by ourselves,' said Crutch. 'We'll also draw less attention.'

'Very well,' said General Talbot. 'You got us this far.'

Crutch and the marines walked through the open city gates.

'It's like they're inviting us in,' said Sergeant Zander. 'Did I mention that I don't like this?'

'You did,' said Crutch. 'You're not the only one.'

The civilians who saw the marines ran down the main street and disappeared deep in the city.

'Looks like they weren't expecting us to take the docks so quickly,' said Sergeant Zander.

'Do you think we caught them by surprise, and that's why they didn't guard the gates?' said Longshot.

'No, I don't,' said Crutch. 'They've known we were coming for weeks. They're prepared.' He pointed to the highest building he could see. 'Let's get up on that roof and get a better view.'

Once they were on the roof, Crutch could see that the whole population close to the city walls had already left or was evacuating.

'I can't see any soldiers or ballistas,' said Sergeant Zander. 'No fortifications or road blocks either. It looks like they're just leaving this part of the city to us without a fight.'

'If they're not planning on fighting here…' said Crutch.

'Then they must be planning on fighting somewhere else,' said Sergeant Zander.

'The palace,' said Crutch. 'Solokov would have them all defending his palace.'

'Fucking coward,' said Sergeant Zander.

'Still, we can't assume anything. We'll get the troops to clear all these buildings to make sure there aren't any Estovians hiding and waiting for a chance to attack us from the rear after we've passed through.'

'Good thinking,' said Sergeant Zander.

'I have a really fast way to clear all these buildings,' said Longshot.

'No,' said Crutch.

'All it will take is a dozen men with burning torches,' said Longshot. 'No one will even have to go inside.'

'No,' said Crutch. 'We're not burning down Teevilgrad.'

'But all these buildings would burn so well,' said Longshot. 'And they're so close together.'

'No!' said Crutch.

General Talbot was surprised when Crutch explained the Estovians had left most of Teevilgrad undefended. He gave the order for the troops to clear the buildings.

'This won't be pretty,' said Sergeant Zander as hundreds of men poured through the city gates and entered the buildings on the other side.

He was right. These men had just watched their friends get slaughtered on the docks. This was their first chance to settle the score.

Instead of opening a door, they'd smash it open. They barged through rooms, destroying anything that could hide an Estovian soldier. They smashed open cupboard doors with axes or swords, overturned beds then smashed them to pieces.

They threw furniture out of the windows, where it smashed below on the streets.

Crutch thought of ordering them to stop, but Sergeant Zander told him it was better they took out their anger on furniture than on people. And if he did order them to stop, then he'd have an army angry at him instead of the Estovians. Maintaining order with thousands of soldiers angry at you would be impossible.

So Crutch and the marines walked into the city, keeping pace with the soldiers clearing buildings. Crutch hated the unnecessary destruction they caused. These were the Estovians' homes and businesses. Lives smashed into splintered wood.

The Estovians were good people. They deserved better.

It was just a flash, but Crutch saw something through an upstairs window of one of the buildings. He ran inside, one step with his good leg, the other driving with his cane.

He took the stairs more carefully. He could move as fast as any man on level ground, but going up stairs was a challenge, no matter how fit he got. If he put the cane down in the wrong spot, it could slip off a step, and he'd be tumbling forwards or backwards.

When he got to the top of the stairs, he could hear them. A woman and a man.

'No,' said the woman.

'Come on, darlin', you'll like it once we get started.'

'No,' said the woman again.

Crutch followed the noise and found one of the Ironborn soldiers pushing a thin blonde woman with blue eyes to a bed in the room. Crutch's mind went to Abagail with her blond hair and her ocean blue eyes. He imagined her being pushed down onto a bed by this filthy pig.

His guts churned with fury. He pulled out his dagger, slipped behind the soldier, and held it to his throat.

'Let go of her, or I swear this knife will go in one side of your neck and out the other.'

The soldier's eyes went white with fear.

'I wasn't doing anything,' said the soldier, releasing the woman.

'I saw what you were doing,' said Crutch.

The soldier looked out of the corner of his eye, recognised Crutch, and his fear turned to desperation.

The woman cowered against the wall. All Crutch could see was Abagail against the wall, cowering from a man like this. Some man they forced her to marry. Some man she didn't want, pushing himself on her like a filthy, rutting boar.

'I should execute you right here and now,' said Crutch.

And he could do it too. Without feeling an ounce of regret. He seethed with anger at this soldier for what he was about to do to the young woman, but most of all because he made Crutch feel something for her.

'Please don't,' said the soldier. 'I've never done this before.' The soldier dropped to his knees, begging. 'I've got a wife and two daughters.'

That made Crutch's anger boil even more.

'Maybe I should let some Estovians loose on your daughters you pig. Downstairs.'

The soldier looked at Crutch, unsure what to do.

'Go downstairs now, said Crutch. 'Wait for me at the front door.'

The soldier didn't have to be asked twice. He ran out of the room, and Crutch could hear his footsteps on the stairs. Crutch put his hand out to the woman.

'What is your name?' said Crutch as he helped her to her feet.

'Larney,' said the woman, still frightened, still looking down.

'You're safe now, Larney. I'm Colonel Crutch. I won't let any soldiers touch you.'

'Thank you,' said Larney.

'Can you help me with something,' said Crutch.

When he and Larney got to the front door of the building downstairs the soldier was there. He dropped to his knees again, hands together, begging.

'Have mercy, Colonel Crutch. She's just an Estovian woman.'

'Shut up!' yelled Crutch.

He looked around. Soldiers stopped and looked over to see what was happening.

'Listen up, soldiers,' yelled Crutch. 'This pig tried to take advantage of an Estovian woman. He tried to push himself on her. We are Ironborn, forged in steel. Not pigs, wallowing in mud.'

The soldiers crowded around, murmuring.

Crutch gave Larney his dagger.

'You do whatever you want to him, Larney,' said Crutch. 'Cut him open like a pig if you want.'

Larney took the dagger, her hand trembling.

'Please don't,' said the soldier, his face wet with tears. 'I wouldn't have hurt you, I promise.'

The soldiers crowding around went silent. Larney stood there with the dagger, the power of life and death in her hands.

She drew back the dagger and stabbed it forward an inch, then stopped. The soldier flinched, and she smiled, her hands still trembling. She stopped in thought for a moment, then she kicked the soldier hard in the groin. And kicked him again and again as he rolled on the ground in agony, clutching at his balls.

She kept kicking, like she was kicking every arsehole man who'd ever done her wrong in her life. Crutch imagined Abagail giving this soldier a kicking. Or giving Young Turd Chudwell a kicking.

She stopped when she was exhausted, her body shaking with anger and fatigue. Then Crutch saw her for what she was. A young woman, barely more than a girl, in the wrong place at the wrong time. Another victim of this war.

Right now, Crutch didn't want to feel anything but angry. There was still plenty more killing to do, and he didn't need feelings about his troops getting killed or civilians getting hurt to cloud his judgement. He was here to get the job done. To rid Teevilgrad and the world of that filthy dog turd Emperor Igor fucking Solokov.

He saw Captain Travis standing nearby at the edge of the crowd of soldiers.

'Captain Travis, who's your most trustworthy man?'

'Sergeant Rogund here,' said Captain Travis.

'Sergeant, I want you to escort this woman back to the Auld Faithful,' said Crutch. 'When you get there, tell Captain Beaumont to place her under his protection. Orders of Colonel Crutch.'

'Yes colonel. Will do, colonel.'

'And sergeant, if anyone touches her, you have my permission to kill them.'

'Yes colonel.'

'Listen up,' yelled Crutch. 'We are here for one thing. To kill Emperor Igor Solokov. You will not harm any civilians unless they attack you first. The next man who touches an Estovian woman will be hanged. Do I make myself clear?'

The crowd of soldiers nodded.

Larney went to give Crutch his dagger back.

'No. You keep that,' said Crutch. 'If anyone tries to touch you, stick it in them.'

Chapter 34
Torn Beyond Repair

Before night fell, the Ironborn troops had established a solid perimeter using furniture and wagons to block all the streets. They set guards just in case the Estovians decided to counterattack.

The buildings were empty of food. Crutch expected most of the Estovians were going hungry. But as night came, feeding his own troops was an issue he'd have to deal with. They could eat the hard tack they carried, but that would not be good for morale after fighting such a costly battle.

'Why don't we just go back to the ships and eat?' said Sergeant Zander. 'We can send three or four squads back at a time. We have thousands of men. A couple of hundred gone won't make any difference, even if the Estovians attack.'

It felt strange heading back to the Auld Faithful and their other ships in the middle of a battle, but General Talbot agreed that was the most practical plan.

They sent back squad after squad through the streets to the docks until it was their turn. As Crutch and the marines walked back through the city, they could see broken furniture in the streets and doors of buildings smashed open with axes.

These were the treasured possessions of Estovians, now trashed and thrown on the cobblestone streets like every part of their lives meant nothing. To the Ironborn soldiers, the lives of the Estovians meant less than nothing, but to Crutch, who'd lived with the people of Teevilgrad, eaten with them and danced with them, he could feel their loss in every broken dresser and every smashed portrait flung into the street.

They passed a hand-sewn rag doll of a girl dressed in tiny clothes also hand-sewn. The rag doll was covered in boot marks, its legs, arms, and head barely held together with thin threads.

Someone's mother had probably spent hours making that doll for a daughter she loved more than the world itself, hunched over for nights in the candlelight after cooking the evening meal. A labour of love, now tossed into the street to be trampled by soldier after soldier.

The rag doll was like the heart of Estovia, ripped and torn at the seams and trampled underfoot. Like Crutch's heart, torn beyond repair.

When they got back to the Auld Faithful Crutch and the marines joined Cedric in the galley to eat. Cedric was thrilled to see them. To Crutch, it felt bizarre to be eating dinner in the middle of invading a country like nothing was happening.

'I put the young woman you sent into my cabin with a guard on the door,' said Cedric. 'I'll sleep in your marines quarters so she can have a place to herself. Is there something special about her?'

'Just an innocent in the wrong place at the wrong time. We'll get her back to her family once the fighting is over.'

'You all look uninjured,' said Cedric.

'Boulder went over the side of one of the buildings the ballista was on,' said Crutch. 'But he held on until we pulled him back up.'

'I held on,' said Boulder, smiling.

'And you've been careful like I asked you to, Damen?' said Cedric.

'As careful as you can be in a war,' said Damen.

'I know you're trying to look after us,' said Sergeant Zander, 'but being careful in battle can get you killed.'

'I'm sorry,' said Cedric. 'When you all disappeared into the smoke on the docks, I was afraid none of you would come back alive. As I get older, I worry more about the people who are closest to me.'

'Thank you, Cedric,' said Crutch. 'We appreciate your concern.'

'Who did you put in charge of the supply office when you left?' said Cedric.

'Why do you ask?' said Crutch.

'In all my time as a captain, I've never witnessed anything like it,' said Cedric. 'The first supply ships arrived already, and whoever sent them anticipated exactly what we'd use on the first day of the invasion.'

'That would be Abagail,' said Crutch.

'You taught Abagail Hastings how to run the supply office?'

'To be honest, she taught me about how the navy office works. I just taught her logistics.'

'She's quite the student. If I had a supply office like this when I was fleet commander, I would have been unstoppable.'

'You were unstoppable. Until you were betrayed at the siege of Crestona.'

'That's debatable,' said Cedric. 'What's not debatable is what a superlative job your Abagail is doing.'

'She's not my Abagail any more,' said Crutch, his anger rising to a boil at the thought of it.

'My apologies, Crutch. It's taking us all some time to adjust to the fact that you're not together any more.'

'Can we just not talk about it,' said Crutch.

'Of course,' said Cedric. 'Since you're my colonel, I do have to tell you our cargo hold is full of food and ammunition. It's the same with all the cargo holds.'

That gave Crutch an idea.

'How much food?'

'Two months at least, for all the troops and all the ships' crews.'

'That's a lot of food.'

'And if what I've seen so far is any measure, I'd expect more will be arriving every day. If this continues, we'll have enough to feed the people of Teevilgrad.'

Crutch sat silent in thought. He knew from his last trip here that in Teevilgrad, food could be the most powerful weapon of all.

Chapter 35
One Tired Finger

An hour before Dawn Crutch ordered the Ironborn troops deeper into the city. General Talbot came with them. The general had told him that it was Crutch's job to take the palace and the general's job to protect the docks and ensure the supplies they needed kept flowing. But the general wanted to see what their troops were up against.

The Ironborn soldiers went slow, making certain that Estovian soldiers weren't hiding in the buildings, waiting to spring some kind of trap or ambush after they passed.

It took most of a day to clear the buildings. The soldiers had lost most of their enthusiasm for destruction after a night of sleeping hard in the streets between sentry duties.

When the palace came into view, Crutch knew immediately why the Estovians hadn't tried to defend their city. They didn't need to.

The Estovians had turned the last hundred yards that led to the palace gates into a killing zone. Ballistas lined the roofs of the buildings. There were bowmen up there too, and piles of large rocks to throw on any Ironborn soldiers who tried to get to the roofs.

Carts, doors, planks, and other solid pieces of wood made a barrier along the road, neck high, that would funnel any soldiers into a narrow line. Holes in the barriers meant the Estovians could shoot through into any soldiers on the road, but Ironborn troops would be unable to shoot back.

The more men Crutch sent into that funnel, the more difficult it would be to get through as dead bodies piled up, blocking the street.

'We'll lose every man we have trying to get to the gates if we try to go through that,' said Sergeant Zander.

General Talbot peered through an eyeglass.

'I think I can see their general, but he's not dressed like a regular Estovian,' he said, then handed the eyeglass to Crutch.

'Is that who I think it is?' said Crutch, looking through the eyeglass then handing it to Sergeant Zander. He prayed it wasn't just wishful thinking playing tricks on his eyes.

'That's exactly who you think it is,' said Sergeant Zander. 'Anton Ivenko. Leader of the true compatriots.'

'General Talbot,' said Crutch, 'could we talk in private?'

It took Crutch an hour to put on his face paint and disguise himself as Sergey Crujge, the merchant from Uraskova and Anton's uncle. When he was done, he took off his uniform and put on the merchant's robes he'd brought with him. He got Boulder to change too.

'I should come with you too,' said Sergeant Zander.

'I thought about that,' said Crutch. 'It's too much of a risk. They trust Boulder, and all he's going to say is, 'I'm a pumpkin.''

'I'm a pumpkin,' said Boulder, grinning.

'We've been away from Teevilgrad too long,' said Crutch. 'You haven't had weeks listening to Estovians, practicing your accent like you did last time. The chance you'll mess up and say something that gives us away is too high.'

'I could just stand there and say nothing.'

'You could, but what if they try to question you or interrogate you? There's no way you could get through that. They already interrogated Boulder. His pumpkin story is solid.'

'I'm a pumpkin,' said Boulder.

'What if they interrogate you?' said Sergeant Zander.

'Then I'm most likely dead,' said Crutch. 'But it's worth the risk if we can get these Estovians to let us through to the palace.'

Sergeant Zander nodded his head. 'You're a brave man, Crutch,' he said.

'So are you,' said Crutch. 'The bravest I've met.'

'Get back from this one alive,' said Sergeant Zander. 'We've come too far for you to die from a knife in the back behind Estovian lines.'

'I don't plan on dying,' said Crutch.

'No one ever plans on dying. It's the attack you don't see coming that gets you.'

Crutch smiled. He owed so much to Sergeant Zander.

'If I don't make it back, thank you for everything,' said Crutch. 'You taught me how to fight, and you saved me countless times.'

'Just returning the favour,' said Sergeant Zander. 'I'd be in the ground a dozen times over if it weren't for you and your walking cane. Say thank you by coming back to us with all your body parts still attached.'

'I'll do my best,' said Crutch.

'You always do,' said Sergeant Zander.

Crutch left the tent hobbling, with Boulder holding one of his arms. This would be the last time he could use this disguise. Once his Ironborn troops had seen him dressed as Crujge, the secret would be out. Even now, there was a serious chance that some spy might sneak over to the Estovian position and let them know who Crujge really was.

The Ironborn banner man raised the white flag of truce, waving it from side to side.

'Surrendering already,' yelled an Estovian from their position. 'Is good idea.'

'Not surrendering,' said General Talbot. 'We have someone who wants to talk to you,' yelled General Talbot. 'And a cart full of food for you as a peace offering. We know you're hungry.'

'Send one man with cart first,' yelled the Estovian voice.

A brave Ironborn soldier walked out into the line of fire, pushing a hand cart full of food.

'Slowly,' yelled the Estovian voice. The soldiers on both sides fell into silence as the Ironborn soldier pushed the cart full of yams, sweet potato, and fruit forward, its wheel creaking as it moved.

'Is far enough,' yelled the Estovian voice.

The Ironborn soldier turned and walked slowly back to safety.

'Now your men,' yelled the Estovian voice. 'Stand where we can see. Then I decide.'

Crutch hobbled out of cover into the cobblestone street, into the line of fire. If the Estovians chose to they could now shoot him full of arrows. There was a long silence.

'He can come to us,' yelled the Estovian voice.

'I'd like to send his bodyguard and my captain so you can negotiate,' yelled General Talbot.

'Make them stand where I can see them too,' yelled the Estovian voice.

'Do I have your word you won't fire on them?' yelled General Talbot.

'You have my word,' said the Estovian voice.

Boulder and Captain Travis joined Crutch in the street. Exposed.

'His bodyguard can come,' yelled the Estovian voice. 'But not the captain. If this is trick, we kill both of them.'

'You have my word, this is no trick,' yelled General Talbot.

'I hope you speak true,' yelled the Estovian voice.

Crutch hobbled forward, with Boulder holding him up under one arm. He stayed hunched over, trying to look as old as possible, but his eyes glanced up from side to side. He could see bowmen, arrows drawn, aiming straight at him. Just one tired finger, and he'd be dead.

Chapter 36
Everyone Loses

When he reached the barricade made of old carts, crates, and barrels, Crutch stopped. Two soldiers pulled a crate aside to make a gap. Inside, Crutch could see Anton.

'Put down your weapons,' yelled Anton. 'This is my uncle Crujge.'

'So nice to see you, nephew,' said Crutch.

'You too, uncle. Come through. We have a lot to talk about.'

Crutch hobbled through the gap in the barricade, with Boulder holding him under the arm. He let out a few raspy coughs.

'Are you okay, uncle?' said Anton.

'Was long trip on ship to get here,' said Crutch. 'Then a long walk from docks. My old legs are weary.'

'We have some walking to do still,' said Anton. 'Would you like to rest first?'

'I am alright with Boulder helping me,' said Crutch.

'Good to see you too, Boulder,' said Anton.

'I'm a pumpkin,' said Boulder, smiling.

'Yes, I remember,' said Anton, smiling back.

'What happened with Emperor Solokov?' said Crutch as they walked past heavily armed komitav officers, ready to fight behind crates and walls.

If the Ironborn troops tried to take these streets, it would be a bloodbath for both sides. And Crutch wasn't sure the Ironborn had enough men to get through them all.

'Once we knew we didn't have numbers to get past Solokov's palace guard, we convinced Solokov that Arch Warden Gragor was behind uprising.'

'And he believed that?' said Crutch.

'Solokov is vain,' said Anton. 'Believes what he wants to believe. Easier for him to believe one man rose up against him instead of entire city of Teevilgrad.'

'I am glad you're alive,' said Crutch.

'You too,' said Anton.

'You are general now?' said Crutch.

'Solokov killed most of his generals,' said Anton. 'I was only one left willing to do job. Here we are.'

Anton led Crutch and Boulder into a large hall. Inside were women and children. He recognised Yelena immediately.

'Crujge, you're alive,' said Yelena, running to him and taking him in her arms. As he held her, he could feel that she was thin. So thin.

'Would have come back sooner if I knew I would get hugs like this,' said Crutch. That feeling of warmth, of having someone to protect and care for, came flooding back to him. A feeling he didn't need right now, but there was no way to push it down.

'Crujge brought food for us,' said Anton.

'You are our angel again,' said Yelena. 'And you brought Boulder.'

The children had already found Boulder and climbed up onto him, with Boulder smiling as they did.

'I'm a pumpkin,' said Boulder.

Yelena laughed. 'Reminds me of better time when we had the soup kitchen,' she said.

'The soup kitchen was best thing I ever did in my life,' said Crutch, and he meant it.

'Solokov burned the kitchen down,' said Anton.

'I heard,' said Crutch. 'Solokov must die, or there will never be peace for Estovia.'

'You speak true,' said Anton.

'Are women and children safe here so close to battle?' said Crutch.

'Is temporary,' said Anton. 'We bring them here when Ironborn invasion starts. Tonight they leave.'

'Is good to get them somewhere safe,' said Crutch.

'Yes. We worry what Ironborn soldiers do to our women if they catch them.'

'Ironborn soldiers will not touch women,' said Crutch. 'Their colonel will hang anyone who does.'

'Really?' said Anton.

'I see with my own eyes,' said Crutch. 'Soldier touches Teevilgrad woman, and colonel gives her a knife, says she can do whatever she wants to him.'

'So she stabbed him?'

'No,' said Crutch. 'She is kind woman.'

'So she didn't hurt him?'

'Didn't say that,' said Crutch. 'She kicked him in balls.'

Anton laughed.

'Many times,' said Crutch. 'He was lying on ground, and she kept kicking him. Was justice.'

'This makes me happy,' said Anton, laughing again.

'Ironborn are good men like you and true compatriots,' said Crutch. 'They don't want war.'

'So this colonel, will he stop invasion?' said Anton. 'Leave Teevilgrad in peace?'

'He wants what you want,' said Crutch. 'What we all want. Emperor Solokov dead.'

'Solokov has many palace guards. And his palace is full of defences and traps. That's why true compatriots call off siege of palace. Even with all our people, is no way we could get to Solokov.'

'Maybe Ironborn troops can do it for you,' said Crutch.

'Uncle, you are crazy.'

'Maybe I am crazy old man, but if you let Ironborn troops past to palace, even if they all die, you have much easier job taking Solokov yourself.'

'Is too dangerous,' said Anton. 'How do we know Ironborn troops won't take over city and kill all our soldiers?'

'How could they? You have strong position here. Many men. If they try to fight you after taking palace, they will not have enough men. You would kill them all.'

'Maybe,' said Anton. But they control docks. They could bring in more men and overwhelm us or wait till we starve.'

'I have been in Ironbay this last year. They have no more troops,' said Crutch.

'Really?' said Anton. 'So Ironbay is as weak as Estovia now?'

'I think so,' said Crutch. 'They might have enough men to take palace, or they might have enough men to fight komitav you lead, but they could never fight both.'

'If they know this, then they should leave Teevilgrad. Leave or die here.'

'Maybe,' said Crutch. 'But they came here to kill Solokov. Just like you, they know this is only way they can end war. They don't want to attack your komitav men. That's why they ask me to talk to you.'

'Could be trick. You are old man, uncle. They might trick you to say what they want.'

'I don't think so,' said Crutch. 'They might not be able to fight your komitav, but I have seen their supplies. They have enough bluefire to burn your city to ground.'

'I have seen this bluefire,' said Anton. 'Is horrible weapon.'

'You talk true,' said Crutch. 'They have plenty of food too. They give you food as peace offering, but they can starve out Teevilgrad if they choose to, now they control docks. They can wait until you are too weak with hunger to fight.'

'Is terrible but you are right. If they have food and docks, they can take all time they want. But we could counterattack.'

'Yes, but then you have same problem Ironborn troops have. Not enough men to win, then control docks. It doesn't matter which way you look at this; if komitav fight Ironborn troops, everyone loses.'

'You talk true,' said Anton.

'Simple solution is take Ironborn food as gift and let them through. Let them into palace to kill Solokov. Then we can all have peace.'

'And city is not burnt down, komitav stay alive. But will the Ironborn honour agreement if we let them through? Will they let us rule Teevilgrad? Or will they take over and become new Solokov? New tyrants.'

'They will have no choice but to let you rule. To take palace and kill Solokov will cost them many men. You could cut off supply to palace and starve them out. Wait for them to come out and kill them all.'

'Maybe we could,' said Anton.

'Is same thing though. Too many good men die. Is better if Ironbay and Estovia work together. Trust each other. Already, there has been too much killing, too much dying. Solokov is one who must die. No one else.'

'You talk true,' said Anton. 'I will think on this and talk to my compatriots. Now we should eat.'

Chapter 37
Evil Magic

Crutch sat and talked with Yelena and a long line of men and women who knew him from when he ran the soup kitchen. He saw Anton's boy, Nikolai, now crawling and smiling happily. He saw Yevgeny, the close friend of Dima, who Arch Warden Gragor and Emperor Solokov had hanged in the people's plaza, declaring the true compatriots and the soup kitchen the enemy of the people.

Crutch struggled to push down his emotions. The last thing he needed right now was to feel anything for any Estovians with so much killing still to be done. But it was hard. These were good, kind people, and he had been an important part of their lives.

It was hard not to be moved by the love and affection they showed him.

After an hour of talking to people, a horse and cart arrived outside the hall. Two burly-looking komitav unloaded four barrels from the back of the cart as the driver, just a teenager, climbed down.

Crutch recognised the boy immediately. That half-starved street urchin he'd coaxed out of the sewers here the last time he was in Teevilgrad was now fit and full of energy.

'Pavee,' said Crutch, making a show of struggling to his feet.

Pavee looked over, and a huge grin spread across his face. He half walked, half ran to Crutch, and enveloped him in a huge hug.

'Crujge. I'm so glad you're alive.'

'You too,' said Crutch. 'Go easy on my old bones.'

'Sorry,' said Pavee, loosening his hug.

'Is alright. Is good to see you,' said Crutch. 'What are you doing here?'

'Me and street urchins and brothers of mercy did like you said. We grew beans up in hills and made volktag beer. We sold it to army, now to komitav. Is good business. No matter how hungry or poor people get, they always have money for beer.'

'You speak true,' said Crutch, laughing, then letting out a few gravelly coughs to keep up his disguise.

'That doesn't sound good,' said Pavee. 'You should sit down.'

'I will,' said Crutch. 'Will you sit with me? Tell me what you've been doing?'

'Of course,' said Pavee, pulling an empty chair over and looking around at people eating as he did. 'Was it you who brought food?'

'Me and the Ironborn navy,' said Crutch.

'The Ironborn navy brought food for people of Teevilgrad? But they are enemy.'

'Not so much,' said Crutch. 'They just want Emperor Solokov dead.'

'I would kill him myself if I could. Still remember when he hanged Dima and Tamiva and burned down soup kitchen.'

'He is evil man and must die,' said Crutch. 'Maybe very soon.'

'Really?'

'Yes,' said Crutch. 'Ironborn troops are ready to attack palace.'

'Will need big army,' said Pavee. 'Anton told me true compatriots didn't have enough men to get into palace last time.'

'You talk true,' said Crutch. 'Many Ironborn men will die getting past gates and walls.'

'There is another way into palace,' said Pavee.

'Really?'

'Yes. I wasn't in Teevilgrad when true compatriots surrounded palace first time, so I never told Anton. There is entrance underground into Solokov's dungeons.'

'There is?'

'Yes. Has iron door, but lock is rusty and door is easy to shake open. When I was street urchin, boys would sneak in there, but none ever came out alive. Sometimes we find bodies of dead urchins at door, twisted, mouth open like they were screaming. Is evil magic down there.'

'But you know how to get to this door through sewers?' said Crutch.

'Of course.'

'Can you make me map?'

'I can,' said Pavee. 'But it is evil. Safer for Ironborn to take on gates and walls than evil that lives in dungeons of Solokov's palace.'

Chapter 38
I'll Bring A Hamper

The marines, General Talbot and Captain Travis gathered around a wooden table in the bottom of an old inn to discuss Crutch's meeting with Anton. A couple of candles flickered in the darkness of the night.

Outside, Crutch could hear the troops. Many now caught what restless sleep they could get. Guards paced by, vigilant, eyes on the komitav and any Estovians.

'Anton says if we deliver him food for the rest of the night, he'll withdraw his troops tomorrow morning,' said Crutch.

'Feeding the enemy sounds like a disastrous idea,' said General Talbot. 'They look like they're on the verge of starvation. They could just be trying to build up their men's strength so they can fight us without collapsing in exhaustion.'

'I don't think so,' said Crutch. 'I know Anton. He doesn't want to fight us. He just wants Emperor Solokov dead.'

'If you're wrong, we could be giving our enemy a huge advantage,' said General Talbot.

'How many choices do we have?' said Crutch. 'If we have to fight the komitav, we won't have the troops to take the palace.'

'Can we bring more men from Ironbay?' said Captain Travis. 'Or get some from the territories?'

'Not enough,' said General Talbot. 'Colonel Crutch is right. We don't have the numbers. I can't believe I'm contemplating feeding the enemy.'

'Solokov is our enemy,' said Crutch. 'Not the people of Teevilgrad or Anton's komitav.'

'If Anton withdraws his troops, we still have to get into the palace,' said Captain Travis. 'Solokov's palace guards have bowmen, and who knows what else ready in defence. They'll cut our troops to ribbons if we try to scale the walls.'

'We might be able to get into the palace through the sewers and the dungeon underneath,' said Crutch.

'Really?' said General Talbot. 'How do you know this?'

'A street urchin I knew from our time in Teevilgrad gave me a map,' said Crutch.

'You have a map from a street urchin?' said General Talbot. 'Sounds a bit thin.'

'We've been in the sewers, general. Just like Ironbay they lead everywhere.'

'But a street urchin?' said General Talbot. 'We can't hinge our whole attack on what a street urchin says.'

'I was a street urchin,' said Crutch.

'My apologies,' said General Talbot. 'I recall you did tell me that the night you saved my life in Ironbay.'

'You're right though,' said Crutch. 'A map and information from one street urchin is not enough to go on. Even if it was, we couldn't send hundreds of men through the sewers then through a dungeon.'

'What did you have in mind then?' said General Talbot.

'Just a small group of men to go into the sewers and the dungeon and see if we can find a way to open those palace gates and let our troops through.'

'A small group?' said General Talbot.

'Yes. I think a squad of marines could do the job.'

'I guess I don't need to ask which squad of marines?' said General Talbot.

'No, you don't,' said Crutch. 'We will need someone who can pick locks, though. And someone who's an expert in castle gates and castle defences. We want to take out as many of those as we can if we can get through.'

'When were you planning on going?' said General Talbot.

'Right now,' said Crutch. 'While it's still dark.'

General Talbot found them a lockpick and a soldier who'd worked with the palace guard in Ironbay maintaining the portcullis and gates. The general also insisted on sending two of the army's best shieldmen with them.

Before they could leave, a messenger came to General Talbot, running fast.

'What is it?' said the general.

'Trouble on the docks, general,' said the messenger. 'Lookouts spotted several ships out beyond the harbour.'

'Did they identify the ships?' said General Talbot.

'No general. They were too far out.'

'Could just be merchant ships,' said Crutch.

'Yes, or it could be the last of Solokov's navy, ready to counterattack. I need to go take care of this,' said General Talbot. 'Colonel Crutch, do you have any suggestions for who I should leave in charge?'

'Captain Travis,' said Crutch without a second's hesitation.

'My choice too,' said General Talbot. 'Captain Travis, you're now leader of the soldiers here. Your primary goal is to take the palace. You're a capable officer. I don't think I need to tell you any more than that.'

'No, you don't, general,' said Captain Travis.

'If I don't get back here before you take the palace, I'm relying on you all to kill Solokov,' said General Talbot.

'We'll find a way to get the job done,' said Crutch.

'I know you will,' said General Talbot. 'You're the finest damn soldiers I've ever seen in my life.' With that, the general turned and left for the docks.

Crutch turned to the marines as they watched the general go.

'Ready for a walk in the sewers?' he said.

'Sounds delightful,' said Quicksilver.

'Can never spend too much time sloshing around in the sewers,' said Sergeant Zander.

'I'll bring a hamper, and we can have a little picnic while we're down there,' said Longshot.

'I like picnics,' said Boulder.

'No offence, colonel,' said Captain Travis, 'but your marines may be the craziest bastards I've ever met.'

'Haven't you heard?' said Longshot. 'Crazy bastard is Colonel Crutch's middle name.'

Chapter 39
No One Will Hear You Scream

The marines and their four new army soldiers crept through the sewers with Crutch in the lead. Crutch had a good idea of where he was from moving through the sewers the last time he was in Teevilgrad.

This time, though, he worried that Emperor Solokov might post guards on the sewer grates to stop Ironborn soldiers from moving through the city this way. Anton could have done the same, and if Anton's men caught them in the sewers, that could throw off their hopes of getting Anton to withdraw his komitav and letting the Ironborn troops through to the palace.

So they crept slowly and silently as they could, now there were ten of them. Boulder was right behind Crutch with his huge shield.

They finally came to the iron door on Pavee's map, drawn with charcoal on a piece of an old rag. Crutch put his ear to the iron door and listened. He couldn't hear anything on the other side. No voices. No movement.

He waved over the lockpick, who pulled out his tools and dropped them onto the stone tiles of the sewer with a clatter. Crutch frowned at him. The lockpick mouthed a, 'Sorry,' and retrieved his tools.

His hands trembled as the lockpick inserted two tools into the lock and moved them around. Crutch could hear the scraping and the clicking of the tools in the lock. He tapped the lockpick on the shoulder and put his finger to his lips. The lockpick nodded and went slower, more carefully, more quietly.

It must have taken less than a minute, but it seemed like it took him forever to get the lock open. The lock made a loud click, and the lockpick smiled, looked over at Crutch, and nodded.

Crutch put his ear back on the door, hoping the noise they'd made hadn't attracted any guards from Solokov's palace. He couldn't hear anything, so he slowly pulled the heavy iron door open.

Inside was a narrow stone corridor. Crutch went through, with Boulder right behind him. The marines and the soldiers followed. In the sewers, there was a dim moonlight coming through the sewer grates. After growing up hiding in the sewers of Ironbay, Crutch could navigate his way without any help.

But this corridor built from stone was dark. He didn't dare get Quicksilver to light a torch. That would be like a beacon to any guards who might be down here. So as the dim light turned to blackness, Crutch felt along the stone wall with his hand. He put Boulder's hand on his shoulder so Boulder could follow without running into him from behind.

He knew the marines and the soldiers behind him did their best to be quiet but he could still hear their soft footsteps echoing in the cramped stone corridor. If anyone was close they could be heard.

Crutch came to a stop with something blocking the corridor. He felt with his hands in front of him. Rough wooden planks. Someone had nailed planks across the corridor. He felt to the sides of the corridor. This was a doorway.

Crutch put his ear to the planks. He couldn't hear anything on the other side. He whispered as softly as he could in Boulder's ear.

'Could you try to pull off one of these planks. Quiet as you can.'

He guided Boulder's hand to the planks. There was the sound of wood splintering then a dim light came through the hole Boulder made by breaking one of the planks in half and ripping it off. This was a doorway someone had planked over.

Clearly, they didn't want whatever was inside to get out. Or they didn't want people to get in.

'Pull the other planks off as quietly as you can,' whispered Crutch. 'Just enough so we can get through.'

Boulder pulled off the planks one at a time until he made a hole big enough to step through. Crutch went first. A torch burned and flickered from somewhere Crutch couldn't see. In the dim light, he could see large stone tiles on the floor and prison cells with iron bars.

A chill went through Crutch as memories of being locked in the prison in Zanithburg came back to him. The prison cells here were empty, but Crutch guessed they were in the bottom of the dungeons. There would be many more cells they'd have to go past.

The rest of the marines came out behind him, and he led them forward, towards the light. The walls here were made of stone. In the dim light in one cell he could see chains, manacles, and dark stains on the stone tiles.

He came to a corner. Staying in the shadows, he peered around. He could see the torch now and more prison cells. He couldn't see any guards or Estovian soldiers, but in one cell was an old woman.

Their eyes met, and Crutch put his finger to his lips. Her eyes were deep black. She smiled when she saw Crutch and nodded.

Crutch crept into the corridor. There were prison cells on both sides. He passed the cell with the old woman, putting his hand to his lips again, then crept to the next corner and looked around. More cells. Empty cells.

'You don't need to sneak around here,' said the old woman. 'The guards won't be back until morning.'

He turned back, and the old woman smiled. A half smile and a half smirk as if Crutch was a stupid child who'd done something wrong.

'I'd rather stay silent,' whispered Crutch.

'No one will hear you,' said the old woman. 'Except your nine friends hiding around the corner there.'

'Are you sure?' whispered Crutch.

'Quite sure,' said the old woman. 'I've been down here quite some time. This is where they torture the poor unfortunates the fat little emperor doesn't like. It's deep enough that they can't hear the screams.'

'They tortured you?' said Crutch.

The lady cackled. 'I'm just a broken down old woman. Why would they torture me?'

'Can we get to the palace gates from here?' said Crutch.

'Oh yes,' said the old woman. 'You can even get to the control room from here and raise the two portcullis that block the entrance.'

'You know how to get there?' said Crutch.

'I should do. I built them,' said the old woman.

CHAPTER 40

I Am Queen Astrid

'You built the portcullis?' said Crutch.

'I built this whole palace. I am Queen Astrid.'

'Queen Astrid? That's not possible. Queen Astrid disappeared over sixty years ago. If she was alive, she'd be over one hundred years old.'

'You're a scholar,' said Queen Astrid. 'What an unexpected delight. I am one hundred and seven years old, if you want to be exact.'

For a few seconds, Crutch was struck dumb. It wasn't possible. No one could live that long.

'Perhaps you could get your lockpick to open this cell and take these chains off me?' said Queen Astrid. 'They do chafe.'

Looking closer, Crutch could see someone had put chains and manacles on the old woman's ankles, wrists, and her neck.

'I don't' know if I want to do that. It looks like someone really didn't want you to get away,' said Crutch.

'The fat little emperor is terrified of anyone who might usurp his rule,' said Queen Astrid. 'Wouldn't be too hard. From what I hear, a commoner with a soup kitchen took a pretty good shot at it just a few months ago.'

The old woman looked at Crutch with dark, knowing eyes and a half smile.

'How do you know I have a lockpick with me?' said Crutch.

'You crept in here quietly. That means you got past that big iron door without breaking it down. Hence, you have a lockpick in your motley group hiding around the corner. Or maybe I can read minds.' The old woman laughed, an unsettling, raspy cackle.

'If I set you free, do you give your word you'll help us open the palace gates?' said Crutch.

'Not only that. I'll help you kill the fat little emperor too. There's nothing I'd love more than to see that fat little turd's head parted from his body.'

Crutch motioned for the marines to come out.

'Get the door unlocked,' said Crutch to the lockpick. 'And take off her irons.'

'Thank you,' said Queen Astrid.

The lockpick fiddled with his tools and the cell door as Sergeant Zander took up a defensive position at the other end of the corridor with Boulder. As soon as Damen came into her view, Queen Astrid's head snapped to him, and her eyes fixed on him.

'Do you know how many guards the palace has?' said Crutch.

'I built this palace, but I haven't lived upstairs for over sixty years,' said Queen Astrid as the lockpick opened the cell. 'I can show you how to get to the throne room, though. I doubt the fat little emperor has found every secret passage I built into the palace.' As she spoke, her eyes never left Damen, who joined Sergeant Zander and Boulder at the end of the corridor.

'You can get us into Emperor Solokov's throne room?' said Crutch.

'Before he even knows you're there,' said Queen Astrid. 'That would make for quite the surprise.' She watched Damen as he peered around the corner of the corridor. Her gaze was like a crocodile waiting for its chance to strike. 'It's been quite the day for surprises.'

'How do I know you're not just making up stories so we'll set you free?' said Crutch.

'You're a sharp one,' said Queen Astrid. 'Why would they put me here in the deepest part of the dungeon, where only one guard comes twice a day? I'm the secret the fat little emperor wants nobody to know about.'

'That doesn't mean you're Queen Astrid,' said Crutch.

'No, I suppose it doesn't. Since you're a student of history, I'm sure you've heard that when Estovia was one of my territories, the empire never fought with Voldheim. What you don't know is why.

'There was a winery in Voldheim called the Hidden Orchard that distilled the most delicious mango wine. The wine only lasted in the bottle for a year, so I couldn't just fill my cellars with it.'

'You could conquer Voldheim and get all the mango wine you wanted,' said Crutch. 'It's not a very convincing reason.'

'You are delightfully clever,' said Queen Astrid. 'Also, I had spies spreading hatred and fear of the Voldheim through the city of Ironbay. Why fight my two biggest rivals when I could get them to destroy each other, then take them both when they're weak.'

'But you didn't take them both,' said Crutch.

'Alas, sometimes the best plans come awry. It seems Ironbay's diplomats found a path to peace before the war reached the level of mutual destruction I'd hoped for.'

Crutch thought about it for a second. She might be a crazy old lady, but she knew a whole lot that only Queen Astrid would know. Or she was an exceptional historian with a great imagination. On the balance of probabilities, she was exactly who she said she was.

'Get those manacles off her,' said Crutch to the lockpick.

'Thank you,' said Queen Astrid, her eyes never leaving Damen.

The lockpick started with the neck collar, which looked like it was made of pure silver. After fiddling for a minute, he finally opened the lock with his tools. Queen Astrid smiled as it came off. Her skin underneath had a thick red welt from years of chafing.

'That's a relief,' said Queen Astrid as the lockpick started on the manacles around her ankles.

Crutch knew if they could kill Emperor Solokov, that would mean the Ironborn troops wouldn't have to attack his palace.

'Can you lead us straight to Igor from here?' said Crutch.

'I'm afraid that isn't possible,' said Queen Astrid. 'When I built the dungeons, I made certain they didn't connect to the royal chambers. Didn't want the commoners getting ideas and locking me in here. Such irony.'

'Can we get there another way?' said Crutch.

'Through the front gates of the palace is the fastest route,' said Queen Astrid.

'Which way do we have to go to get to the control room for the gates?' said Crutch.

'You young commoners,' said Queen Astrid. 'Always in such a hurry. We go to the left first, but it's not possible to get there with directions or a map. I'll have to come with you to help you open the secret doors.'

The lockpick got off the manacles around her ankles and her wrists.

'Free at last,' she said.

She went to stand, and her legs gave out from under her. She flopped back onto the stone tiles of the cell.

'Perhaps you could get one of your men to help me walk,' said Queen Astrid. 'Perhaps that strong young man.' She pointed at Damen.

Crutch couldn't understand why she'd pick Damen instead of Boulder, but right now he just hoped she really did know how to get into the control room for the gates to the palace. If she did that would save the lives of hundreds of Ironborn troops.

If getting Damen to prop her up while she walked was what it took to get her help, then it would be worth it if she could get them into that control room.

'Damen, could you help Queen Astrid here to walk?' said Crutch.

'Of course,' said Damen, coming into the cell. 'Take my hand, your majesty.' He pulled Queen Astrid to her feet then held her under the arm.

'So strong,' said Queen Astrid, smiling and patting Damen on the hand. 'Is it Prince Damen?'

'No, just Damen, your majesty.'

She looked at him and shook her head. 'The things we tell our children.'

'Are you able to walk?' said Crutch. 'I'd like to get those gates open before the sun comes up.'

'Oh, I can walk,' said Queen Astrid, 'with Prince Damen here helping me.' She patted Damen on the hand again.

'It's just Damen.'

'Yes, you told me that, my prince.'

Crutch shook his head. If she really was Queen Astrid, she would have been in this dungeon for decades. It was amazing she'd retained even the slightest semblance of sanity being chained all that time. If calling Damen a prince was the worst of it, then they'd be lucky.

'Which way do we go?' said Crutch as they came to the end of the corridor.

'There's an underground passage to the control room,' said Queen Astrid. 'But we have to get to it first. The fat little emperor will have guards.'

'We can take care of guards,' said Damen.

'I'm sure you can, my prince,' said Queen Astrid, patting Damen's hand. 'So strong.'

'Whoever we have to deal with, we have to kill quietly,' said Crutch. 'We don't want half the guards in the palace fighting us.'

'Why ever not?' said Queen Astrid. 'Sounds like that would make quite the adventure. I could see Prince Damen here in action.'

'If it's all the same to you, your majesty,' said Crutch, 'I'd rather fight the palace guard with the Ironborn troops, who I hope are now forming outside the palace gates.'

That was another problem Crutch had to consider. Had Anton withdrawn his men while they were here and let the Ironborn troops through?

'An army of men storming the palace of the fat little emperor,' said Queen Astrid. 'That would be a delight to witness. To the control room, then.'

'Quietly,' said Crutch.

'Yes, quietly,' said Queen Astrid. 'We need to go left here.'

The marines and Queen Astrid turned left and crept along the corridor. The Queen's smile never left her face as Damen helped her walk. She kept looking at him as if he was her recently reunited lover.

At the end of the corridor, they came to an old iron door. Crutch nodded at the lockpick, who worked at it silently with his tools and had it open in seconds. Crutch could hear the sound of dripping water in the distance and the breathing of the marines around him.

'Seems all that coin I spent on fancy locks were a total waste,' said Queen Astrid, her voice echoing loud in the corridor.

Crutch put his finger to his lips.

'Sorry,' said Queen Astrid, smiling at Crutch, still talking at full volume. 'Quietly.'

Crutch put his finger to his lips again. How could he get her to shut up? Queen Astrid put her old, bony finger to her lips and nodded her head. She waved her hand, motioning for everyone to go through the door.

Crutch slowly opened the door and peered into the dimly lit corridor ahead. It was empty. He crept forward with Boulder and his huge shield right behind him. After fifty yards, the corridor turned right and he could hear voices.

Chapter 41
A Life Dodging Arrows

Crutch peered around the corner and could see two Estovian guards twenty yards away in front of a door made of iron bars. They were relaxed, chatting casually with each other.

Crutch ducked back, pointed at Longshot, and signalled with his fingers. Two guards, twenty yards. Longshot nodded, pulled his bow from his shoulder, and notched an arrow as he squeezed past the marines and Queen Astrid.

Queen Astrid looked at his drawn weapon, and her dark eyes got a little wider, as if she were a child spotting a pony ride at a fair.

Longshot crept to the corner, peered around, then stepped into the corridor and let an arrow fly. Crutch heard one body drop, heard the second guard begin to say something, but before he could Longshot already had a second arrow drawn and fired.

Crutch came into the corridor just as the second guard slumped to the ground. The marines moved fast, advancing down the corridor.

'Splendid shooting,' said Queen Astrid from behind Crutch. She knelt down and put her hand on one of the dead guards.

'Such a waste of a young life,' she said.

Crutch scanned ahead of him. There were prison cells here. Some of them were empty, but some of the cells had starved, decrepit prisoners who looked like they hadn't seen sunshine for years. They came to the bars and begged for food. The marines shared the hard tack they had on them.

'Can we let them out?' said Damen.

'Not yet,' said Crutch. 'That would alert the guards.'

They kept moving, telling the prisoners as they passed to stay silent and they'd be released soon. They went down another long stone corridor and came to a tee junction.

'Left here,' said Queen Astrid.

After going left and walking for fifty yards, Queen Astrid told them to stop.

'It's here somewhere,' she said, feeling along the wall with her hands. 'There it is.' She guided Damen's hand to a spot on the wall and said, 'Push there as hard as you can, my prince.'

Damen pushed, and Crutch heard a grinding sound like two huge stones moving on top of each other. Queen Astrid smiled as an entrance into a dark corridor was revealed behind the wall.

'Through here,' she said. 'There are stairs that will take us to the surface.'

'Where do they come out?' said Crutch.

'In the courtyard, just inside the gates,' said Queen Astrid. 'We'll be around fifty yards from the control room.'

'A courtyard full of Solokov's palace guards,' said Crutch.

'You can't make an omelette without breaking a few eggs,' said Queen Astrid. 'All you fine, strapping young men look like you're well equipped to do some killing. It's only fifty yards.'

Crutch didn't like it, but he really didn't have a choice. Their best chance of taking the palace and killing the emperor was to get those gates open.

He moved into the dark corridor, feeling the wall with his hands and searching for the stairs with his feet. Years of moving around in the sewers of Ironbay in the dark made this kind of movement second nature. As his foot hit the first step, he put Boulder's hand on his shoulder and started up.

As they climbed the steps in the dark, Crutch could hear voices above them. They got louder the higher he climbed. After climbing for a couple of minutes, Crutch's head hit hard stone. He felt around above him. He couldn't find a handle or a door.

'How do we get out?' he whispered.

'It's a large block of solid stone,' said Queen Astrid. 'You have to push up to lift it off.'

And as soon as he did that, any guards in the courtyard looking in their direction would see them. He could hear muffled voices. They could be close. They could even be standing on the stone they had to move to get out.

'As soon as we get this stone off, we have to be ready to fight,' whispered Crutch. 'We'll sneak out if we can, but it's more likely we'll have to fight our way to the control room.'

'It all sounds so exciting,' said Queen Astrid.

'Can you guide us to the control room, Queen Astrid?' whispered Crutch.

'Of course.'

'They'll have arrows and spears,' whispered Crutch. 'You'll be in danger.'

'I am a queen. I've spent my whole life dodging someone's arrows. A few of the fat emperor's guards don't frighten me. I'm looking forward to a little fight out in the open air.'

She was brave. Or crazy. Probably both.

'Thank you,' whispered Crutch. 'Boulder and I will push this stone off, and then we go. Move fast and use your shields. Expect them to fire at us.'

The marines and the soldiers whispered their assent. Crutch pushed up on the stone, with Boulder doing the same. He could feel it shifting then they slowly slid it up and to the side. It was still dark outside, but the first light of dawn was just breaking through the clouds.

Crutch clambered up onto stone tiles, with Boulder right behind him. He looked around and could see some of Emperor Solokov's palace guards on the other side of the courtyard. Worse, lining the walls above him were more guards. In the faint light, he could see crossbows leaning against the battlements.

They had come up close to the middle of the courtyard. They had to get away from here before they were filled full of crossbow bolts.

'Make a circle of shields as you come out,' whispered Crutch.

The marines and the soldiers came out fast. Boulder already hovered over Crutch with his shield up when the first Estovian shouts echoed around the walls.

'Enemy in courtyard,' yelled one palace guard.

'Kill them! Kill them all!' yelled another.

Chapter 42
The Fun's Just Beginning

Queen Astrid came up as the first crossbow bolts fired down on them. Crutch heard two clatter against Boulder's shield. Across the courtyard, Boulder could see a group of palace guards with shields and spears forming up and heading their way. They wouldn't live long if they stayed here.

'Which way is the control room?' said Crutch.

Queen Astrid smiled like she was at a party, and the dancing had just begun. 'Are you sure you don't want to stay and fight?' she said. 'The fun's just beginning.'

'If we stay here, we have about sixty seconds to live,' said Crutch. One of the Ironborn shieldmen next to him took a crossbow bolt in the throat and fell to the stone tiles of the courtyard, clutching it and wheezing, blood running out of his mouth.

'Life is a little overrated if you want my opinion,' said Queen Astrid, watching the dying Ironborn soldier with a happy grin. She patted him on the shoulder. 'There, there. Sleep quietly now, child.'

The marines and the rest of the soldiers closed around the gap the dead soldier made in their shield circle.

'We don't have time for philosophy,' said Crutch. 'Where is the control room?'

'You young people,' said Queen Astrid. 'Always in such a hurry, racing off and forgetting to partake in all the joys and excitements available to you.'

Crossbow bolts rained down now, bouncing off their shields. The first group of Estovian palace guards Crutch saw was now only twenty yards away, moving in formation with shields up and spears out. Two more guard units formed up. This crazy old queen was about to get them all killed.

'Stop playing games,' yelled Crutch. 'Where is the bloody control room?'

'Is that any way to speak to your queen?'

Crutch released the blade on his walking cane and put it to her neck.

'Tell me where the control room is now or I'll cut your throat and leave you here to die…your majesty.'

Queen Astrid smiled.

'What a wonderful instrument of death you have there,' she said, looking at the blade of the walking cane. 'All you had to do was ask nicely. That's the control room there. That red brick tower with the black iron door.'

'To the black iron door,' said Crutch to the marines. 'Shield circle. Stay in formation.'

He'd barely given the order when another soldier beside him took a crossbow bolt to his arm. His shield dropped for just a second, and Crutch felt a crossbow bolt whiz past his neck.

'Keep those shields up!' yelled Sergeant Zander. 'Move. Now. To the black iron door.'

'I'm okay,' said the soldier as Sergeant Zander looked at him. The soldier broke off the crossbow bolt in his arm.

They moved together fast in a tight circle, shields out, with Crutch, Queen Astrid, and the lockpick in the centre. The excitement or the danger must be helping. Queen Astrid didn't need Damen's help to walk now. She went fast enough under her own legs.

'I don't suppose you know where we could find a key to the door?' said Crutch, glancing behind them to see the unit of palace guards with their shields and spears closing the gap between them.

'I'm a queen, not a locksmith.'

'Longshot, can you slow down those guards?' said Crutch.

'Will do, colonel,' said Longshot, slinging his shield on his back and moving to the centre of the shield circle just as they made it to the iron door.

'Get that door unlocked,' said Crutch to the lockpick.

'Yes, colonel,' said the lockpick, pulling out his tools and starting on the lock.

Crossbow bolts rained around them, the heavy thunk of them against their iron shields a constant reminder of the death that awaited them if they made the smallest mistake.

Longshot pulled back his bow, took aim and fired at the guards who were now less than ten yards away. He got an arrow through their shields and one of the guards went down but they didn't even pause. Two more units of palace guards advanced on them from each side. In a few seconds they'd be overrun.

The soldier next to Crutch, who'd already taken a crossbow bolt to the shoulder, made a wheezing sound and dropped to his knees, still holding his shield up. Crutch looked over and saw he'd taken a crossbow bolt to the chest.

Crutch grabbed the shield before he could fall and kept the shield wall in front of them intact. Queen Astrid kneeled next to the soldier and put her hand on his chest as he fell back to the stone tiles of the courtyard.

'He's dead,' she said.

'Get that door open!' yelled Sergeant Zander.

'It's unlocked, but it won't open,' said the lockpick. 'There must be a bolt on the other side.'

'Boulder, open that door,' said Crutch.

'Okay,' said Boulder, going to the door as the other marines closed in the shield wall as he went.

The rain of crossbow bolts had stopped, but that was no cause for celebration. Crutch saw the first line of spears from the unit of palace guards coming towards them.

'Open that door now!' yelled Crutch, deflecting off the head of a spear with his shield.

Beside him, Queen Astrid had a huge grin on her face, like she was a mother thrilled at how a birthday party she'd planned was going for her children.

The palace guard in front of him pulled back his spear and thrust again, this time going lower, aiming for Crutch's legs. Crutch barely kept the spearhead from skewering him.

'Now!' yelled Crutch.

Crutch heard the creaking of the hinges on the iron door, the banging and groaning of something like a bolt straining on the other side. This would make one hell of a place to die. He could hear the stories they'd tell. Got all the way into the courtyard of Emperor

Solokov's palace and were thwarted by a simple iron door. Not even the door to the palace.

He heard Boulder grunt and wheeze, then he heard something give, and the door was open.

'Get inside!' yelled Crutch as he pushed away another thrust from the spear of the palace guard in front of him.

To his right, Crutch heard one of Solokov's palace guards yell, 'Die Ironworm scum!'

The lockpick had moved out of Boulder's way to let him get at the iron door. Crutch tried to the lockpick's shoulder, but he was too late. The lockpick took an Estovian spear to the guts. He fell back, and Queen Astrid caught him as he went down. The crazy old lady had a wild grin on her face.

'Drag him inside with us,' said Crutch to the one soldier left standing.

'Too late,' said the soldier. 'He's dead.'

Crutch and the marines retreated backwards. Boulder let Crutch go past him and took the first line of defence. Sergeant Zander had a hold of Crutch's shirt, guiding him from behind.

Boulder deflected the spears with his shield so hard the Estovians holding them slipped and fell.

'Good work, Boulder,' said Crutch. 'Keep them off balance.'

Crutch saw the iron door as he passed it moving backwards. Somehow Boulder had bent a solid bar far enough to make the door give way. He'd ripped one of the metal hinges loose too. The door hung on the remaining hinge at the bottom.

There was no way they could close that door behind them. They'd have to make a fighting retreat all the way up the tower, with the palace guards following them. Unless Crutch came up with another idea.

'Stairs,' said Sergeant Zander from behind him.

Crutch grabbed Boulder's shirt and started pulling him along, just like Sergeant Zander did for him. Boulder pushed off one Estovian spear with his shield, grabbed another with his hand, and yanked it out of the palace guard's hands.

There was a look of surprise in the guard's eyes when he lost his spear. The surprise quickly changed to shock as Boulder rammed the blunt end of the spear through his throat with sickening force.

But the Estovians didn't stop. Crutch could see thirty or forty of them outside, all waiting for their chance. Crutch took his first step backwards up the stairs.

'Stairs behind you now,' he said to Boulder.

They couldn't get up these stairs alive with so many Estovians behind them. It was just a matter of time before one of them slipped and the guards overran them. And when they got to the top of the stairs, Crutch expected there'd be more palace guards armed and ready to fight.

'Quicksilver, light these guards up,' yelled Crutch.

'You sure?' said Quicksilver from a few steps above him and behind him.

'I can't believe I have to ask you twice,' said Crutch. Crutch had to hope they didn't burn themselves in a fire of their own making. This tower was made of brick, so he figured their chances were better than average.

A ball of bluefire sailed over Crutch's head and landed at the feet of the Estovian palace guards. Then another. The guards didn't react. Clearly, they'd never seen what bluefire could do.

'Five seconds,' yelled Quicksilver.

Boulder was still way too close. If that bluefire went off now, he'd be burned to a cinder.

'Four,' yelled Quicksilver.

'Get up those stairs!' yelled Sergeant Zander. Crutch could hear the marines clearing the stairs above him and started going back, pulling hard on Boulder's shirt.

'Three!' Quicksilver's voice had an edge of panic he'd never heard before. Boulder was still close. Way too close. One of the Estovians kicked a ball of bluefire as he moved forward. It rolled towards Boulder's feet.

'Two! Get Boulder up the stairs!' yelled Quicksilver.

Crutch knew it was too late. The ball of bluefire was about to set them both on fire. There was just one chance. Instead of going back, Crutch went forward.

'One! What the fuck are you doing, Crutch?'

Chapter 43
Never A Good Day To Die

The ball of bluefire was right between Boulder's legs now. Boulder looked down, fear on his face.

Crutch came behind Boulder, balanced on his cane, and kicked the ball of bluefire as hard as he could. It rolled back, bouncing between the legs and the feet of the palace guards.

He grabbed Boulder and pulled him back up one step of the stone stairs, then two, then the world around them exploded in blue flames. Crutch and Boulder cowered behind Boulder's huge metal shield, flames roaring around the edges.

When the flames stopped, Crutch peered around the shield and saw palace guards on fire, running into walls, flailing, screaming. One lay near their feet, moaning; the clothes burned off his body.

Queen Astrid went down the steps to him and kneeled next to him, placing her hands on his burnt flesh.

'Poor boy,' she said. 'You sleep now.'

The palace guard went silent.

Behind him, Crutch could hear swords ringing. The rest of the marines must be engaging the guards at the top of the tower.

'Are you okay, Boulder?' said Crutch.

The hair on the top of Boulder's head looked black and singed, but by some miracle, his body didn't look like it had been burned.

'I'm okay,' said Boulder. 'Your hair's black, Crutch.'

Crutch felt the top of his hair. It must have been burnt by the fire, just like Boulder's. Crutch felt the rest of his body. No burns. Nothing bad enough that he could feel it in any case.

'That was scary,' said Boulder.

Crutch looked in front of him, where the palace guards burned. More would be coming. They'd push past their burning compatriots and kill any Ironborn they found in this tower. Crutch and the marines had to finish the job they'd started.

'Come on, Boulder. We need to get those palace gates open.'

'Okay,' said Boulder.

'You too, Queen Astrid,' said Crutch, looking at Queen Astrid who tended to the burned Estovians. 'It's not safe here.'

'But they're so young,' said Queen Astrid, looking at Crutch with a strange mix of disappointment and excitement.

Combat has a strange effect on people. He couldn't leave Queen Astrid here. The Estovians would kill her, even if she was helping their men. And if she did know how to get to Emperor Solokov in the palace, he needed her with the marines, alive.

'We have to go,' said Crutch. 'Leave them.'

'It's such a horrid waste,' said Queen Astrid, heading up the stairs. The excitement of battle had given her strength. She walked the stairs easily now. He'd seen that before on the Kona Track. Men with feats of strength in battle that seemed impossible. Then they'd collapse in exhaustion afterwards.

They moved up the winding stone staircase of the tower. When they rounded the first bend, Crutch could see Damen and Sergeant Zander engaging two guards at the top of the stairs. Longshot was behind them with his bow but couldn't get a shot off with the marines and the tower guards all using shields.

Crutch could see a total of four palace guards at the top of the stairs. They were all armed with swords, not spears. The marines should be able to take four guards, but if more Estovians came from the bottom of the tower, there was no way the marines could survive that.

'Quicksilver, Longshot, get down behind us and stop any Estovians who try to come up those stairs, said Crutch. Use fire if you have to.'

Quicksilver smiled. 'Yes colonel. I'll burn 'em to ash.'

'Come on, Boulder,' said Crutch. Let's give Damen and Sergeant Zander a hand.'

'Okay,' said Boulder.

They advanced up the steps. When Crutch was behind Damen, he released the blade on his walking cane. Time to use some tricks he'd learned from the Estovian soldiers.

The Estovian guards were good fighters, but using just swords there was no way the guards in the second line could help their compatriots in the first line. Or defend them.

Crutch stabbed past Damen at the guard he fought, using his walking cane like a spear. The guard raised his shield to block the first stab, lowered it to block the second, and Damen went straight over the Estovian's shield with his sword and thrust it straight into his neck.

'Just like training,' said Damen. 'Thank you, colonel.'

'It's not over yet,' said Crutch as another guard moved in from behind his dead comrade, ready to fight.

From down the stairs, Crutch heard Quicksilver yelling.

'Come on, you Stovie bastards. I'll burn the lot of you.'

He could smell the burning and feel the heat of the fire below him. Quicksilver must be using more bluefire.

The guard falling had left a gap at the side of the Estovian Sergeant Zander fought. Crutch moved over, waited until Sergeant Zander launched an attack, and stabbed the guard in the foot with his walking cane.

This guard knew how to fight. He fought as if cold steel hadn't just sliced into his foot. But against a trained killer like Sergeant Zander, any distraction was likely to be your last.

Sergeant Zander pushed forward as Crutch stabbed at the guard's feet again. This time, the guard was wise to Crutch's attacks and used his shield to fend them off. Sergeant Zander thrust at his feet too and the guard smiled. There was no way he would get stabbed in the feet by either of them.

He was so fixated on Sergeant Zander and Crutch the guard didn't see Damen's sword until it was buried in his side. Just like training. It's always the attack you don't see coming.

As the guard fell, Sergeant Zander thrust his sword through his head to be sure. Then he stepped on his dead body and plunged his sword into the side of the guard Damen fought.

Just two Estovian guards left, and Boulder could get into the control room now.

From below him, Crutch heard Longshot.

'There's too many of them, Crutch. We can't hold them much longer.'

Quicksilver must be out of bluefire. How much had he used down there?

'We only need one more minute,' yelled Crutch.

'You'll have it,' yelled Longshot.

Boulder pushed past Sergeant Zander and Damen and used his shield as a weapon. He smashed one guard in the face so hard, the guard smacked back against the brick wall behind him. Then the guard looked up in panic as he saw Boulder advance on him with the shield.

Boulder swung back and smacked the shield into the guard's head. Only one guard left.

The last guard should have surrendered. He was up against four marines who obviously knew how to fight. But Crutch got a lesson in just how fanatical Solokov's personal palace guards were.

The guard stood his ground with his back to a brick wall, shield up, and sword ready.

'Lay down your weapon,' said Crutch. 'You don't have a chance.'

'Come get me, Ironworms,' said the guard. 'Is good day to die.'

Damen moved in, thrusting and parrying with his sword. Crutch went in behind him, stabbing high with his walking cane while Damen went low. The Estovian could fight, at least. He stopped every attack.

Sergeant Zander came in from the side and thrust his sword clean through the guard's head and out the other side.

'It's never a good day to die,' he said.

Chapter 44
We Die Like Men

Now they had another problem. The soldier who knew how to run the chains and levers in a control room was dead. Through a barred window, Crutch could see the gates.

In the light of dawn, he saw Ironborn troops forming up, ready to fight. So Anton and the komitav had let them through.

He went to the bewildering array of levers and wheels in the room.

'Does anyone know how to get the gates open and those portcullis raised?' said Crutch.

Quicksilver and Longshot appeared on the stairs.

'Your minute's up,' said Longshot.

'I'm out of bluefire,' said Quicksilver. 'And there are at least twenty Estovians coming up those stairs.'

Crutch pulled on the first lever. Nothing.

He pulled on the second. Nothing.

Then he pulled on the third. Still nothing.

Boulder and Sergeant Zander met the first Estovian guards at the top of the stairs. Boulder hit the first guard who got near him so hard he fell back and knocked down two guards behind him, their weapons and shields clattering on the stairs as they fell amongst each other.

Quicksilver came over to help get the gates and the portcullis open.

'Try the wheels,' he said.

Crutch tried to turn one of the three wheels.

'It won't move,' said Crutch.

Quicksilver pulled on the wheel with Crutch, but even together they couldn't get it to turn. Crutch looked over and saw Boulder smashing a guard with a shield, still holding the Estovians at the top of the stairs. There was no way he could help.

'We can't hold them much longer,' yelled Sergeant Zander. 'You need to get those gates open now.'

Queen Astrid stood in the control room behind all the fighting with a crazy grin on her face.

Longshot pulled his sword and joined Sergeant Zander at the top of the stairs, prodding between him and Boulder, making it as uncomfortable for the Estovian guards as he could. But Crutch could see they were on borrowed time. At any second, they'd be overwhelmed.

'You turn this wheel while I pull the lever,' said Crutch.

'Will do, colonel,' said Quicksilver.

Crutch grabbed hold of the first lever and pulled it back. Quicksilver turned the first wheel, and it moved. Crutch looked out the barred window and saw the gates at the front of the palace move an inch.

'It's working,' he said. 'Keep turning that wheel.'

Quicksilver turned hard, sweat coming off him. Behind them, Crutch could hear Sergeant Zander and Boulder fighting the Estovian guards. Then the palace gates were open enough for the Ironborn troops assembled outside to start coming through.

They advanced in a shield wall, arrows from the Estovian palace guards bouncing off their shields. To get into the courtyard, they'd have to go through a tunnel blocked by a portcullis. With that portcullis shut, the Ironborn troops would be trapped and shot to pieces by the Estovians.

'Turn the next wheel,' said Crutch as he pulled the second lever.

Quicksilver pulled hard on the second wheel, and Crutch could see the portcullis lift an inch. The Ironborn troops kept moving forward through a hail of crossbow bolts and arrows. For a brief second, as one shieldman went down with a crossbow bolt to the head, he saw Captain Travis, calling out orders, keeping his troops in formation, keeping them disciplined.

It was just a glimpse, then another shieldman blocked up the gap.

Quicksilver pulled on the wheel hard, his muscles straining, his breathing heavy. Then the portcullis was up.

'The third wheel,' said Crutch, pulling on the third lever. Crutch hoped this lifted the portcullis that blocked the way from the courtyard into the palace.

Quicksilver moved to the third wheel and pulled hard.

They couldn't see the portcullis to the palace from here, but Crutch heard a scraping sound. He hoped that was the portcullis lifting.

'Keep going,' he said. 'I think it's working.'

Quicksilver wrenched on the wheel as hard and as fast as he could, his muscles straining with the effort.

Behind them, the Estovian guards pushed back the marines. If they got enough guards up those stairs, they could surround the marines, and then it would just be a matter of time before they were all dead.

'That's as far as it will go,' said Quicksilver.

'That will have to be enough then,' said Crutch. 'Let's find a way out of this room.'

Crutch scanned the walls. There was only one window, and it had solid metal bars sunk deep into the brick wall at the top and the bottom.

'Quicksilver, take Boulder's place in the line,' said Crutch. 'Let's see if he can bend these bars.

Quicksilver nodded and took Boulder's place, with the marines fighting the Estovian guards in a line four wide. Damen, Sergeant Zander, Longshot, and Quicksilver tried to hold back the Estovian guards, but it was obvious there were too many of them.

They needed to get out of this room now.

Boulder came to the iron bars, put down his shield, and grabbed two of the bars. His muscles strained as he tried to pull them apart, tried to bend them.

Nothing.

'Try pulling them out of the wall,' said Crutch.

Boulder put his feet against the brick wall and pulled in, hanging on to the bars.

Nothing.

The bars didn't rattle, didn't move. Not even a fraction of an inch.

'They won't move,' said Boulder.

Outside the window, through the bars, Crutch could see hundreds of Ironborn troops pouring through the open palace gates.

If they could just get out there, they had a chance. But there was no way out there.

They would die here in this stinking control room. If they died, they could at least die fighting.

'Let's join the line,' said Crutch.

Boulder took up his shield, and Crutch moved in behind the marines with the blade on his walking cane drawn. Crutch prodded at the guards, distracting them as well as he could.

Damen was a deadly force of destruction, but these palace guards were highly disciplined, well trained, and there were just too many of them.

When one guard fell, the guards behind him would pull him out of the way and reform the line in seconds. And more guards kept coming up those stairs. A few more seconds, and they'd be surrounded, and it would all be over.

Crutch tried to think of a way out of this, but he had nothing. He looked over and saw Queen Astrid grinning. The old lady must have completely lost her senses after being locked up all those years. Didn't she know that losing this battle meant certain death for her too?

'Anyone have any ideas?' said Crutch as they were pushed back inch by inch.

'Hold this room long enough for all the Ironborn troops to get through the gates,' said Sergeant Zander.

'And then?' said Crutch.

'Then we die like men,' said Sergeant Zander.

When Sergeant Zander saw the only option as dying in battle, you knew you were in serious trouble.

'Dying like men it is,' said Crutch. 'Let's hold these Estovians off as long as we can. Don't let them get to the controls for the gates. Do we stand together?'

'Yes, colonel,' said the marines in unison.

'Are we willing to die together?' said Crutch.

'Yes, colonel,' said the marines in unison.

'Magnificent,' said Queen Astrid, smiling like she was watching a performance at a royal party. If she could, Crutch swore she'd be quite at home, sipping a cup of tea, watching them all die. Didn't she understand she was about to die too?

Chapter 45
At Your Service

The Estovian guards pushed forward, and the marines pushed back just as hard. Every second of time they could buy meant more Ironborn troops coming through those gates and hopefully into the palace to kill Emperor Solokov.

'Push men,' yelled Crutch. 'Push 'em back!'

With a mighty, coordinated heave, the marines pushed the Estovians back a foot. But the Estovians immediately pushed back even harder. Foot by foot, the marines were losing this battle.

Their backs were almost to the levers of the control room. So this is where it ends, thought Crutch.

Then something wonderful happened.

Roof tiles showered down from above them, and spears came through the roof straight into the heads and the shoulders of the Estovian guards in the front line. The single guard left standing in the first line, Damen ran through with his sword.

Then smashed roof tiles and the spears came down again, into the Estovian guards in the second line. Stabbing, plunging into their bodies, fierce, bloody, merciless.

'Marvellous show,' said Queen Astrid. She applauded, three fingers tapping against her palm in the royal fashion.

Ironborn soldiers dropped through the roof above them and joined the battle.

'Into them,' yelled their Captain as he dropped into the control room. More Ironborn soldiers dropped through the roof. Too many for the Estovians to hold back.

'Captain Travis,' said Crutch.

'At your service,' said Captain Travis.

'How did you know we were here?'

'When I saw the bluefire coming out of this tower, I figured that would be you marines working on getting the gates open. So I got the men into formation. I saw a pile of Estovians going into this tower and thought you might like some help.'

'Thank you,' said Crutch. 'You got here just in time.'

'Glad to be of service,' said Captain Travis.

The Ironborn troops kept coming through the roof.

'Those are the controls to the gates and the portcullis there,' said Crutch. 'We need to occupy this tower to keep them open.'

'Consider it done,' said Captain Travis, turning to one of his soldiers. 'Sergeant Rogund, you're in charge of holding this tower. Don't let any Estovians get to those levers and wheels there. I'll give you thirty men.

'Yes, sir,' said the Sergeant.

Crutch looked out the iron bars of the window and saw Ironborn troops flooding through the gates. Solokov had to know he was in trouble now. What would his next move be?

Whatever it was, he couldn't do anything about it stuck here in this tower.

'Marines, we need to get out of here and into the courtyard,' said Crutch. 'You coming with us, Captain Travis?'

'You couldn't stop me,' said Captain Travis.

'What about Queen Astrid?' said Sergeant Zander.

Crutch looked over at Queen Astrid, who kneeled at the body of one of the Estovians.

'Bring her with us,' said Crutch. 'We'll need her to get to Solokov in the palace.

The Ironborn soldiers on the roof dropped ropes so the marines could climb to the rafters. They made a rope harness for Queen Astrid, who giggled happily as they hauled her up. From the roof of the tower, Crutch could see the battle in the courtyard.

The portcullis to the palace was half open, but the palace guards fought in force to stop the Ironborn troops getting to it. Palace guards also shot from the first floor of the palace with crossbows and arrows.

The Ironborn troops moved in shield walls, but when they got close to the troops near the gates, they were easy targets for the bowmen and crossbowmen on the first floor of the palace. The courtyard rapidly became a killing field.

'What a sight,' said Queen Astrid, grinning.

'We need to make the Estovians in front of that portcullis break,' said Crutch. 'Any ideas?'

'If I had some bluefire, I'd make 'em break,' said Quicksilver. 'But I'm out.'

'I can't shoot them from here,' said Longshot. 'They're moving, and they're too close to our own troops.'

'I say we get down there and cut a path through them ourselves,' said Damen.

'Damen's right,' said Sergeant Zander. 'Our best chance is to use the spear formation and push through them. With Ironborn soldiers behind us, every Estovian we push aside as we go forward will be cut to pieces.'

'That sounds like a splendid plan,' said Queen Astrid. 'Well done, Sergeant Zander.'

'Let's get down to the courtyard,' said Crutch. 'Are you with us, Captain Travis?'

'All the way to Solokov,' said Captain Travis.

Crutch and the marines climbed down the ropes on grappling hooks Captain Travis's men had thrown up to get onto the roof. Captain Travis and a couple of his soldiers lowered Queen Astrid, then climbed down too.

'Do you all remember the spear formation?' said Crutch.

The marines nodded. Way back when war first broke out between Ironbay and Estovia, the marines were caught in a crush of rioters in Ironbay. Sergeant Zander designed the spear formation to drive through a rioting crowd.

Sergeant Zander would go at the head of the spear, pushing anyone in front of him aside. Behind him, on either side, marines would kill or push away the men Sergeant Zander had pushed through.

By moving fast, you could move twenty or thirty yards forward through a crush of rioters. But the spear formation had its problems.

Crutch had tried it on the Kona Track against trained Estovian soldiers, and the enemy weren't so easily pushed out of their formations. They'd been drilled for years to keep their shield walls tight.

So it might not work at all.

Worse still, you could push forward twenty or thirty yards and end up surrounded by the enemy. If this was going to work, the Ironborn troops behind them had to fight to tear the Estovians pushed to their sides to pieces.

Before they could even employ the spear formation, they had to get across the courtyard under the fire of enemy bowmen and crossbow men, over the blood and fallen bodies of Ironborn soldiers and Estovian palace guards.

And if they were to have a chance of getting to Emperor Solokov in the palace, they needed to do it while keeping Queen Astrid alive so she could show them how to get to him.

'Form up with shields,' said Crutch. 'Queen Astrid in the middle. Keep her protected. Boulder, pick up the first axe you see. When we get to the Estovians, I want you to cut them to pieces.'

'But it's my job to keep you safe,' said Boulder.

'We'll be surrounded by Estovians when we get to that portcullis,' said Crutch. 'The best way to keep me safe is to kill as many Estovians as you can.'

'Okay, Crutch,' said Boulder.

'Captain Travis, get your troops to follow behind us. When we start pushing through them, the Estovians will try to attack us from our flanks. We're relying on you to stop them from doing that.'

'We'll cut them to pieces,' said Captain Travis.

'Splendid!' said Queen Astrid, her eyes wide with excitement and a huge grin on her face.

The old lady seemed to be as mad as a hatter. He hoped she really did know how to get to Emperor Solokov in the palace. If they could get through the entrance, stumbling around in there with no idea where they were or where the emperor was would likely be the last thing they ever did.

'We go,' said Crutch.

Sergeant Zander was at the head of the spear. Boulder was at his left, carrying his massive shield, and Damen was at his right, also with a shield. Crutch, Longshot, and Quicksilver came behind them, with Queen Astrid in between them.

As they moved forward over the courtyard and through the Ironborn troops, Sergeant Zander yelled, 'Move aside then follow us in.'

Behind them, Crutch could hear Travis yelling, 'Cover the flanks.'

The Estovians saw them coming. Crossbow bolts and arrows started hitting their shields when they were twenty yards from the portcullis. Boulder and Damen covered Sergeant Zander with their shields at the front.

Once they reached the Estovian guards, their bowmen and crossbow men couldn't fire on them without risking hitting their own men. Damen and Boulder opened their shields, and Sergeant Zander pushed the first Estovian guard to his left, moving forward fast.

Boulder hit the guard with his shield so hard he was flung into the wall of the palace, where he slumped onto the stone tiles. Sergeant Zander grabbed the spear of the next Estovian guard and heaved him to the right. As he went sideways, the guard's shield came down and Damen stabbed him in the head with his sword, then used his momentum to push him out of the way.

They were ten yards from the half-raised iron portcullis that led into the palace. Crutch didn't expect Solokov's highly trained palace guards to make this easy.

Sergeant Zander pushed the next Estovian guard to his left, but this guard was ready for it. He waited until Sergeant Zander pushed him, anticipating the move, then thrust his spear straight for Sergeant Zander's guts.

The guard didn't anticipate Boulder using an axe he'd picked up on his push through the courtyard. Boulder swung down through the palace guard's shield with such force it bent the iron and kept right on going. The axe went straight through the palace guard's spear arm, taking it off above the wrist.

Boulder followed through by smashing the guard with his shield. The guard flew back and smashed his head against the bottom iron bars of the half-raised portcullis.

They were seven yards away now, but the palace guards reformed into a triple row; swordsmen with shields at the front, spearmen just behind them, and another row of swordsmen behind them.

Trying to use the spear against that formation would be suicide. Crutch needed another idea, and he needed it now or Sergeant Zander, Damen, and Boulder would be dead in a few seconds, and the rest of the marines shortly after.

How could he use that formation against them? He looked again and realised that by forming up in a triple line, the Estovian guards had left space on the left side of their line. Worse for them, being backed against the half-raised portcullis would make it hard for them to manoeuvre quickly. It's always the attack you don't see coming.

'Halt!' yelled Crutch.

Sergeant Zander stopped, Boulder and Damen closed shields in front of him, the Estovians prodding at them with their spears.

'Captain Travis,' said Crutch. 'Bring your best ten men. We're taking that left flank.'

Captain Travis looked at the gap on the left flank of the Estovians, smiled, and said, 'Yes, colonel.'

The Estovian guards in the back row were pressed against the half raised portcullis, which came down to around waist height. That meant they couldn't move back easily. They'd have to duck, and then they'd be separated from the guards in front of the portcullis.

That also meant if they could stop the guards from moving forward, they'd be vulnerable from the side. There was no way they could form an effective shield wall to protect their flank pressed up against that portcullis. If they could break one shieldman, they could cut through the guards from the side and leave them in disarray.

Crutch and Captain Travis led from the front, moving fast. They didn't want to give the Estovian guards a chance to realise their mistake and change formation.

Captain Travis got to the shieldman and thrust high with his sword. Crutch went low with the blade of his cane. The shieldman was good. He parried off both attacks with his shield. An Estovian shieldman behind him was distracted by one of Captain Travis's men moving beside Crutch to attack from beside him. That would help. The shieldman didn't have anyone to support him.

Crutch went low again, and Captain Travis did the same. Crutch immediately saw what Captain Travis had in mind. The shieldman would assume the man with a sword was the biggest threat. As the shieldman pushed his shield down low, Crutch switched his attack and thrust the blade on his cane straight into the head of the shieldman.

Captain Travis pushed the shieldman's body aside as he fell.

'Into them,' he yelled.

His men pushed in from the side, and the Estovian guards began to panic. With the marines attacking them from the front and Captain Travis, Crutch, and his men taking them from the flank, it was impossible for them to defend themselves.

Crutch kept moving, stabbing at every Estovian guard he could, concentrating to maintain his balance as he stepped over the dead guards and their blood on the stone tiles. The guards wouldn't hold for long now.

He looked for their next goal, the inside of the palace. Beyond the portcullis, he couldn't see any guards, but he expected Emperor Solokov would have plenty of surprises for them. As the last Estovian guard in front of him fell, Crutch looked behind him.

Out in the courtyard, Ironborn troops skirmished with a handful of Estovian guards they had surrounded. The guards wouldn't last long.

Closer, Queen Astrid kneeled next to a dying Ironborn soldier. She spoke softly with her hands placed gently on the soldier's chest. She stayed there until the soldier took his final breath, then she got up and walked to another wounded soldier, this time an Estovian.

Crutch turned back to see the last of the Estovian guards at the portcullis go down. Ironborn soldiers began stooping down to get under the half-raised portcullis.

'Damen,' said Crutch. 'Get me Queen Astrid. We'll need her to navigate the palace and get to Emperor Solokov.'

'Yes, colonel,' said Damen.

Queen Astrid kneeled over another Ironborn soldier as Damen got to her. Queen Astrid looked up, smiled, patted Damen's hand, and came with him.

Crutch turned and bent to go under the portcullis himself. Ahead was a long tunnel made from stone bricks.

'Wait!' yelled Crutch before the Ironborn soldiers could enter the tunnel. Getting men killed unnecessarily was not part of the plan for taking the palace.

Damen and Queen Astrid got to Crutch. Queen Astrid had a manic grin on her face, and she wasn't hobbling any more. The excitement of battle must have perked her up.

'What's in that tunnel ahead?' said Crutch.

'I can't tell you with any certainty what's in there now,' said Queen Astrid, smiling.

She was enjoying this. Crutch decided to play her game. If it meant saving lives, it was a small price to pay.

'After you had the tunnel built, what did you put in there?' said Crutch.

'Twenty guards with pikes and spears above the tunnel. There are some lovely holes in the ceiling they can poke their weapons through. They're the most marvellous little murder holes. I'm very proud of them.'

'Is there any other way into the palace,' said Crutch.

'Oh no. That would spoil all the fun,' said Queen Astrid.

'Any ideas, Sergeant Zander?' said Crutch.

'Murder holes in the ceiling can be a real bastard,' said Sergeant Zander. 'You can't fire through them. If you try to stick a weapon up there, the guards can just stand away from the hole. And once you're under any of the holes, the guards can stab and prod at you with their weapons.'

'Isn't it marvellous!' said Queen Astrid.

'Our best chance is to grab the guards' weapons as they stab at us and break them in half or pull them out of their hands,' said Sergeant Zander. 'Then hope they don't have too many spare pikes and spears up there.'

'Oh, they will,' said Queen Astrid. 'I made racks full of them.'

Crutch frowned. 'Any other ideas,' he said.

Before anyone else could speak, Crutch saw it out of the corner of his eye. A streak of orange falling to the courtyard outside.

Crutch dropped to the ground and saw Queen Astrid turn to face it.

The courtyard exploded in orange flame.

Chapter 46
Please Don't Be Dead

For an instant, Queen Astrid stood there, grinning, then she was flung like a rag doll along with Crutch, the Ironborn soldiers, and the marines down the tunnel until they hit the stone wall at the other end.

For a few seconds, the world went black, then Crutch forced his eyes open.

The smell of burning flesh made Crutch gag and his eyes water. He looked, and he saw Ironborn troops on fire out in the courtyard.

Some were mercifully dead already; some were burning to death.

A buzz went through his ears. He looked at the marines in a pile around him. He opened his mouth to speak, but he couldn't hear any of the words come out.

Crutch saw Boulder lying on his back, his massive shield now coated in black. Crutch crawled to him and shook his shoulder.

Please don't be dead, Boulder. Please don't be dead.

Boulder didn't move. Crutch shook his shoulder harder. Boulder's eyes came open for a second, then fluttered shut.

Crutch looked up to see Sergeant Zander push up to his hands and knees, then fall to his stomach again. The back of his uniform was jet black.

Longshot lay on his side. He was still, then he coughed.

Queen Astrid was the first to stand as if she hadn't just been flung thirty yards into a solid stone wall. She got up, smiling, and said something Crutch couldn't understand.

Quicksilver stood up next to her, and they both smiled like they were chatting at a party.

The buzzing in Crutch's ears began to subside.

'That was magnificent,' said Queen Astrid.

'I know,' said Quicksilver.

'Don't just stand there,' said Crutch, grabbing his cane and pulling himself to his feet. 'Help the wounded.'

'Of course,' said Queen Astrid. She went to the first soldier she could find, kneeled down, and placed her hands on him. 'No life left in this one.'

Quicksilver kneeled at Longshot's side, shaking him.

Crutch balance on his walking cane and kneeled next to Sergeant Zander, whose eyes were open but unfocused.

'Come on, sergeant,' said Crutch. 'We can't stay here. You have to get up.'

Sergeant Zander just lay there, his breath coming in long gasps. They couldn't stay here. The Estovian guards in the room above them knew they were here and would know they were helpless. If they didn't get up they'd die. Crutch grabbed Sergeant Zander's shoulder and shook him as hard as he could.

'Come on, soldier,' yelled Crutch. 'Get on your fucking feet.'

Sergeant Zander's eyes focused. 'Where are we?' he said.

'We're through the tunnel in Solokov's palace,' said Crutch. 'His guards will be coming for us.'

'Fuck,' said Sergeant Zander, groaning as he pushed himself up and got to his feet.

'Can you help me get the other men moving?' said Crutch.

'Yes,' said Sergeant Zander. 'Yes, colonel.' Sergeant Zander half walked, half stumbled to where Damen lay, and shook his body.

Crutch saw Captain Travis on his knees, struggling to get to his feet.

'What happened, colonel?' he said, when he saw Crutch.

'They used orange fire,' said Crutch. Crutch looked out in the courtyard. As far as he could see, there were dead Ironborn soldiers. The Ironborn soldiers who weren't dead were on fire. Crutch couldn't see him, but somewhere out there was Young Lord Talbot. General Talbot had paid a high price for this invasion.

Captain Travis looked out there too.

'I have to help them,' he said.

Crutch grabbed him before he could move.

'You can't go through the tunnel,' said Crutch. 'The Estovian guards above us will cut us to pieces through those murder holes.'

Captain Travis looked up and nodded.

'We have to kill Solokov with the men we have here,' said Crutch. Right now, that was not an inspiring thought. They had a handful of marines and soldiers, most still lying unconscious on the stone tiles, and an old lady who said she knew how to get to the emperor but was as mad as a hatter. 'Solokov's guards will know we're here. They'll be coming. We have to get these men up.'

'Yes, colonel,' said Captain Travis. He grabbed the soldier lying closest to him and said, 'Get on your feet, soldier.' No response. Captain Travis rolled him over, and saw that he was dead.

Crutch went back to Boulder, who was still lying there on his back with his shield on top of him.

'Come on, Boulder,' said Crutch. 'You have to get up.' He shook Boulder's shoulder. Nothing but a few deep, raspy breaths. Crutch put his mouth next to Boulder's ear. 'Grandma says you have to get up now.'

'Grandma?' said Boulder, his eyes flickering.

'Get up now,' said Crutch. Crutch didn't know how long it would take for the palace guards to get to them here, but he knew it wouldn't be long.

'Can't I sleep a bit longer, grandma,' said Boulder. 'I'm tired.'

'Get up now!' yelled Crutch.

Boulder's eyes opened.

'Crutch, where's grandma?'

'She's safe in Ironbay. We're in Teevilgrad, in the palace. You have to get up now. Estovian guards are coming.'

'Okay,' said Boulder, lifting his shield and rolling on his side. As he pushed up onto his legs, he dropped his shield, his knees went out from under him, and he fell on his face. 'My legs are funny.'

'You're just woozy from being knocked out,' said Crutch. 'You can do it. Push yourself up with your arms, then get to your feet slowly.'

'Okay,' said Boulder, pushing himself up. It was so slow it was painful to watch.

Crutch was terrified now. They didn't have time for this. He could hear footsteps coming from a distance and the sound of steel on steel. Most likely guards marching with swords and shields.

Boulder finally found his feet. Crutch went to Queen Astrid, who kneeled at the side of another dead soldier.

'Is there some way from here into the palace the guards don't know about?' said Crutch.

Queen Astrid looked up and smiled. 'There could be,' she said.

'We don't have time for games,' said Crutch. 'Guards are coming, and they'll kill us all if we're still around when they get here.'

'You young commoners,' said Queen Astrid. 'You're always so impatient. Rushing from one place to the next like there's somewhere special you should be. You know sooner or later you all end up in the same place.'

'Enough of the riddles,' said Crutch. 'Do you really want to die?'

'I'm a hundred and seven years old,' said Queen Astrid. 'Death holds no fears for me. You should try it.'

Crutch had enough of this. They couldn't stand around while this crazy old lady talked in riddles.

'If you're not going to help us, we'll find a way to Solokov ourselves,' he said.

'The fat emperor,' said Queen Astrid. 'In all this excitement, I forgot you came here to kill him. Of course, I'll help you. This way.'

Queen Astrid sprung to her feet and walked into the only stone corridor that led deeper into the palace. Crutch stood there, stunned. What was this? She turned and looked at Crutch, the marines, and the half dozen soldiers now standing.

'Are you coming?' she said.

'In formation,' said Crutch. 'Follow Queen Astrid.'

'That's quite impressive,' said Queen Astrid, watching the marines and the soldiers form up. 'You don't even raise your voice, and your men follow you. That kind of leadership and respect is rare, you know. There's something special about you, Colonel Crutch.'

'Can we go?' said Crutch.

'You know you shouldn't rush a queen,' said Queen Astrid. 'It isn't proper.'

Crutch could hear guards coming, the sound of metal on shields getting closer.

'If we don't go now, queen or not, you'll just be another corpse.'

'They won't kill me,' said Queen Astrid. 'But since you are in such a hurry, we need to head down this corridor. If it's still here, there'll be a passage that leads to some stairs about fifty yards down.'

'Thank you,' said Crutch, and turned to the soldiers. 'Two shieldmen at the front to protect the queen.'

'I feel so safe now,' said Queen Astrid as the shieldmen moved in front of her with the marines behind.

'How do we find this passage?' said Crutch after they'd gone fifty yards down the stone corridor.

'It's hidden in the stone wall,' said Queen Astrid. 'We have to feel for it.'

'Palace guards,' said Captain Travis.

Crutch looked up and saw Estovians moving together, shields up, coming around a junction in the corridor in front of them. He could already see ten of them, but from the sound there were a whole lot more.

They were two wide, with spears bristling in front of them like a promise of death. More guards than they could fight and get out alive. And right now, his men were all still woozy from being slammed into a stone wall by a blast of orange fire.

'We need to find that passage now,' said Crutch. 'Longshot, see if you can give those Estovians something to think about. Buy us some time.'

'Yes, colonel,' said Longshot, unslinging his bow.

'Help me find this passage,' said Crutch to the other marines as he heard one of Longshot's arrows bounce harmlessly off an Estovian shield.

'It will feel like a loose stone brick,' said Queen Astrid. 'You push it in, and the wall opens like a door.'

Crutch pushed on every stone brick in front of him, starting as high as he could reach, going all the way down to the floor. Nothing.

He glanced over and saw Longshot hit an Estovian guard in the helmet with an arrow. The arrow glanced off and hit a guard behind him in the shoulder. The Estovian guards didn't even pause. They just kept coming, like the Estovians did all those years ago on the Kona Track.

'Hold them back!' yelled Captain Travis to his soldiers. 'Shieldmen at the front, spears behind.'

'This is so exciting,' said Queen Astrid, a wild look of glee on her face.

Crutch began to question the wisdom of trusting this woman. If there was no passage, they'd die right here in this corridor.

The Ironborn and Estovian shieldmen came together with a clanging of metal on metal. An Ironborn soldier pushed his spear past the shield of an Estovian and into the guts of the Estovian guard behind him.

One of the Estovian shieldmen reached over his shield with his sword and stabbed an Ironborn soldier on the front line straight through the face. The Ironborn shieldman crumpled, his blood staining the stone tiles underneath him. Another Ironborn soldier grabbed his shield as he fell and took his place immediately.

Captain Travis had trained his men well, but in this type of combat, with no quarter given and no way to retreat, those soldiers wouldn't last more than a minute or two. The Estovians pushed forward, not caring about the risk of being stabbed or cut by Ironborn swords and spears.

Crutch saw another Ironborn soldier run through with a spear. He had to find this passage now.

He ran his hand over row after row of stone bricks, pushing every one. Nothing. He could hear the clash of steel around him, getting closer. He used two hands, his walking cane clattering as it fell to the stone tiles. One stone brick after another. Still nothing.

'Where the hell is the brick?' he said punching the wall with his fist.

Chapter 47
My Feeble Old Mind

And it moved. The brick moved! He pushed harder on the brick he'd punched and pushed all the way in, and the wall shifted in just a fraction of an inch.

'That's it,' said Queen Astrid, grinning. 'Now you push the wall in.'

'Help me push,' said Crutch to Boulder, who was standing beside him with his shield up.

Boulder pushed on the wall, with Crutch and Sergeant Zander helping. Crutch could hear the grinding of stone on stone, and a door-sized part of the wall moved in. They kept pushing until it was wide enough to get through. On the other side was a dark tunnel.

'Through the door,' yelled Crutch. 'Fighting retreat.'

The marines and Queen Astrid went first, moving into the darkness of the tunnel. Captain Travis and the marines came after them, moving backwards with shields up.

The palace guards increased the intensity of their attacks. Clearly they didn't want Ironborn to escape through the tunnel.

'As soon as our last soldier is past the door, help me push it closed,' said Crutch to Boulder.

'Okay,' said Boulder.

By the time the last Ironborn soldier passed, an Estovian guard was already next to the door. Boulder and Crutch pushed with all their strength. The guard tried to stab at them with his sword, but they kept behind the door and kept pushing. The Ironborn soldiers held him off with their own spears and shields.

It was harder to get the door closed with Estovian guards behind the first guard pushing against them. Sergeant Zander and Captain Travis pushed from behind as well as they could to help. With a huge heave, the door finally moved back into place.

As the door shut, the Estovian guard's leg was crushed between the stone wall and the door. He screamed in pain, but he was trapped. The door was shut.

And they were in total darkness.

'A little light, Quicksilver,' said Crutch.

'I'm on it,' said Quicksilver, his voice echoing in the tunnel. Crutch could hear the striking of a match, then light filled the tunnel from the burning torch Quicksilver carried.

An Ironborn soldier lay on the stone tiles of the tunnel, Queen Astrid kneeling next to him.

'He's dead,' said Queen Astrid.

'Must have taken a spear,' said Captain Travis.

'Or a blow to the head,' said Sergeant Zander.

Crutch noticed there was no blood around the soldier. It wasn't something they had time to worry about right now. The Estovian guards had seen them open the door to this tunnel. It wouldn't be long before they found the right stone and pushed that door back open.

And if the Estovian guards knew where this tunnel led, they might just wait for them at the other end.

Sergeant Zander took a spear off one of the Ironborn soldiers and jammed it under the door. Then he took a shield and jammed that under the bottom of the door too.

'That won't hold forever, but at least it will slow them down once they find the brick that opens the door,' he said.

'How do we get to Emperor Solokov from here?' said Crutch, helping Queen Astrid get up off her knees.

'All these secret tunnels can get us to the fat little emperor,' said Queen Astrid. 'If we can find the stairs.'

'Will that be hard?' said Crutch.

'I assumed finding that first door would be easy,' said Queen Astrid. 'Perhaps my memory isn't as clear as it once was.'

'So the door to the stairs is hidden too?'

'Yes.'

'Do you remember where?' said Crutch.

'A little further along this passage.'

They moved on, their footsteps echoing off the low stone ceiling. Behind them, they could hear the palace guards trying to get through the door they'd escaped through.

'It's somewhere here,' said Queen Astrid, running her hands along the stone wall.

'Everyone feel for a loose stone,' said Crutch. 'Start at the top of the wall as high as you can reach and feel down to the bottom.'

The marines and the soldiers stood shoulder-to-shoulder running their hands over the wall. After a few seconds, there was a sound like air forced through a pipe. One of the soldiers grunted, then staggered back.

'What was that?' said Captain Travis.

'Sorry,' said Queen Astrid. 'I forgot about those.'

'Those what?' said Crutch as the guard slumped to the stone floor, with Queen Astrid kneeling down to help him. 'What's wrong with him?'

'Poison darts,' said Queen Astrid. 'Couldn't have just anyone coming up the hidden stairs.' She looked up at Crutch with a forced smile as the guard took his last breath. 'Sorry.'

'Keep your shields against the wall as you search,' said Crutch. 'Are there any more surprises we should know about Queen Astrid?'

'Nothing I can think of off the top of my head,' said Queen Astrid, getting back off her knees with surprising ease given how decrepit she looked when they first found her. 'As I mentioned earlier, my memory may not be entirely accurate.'

'Seems that poison darts shooting out of the walls is something you'd recall fairly easily,' said Crutch.

'And yet it slipped my feeble old mind,' said Queen Astrid, grinning and tapping the side of her head. 'It has been a long time since I was in these passages.'

'Found something,' said one of the soldiers. 'There's a loose stone here. I think I can just push it in.'

'Wait,' said Crutch, but he was too late. The soldier was already pushing the loose stone. A stone door swung open in front of him. A huge crossbow bolt shot from beyond the door and went straight through the soldier's upper chest, slamming him into the wall behind him.

His shield clattered to the stone floor as he hung suspended on the bolt that was now embedded in the stone wall.

'You poor thing,' said Queen Astrid, stroking his face with her hand as he gurgled and spat blood from his mouth. In seconds, he was dead. 'Sorry again,' she said. 'I completely forgot about that contraption.'

'Are there any more *contraptions*?' said Crutch.

Queen Astrid screwed up her face like she was trying to work out which dress to wear to a royal ball. 'No. I think that's the last of them.'

Crutch peered through the door, the light from Quicksilver's torch revealing a set of stairs leading up in the flickering shadows.

'What's at the other end of the stairs?' said Crutch.

'The queen's chambers,' said Queen Astrid. 'It's the safest place in the palace. If I was a betting woman, and I do like a little flutter, I'd say the fat little emperor will be there, hiding like a rat.

'No more contraptions or poison darts or blades, swinging from the ceilings or huge rocks or logs are gonna fall on us?' said Crutch.

'Not that I can recall,' said Queen Astrid. 'But I do like the way you think.'

'Up the stairs,' said Crutch. 'Shields at the front. Be careful.'

They climbed the stairs in single file up the narrow stairs as quietly as they could. Crutch listened for any sounds up ahead and watched for wires or anything else that might signal another hidden trap.

When they reached the top Crutch turned to Queen Astrid.

'What's behind the door?'

'That should be the queen's chambers,' said Queen Astrid.

'So Emperor Solokov is likely to be there?' said Crutch.

'When I built this palace I made the queen's chambers the safest place to retreat to if the palace was under attack. This is the most likely place that coward would be given the circumstances.'

Crutch put his ear to the stone wall at the top of the stairs and tried to listen. Nothing. Either there was no one on the other side or the stone wall was too thick to hear through.

'How do you get it open?' said Crutch.

'Somewhere in the wall there's a loose stone,' said Queen Astrid.

'How did I know she was going to say that,' said Sergeant Zander.

'Is there another trap that will kill our men when we find it?' said Crutch.

'It should be perfectly safe,' said Queen Astrid, grinning. 'But my memory is not what it used to be.'

'Great,' said Crutch. 'I'll search the wall myself.'

'No, you won't,' said Sergeant Zander. 'We can't afford to lose you, colonel. I'll do it.'

'We'll do it together,' said Crutch.

Sergeant Zander looked at him, then nodded. They stood in front of the wall, cramped shoulder to shoulder, and ran their hands over the stone bricks, searching in the flickering torchlight for a loose brick.

Crutch tried not to think about the fact that at any second a poison dart, or a crossbow bolt, or something else might come shooting out at them.

'Found it,' said Sergeant Zander.

'Don't press on it,' said Crutch. 'Get a shield in front of you first.'

An Ironborn soldier passed Sergeant Zander a shield. Sergeant Zander held it up in front of him and reached around, pushing on the stone, his eyes squeezed half shut, expecting the worst.

And nothing happened.

'Push it further,' said Crutch.

Sergeant Zander pushed again. Nothing again.

'That's as far as I can get it to go,' said Sergeant Zander.

'Let Boulder get in there and try it,' said Crutch.

They squeezed around each other on the narrow stairs until Boulder was up against the wall with his shield in front of him.

'Push on that stone there,' said Crutch.

'Okay,' said Boulder. He pushed on the stone, and nothing happened.

'Push it with everything you've got,' said Crutch.

'Okay,' said Boulder, his shoulders flexing. Crutch could hear stone grinding on stone, then the wall in front of them collapsed, leaving a door-shaped hole and a pile of stone bricks.

For a second, Crutch was blinded by bright sunlight coming through the opening. When his eyes focused, he saw twenty fully armed palace guards and Emperor Solokov standing among them.

Chapter 48
I Am Magnificent

'The fat little emperor,' said Queen Astrid from behind Crutch. 'I've waited so long for this day.'

'Through the door and into formation,' said Crutch. 'Now!'

Quicksilver already had his bow out, shooting arrows before Solokov's guards could get their shields up. The first arrow caught a guard in the back. The second was aimed straight at Solokov, but a guard moved his shield up before it could land, and the arrow clattered to the tiled floor.

Solokov turned and looked straight at Crutch, raised his hands, and the world around them stopped like they were frozen in a painting. Crutch tried to move his hands, his arms, his legs, but he couldn't shift them more than a fraction of an inch.

A dark shadow spread around Solokov's feet, and the air in the room hummed and crackled with an evil energy.

Crutch could feel something pushing into his mind, like a large beast breaking down a door, forcing its way in. Then it was inside him, invading his thoughts, speaking to him.

'*So we meet, Crutch. I expect someone stronger. You can't even walk without cane.*'

Solokov. How had he gotten into Crutch's mind?

'*Strong enough to kill your army and strong enough to kill you,*' said Crutch inside his head.

'*You are weak,*' said Solokov, talking in Crutch's mind.

The black shadow around Solokov's feet spread, inch by slow inch. It reached the palace guard closest to Solokov. The guard's eyes went wide with fear as the blackness enveloped him. His mouth opened in a silent scream, and his body shrivelled, shrinking into an empty husk, still standing frozen in time.

Another voice pushed at the edges of Crutch's mind, then forced its way in.

'Think you're so strong, you fat little toad,' said Queen Astrid, talking in Crutch's head, talking to Solokov. *'You can't even control the power. You're killing your own guards.'*

'I can get more guards,' said Solokov. *'There are always more Estovians willing to protect their mighty emperor.'*

'Not as many as you think,' said Crutch. *'Your soldiers stood aside and let us walk right into your palace.'*

'Lies!' said Solokov. *'My people love me. They'd all happily die for me.'*

The black shadow around Solokov shrank back for a few seconds, then expanded again and spread further. It reached another of his guards, this one holding a shield. The skin on the guard's face turned wrinkled, then shrank in seconds; the life sucked from him.

'You are totally clueless, you fat little toad,' said Queen Astrid. *'The power will consume you and eat you alive.'*

'I know enough to hold you,' said Solokov. *'And to kill you all.'*

'Congratulations,' said Queen Astrid. *'You can hold an old woman, and you can kill your own guards. Ironbay and its territories must be quaking in fear.'*

Crutch watched that black shadow creeping slowly, sucking the life from everything it touched. Queen Astrid's bluster aside, if it got to the soldiers and the marines, they'd all be dead. He had to do something.

'If your people love you so much, why did your komitav stand aside and let us through to the city gates without a fight?' said Crutch.

'More lies,' said Solokov. *'My Komitav died gloriously protecting their emperor.'* The black shadow shrank back again.

'Your advisors would tell you that?' said Crutch. *'I notice none of them are here with you. They're long gone. Probably hiding somewhere safe, waiting for you to die.'*

'Your lies don't fool me,' said Solokov, his voice now screaming in Crutch's head.

'Where are your advisors then?' said Queen Astrid. 'If they love you so much, they'd be right here with you.'

The black shadow shrank even further. Crutch could see two Ironborn soldiers, with Damen and Captain Travis, moving slowly to his right, like they ran through molasses, heading for Solokov.

'They prepare magnificent victory parade for when my Estovian army conquers Ironworm invaders,' said Solokov, sneering at Queen Astrid.

'You can't be that stupid,' said Queen Astrid. 'They're long gone, hiding out in the country in civilian clothes. They left you here to die.'

Captain Travis moved faster now, with his last two soldiers and Damen right behind him. They headed for Solokov's left. But they were still slow. So slow. The black shadow of death flickered and spread out again, just inches from Captain Travis's feet.

'Remember the true compatriots?' said Crutch. 'Remember how they painted Igor's kitchen on the wall in the People's Plaza? You couldn't even give out half a dozen crates of food to your people without getting hundreds of them killed.'

'Was great act of generosity,' said Solokov.

'Was burning down the true compatriots hall and the soup kitchen a great act of generosity?' said Crutch. 'You were scared of old women and street urchins who fed more Estovians in an hour than you could feed in your entire rule as emperor.'

Out of the corner of his eye, Crutch saw movement from behind and to the far right of Emperor Solokov. A pair of hands coming through the window.

'Terrified of old women,' said Queen Astrid with a cackle. 'That sounds like the fat little emperor I know.'

'I am not scared of you,' said Solokov, his hands trembling. 'I beat you. Put you in irons.'

'You keep telling yourself that you fat little slug,' said Queen Astrid. 'Look at you shaking like a leaf. You're terrified of me, a feeble old woman.'

'I am not scared of anyone,' yelled Solokov in Crutch's head. 'I am magnificent Emperor Solokov. Glorious ruler of Estovia.'

'Ruler of no one,' said Crutch. 'All we had to offer your komitav was a few wagons full of food, and they were happy to let us *through to the palace gates. Your loving, loyal komitav are outside waiting for your head, waiting to take over the rule of Estovia.'*

Captain Travis was just a couple of feet from Solokov now, drawing back his sword, ready to strike. His two soldiers and Damen were right behind him. If Crutch could just keep Solokov distracted for a few more seconds.

'*No,*' said Solokov, his voice in Crutch's head less certain now. '*My komitav love me.*' The shadow around Solokov was tiny now, barely past his feet.

'*It was your own komitav who started the riots,*' said Crutch. '*They told you it was Arch Warden Gragor, but it was the komitav all along. They want you dead.*'

Captain Travis's sword was inches from Solokov, slowly swinging from behind him, towards the back of his neck. Could it even kill him swinging so slow? Crutch hoped Captain Travis kept his sword razor sharp.

Solokov's eye was drawn to the movement behind him. He saw Captain Travis, the two Ironborn soldiers, and Damen.

'*Tricks and lies,*' he yelled into Crutch's head. '*You think I am stupid fool; believe your stories?*'

The shadow spread out from Solokov, enveloping Captain Travis, his soldiers, and Damen in blackness. Captain Travis was the first to fall, his eyes wide with terror, his mouth open in a silent scream. The two Ironborn soldiers fell behind him; their bodies turned to shrivelled husks.

Horrifying images took over Crutch's mind. He saw One-eye swinging on the gallows in Ironbay, gasping for air, trying to take a breath that wouldn't come.

He saw Alfred pushed down the Kona Track into a trap, screaming in pain.

Saw an Ironborn reservist pushed under the Estovian soldiers on the track, pain and fear in his eyes as he was crushed under their advance, then speared as they marched over him.

He saw Zak, the deckhand on the Auld Faithful, sucked dry by the shadow wraith, felt the shadow wraith clutching him, sucking the breath from his lungs.

He saw an army of skeletons in Yavenland, the dead walking, teeth gnashing and snapping at him, desperate to bite him, to tear his flesh from his bones.

Queen Astrid laughed. *'It's happening already, you fat slug. The power is eating you alive. Your mind is too feeble to control it.'*

'I have total control,' yelled Solokov, his whole body trembling now, sweat dripping from his face, his lips sneering. *'I am magnificent emperor of Estovia, stronger than anyone.'*

'Really?' said Queen Astrid. *'You should tell Prince Damen that.'*

'More lies and tricks,' said Solokov. *'Ironbay has no prince.'*

'Are you sure about that?' said Queen Astrid, looking towards Damen, who still moved, still very much alive, even though the shadow spreading out from Solokov was all around him.

Panic spread across Solokov's face, then rage as Damen advanced, slowly. So slowly. His shield up and his sword drawn.

Crutch thought about Captain Travis, his wife Tilly, and his son Timothy back in Ironbay. Another boy who'd never know what it was like to have a father who cared for him, never have a father to guide him as he grew into manhood.

He thought about his own life as a street urchin, struggling to find a way to survive, having to learn every one of life's lessons the hard way instead of having the guiding hand of someone who'd walked down that path before him.

He thought of the fear, the hunger, the loneliness he'd endured, and something in his mind snapped.

He could move again. Slowly, but he could move. After all the killing he'd done in Teevilgrad, there was still one piece of killing that he had to do. Step by laborious step, he headed for Solokov, for the filthy scum who'd murdered so many good people.

When Crutch moved, Queen Astrid looked at him with surprise, then grinned.

'You can't even control the cripple,' she said. *'You're a weak little slug.'*

Crutch moved step by step closer to Solokov, whose eyes were wide with fear. Damen advanced on him too. Damen's sword was back, ready to strike.

'Say goodbye to your head you fat little slug,' said Queen Astrid.

'No!' screamed Solokov. *'I am magnificent, powerful emperor.'* The shadow that flickered at his feet now flowed out,

enveloping Crutch and Damen, passing over them like the shadow of death.

The inside of Crutch's head exploded with sound. One-eye and Tamiva and Lena and Dima all screaming at him at the top of their lungs at the same time. His own mouth opened in a silent scream, his eyes wide. Damen and Queen Astrid were the same, mouths open in a scream that made no sound, eyes wide in terror.

'*Now you die!*' screamed the voice of Solokov in Crutch's head. Every drop of blood, every muscle, every fibre of Crutch's being flooded with fear and pain. The world in front of him went in and out of darkness like the flickering of torchlight in the dark, putrid caves of Damnation Rock.

So this was how they died. All the crewmen taken by the shadow wraith. All the Estovians taken by the spirit keeper on the Kona Track. Captain Travis. This was how they died. How he died.

As his vision flickered, Crutch saw Solokov smiling in triumph, blackness flowing from him, around him. Crutch had come so far, fought so hard, and it would all end here with this petty tyrant.

'*I am magnificent,*' yelled Solokov, his arms in the air, his face wild with glee, clouds of blackness swirling around him.

A sword blade appeared through Solokov's chest, and the shadow and the darkness fell away as quickly as it had come.

'Magnificent that!' said Young Lord Talbot from behind Solokov as he drew his sword out of the emperor's chest.

Solokov dropped to his knees, clutching at his chest with his hands. Blood ran from the wound.

Crutch was free. He could move again, breathe again.

'You've lost your tether, you fat little slug,' said Queen Astrid from behind him. 'You're so weak, it's pathetic.'

Crutch released the blade on his cane and held it to Solokov's throat.

'Wait!' said Solokov. 'I can give you gold.'

'Gold stolen from the people of Teevilgrad,' said Crutch. 'I don't think so.'

'I can give you ships, land, anything you want,' said Solokov. 'Please don't kill me.'

'We destroyed your ships,' said Crutch. 'And the land you want to give me doesn't belong to you. Why don't you just die with some dignity, *magnificent emperor?*' Crutch spat out the last words and pushed the blade at Solokov's throat.

'I can tell you who spy is in Ironbay palace,' said Solokov.

Crutch paused for a second. Who was it that fed information to the emperor? Who got Saldoria burned? Was it worth enough to keep Solokov alive?

'No,' said Crutch. 'I can work that out myself.'

'You can't kill me,' said Solokov. 'I am emperor. You are just filthy commoner.'

'Indeed I am,' said Crutch, leaning in close so his face was inches from Solokov's. 'Just a filthy street urchin with a bad leg and a crutch. You never see us street urchins because you don't wanna look. But you're looking now.'

Crutch thought about Dima hanging by a noose in the people's plaza. He thought about the little street urchin, Tamiva, with his neck cut by Arch Warden Gragor. He thought about all the street urchins they fed in the true compatriots soup kitchen and how Solokov had burned that soup kitchen down without a thought about how those street urchins would find their next meal.

'This is for Dima and Tamiva,' said Crutch and pushed the blade of his walking cane through Solokov's throat. 'And for every other street urchin you starved or killed.'

The emperor's eyes went wide, a gurgling came from his throat as blood spurted over his chest. Crutch pulled the blade out, and Solokov dropped to his back, blood spreading in a pool on the polished tile floor around him.

Around Crutch, the marines moved. They were alive.

Queen Astrid walked to Solokov and stood over him, sneering.

'Don't look so magnificent now,' she said, made a hacking gurgle in her throat and spat a huge glob of green spit onto his face.

'Is it over?' said Young Lord Talbot. He was covered in blood, the back of his hair singed black.

'The guards are all dead,' said Sergeant Zander as he moved around the room, checking bodies. 'Solokov killed all of his own men with whatever that dark magic was.'

'It's over,' said Crutch to Young Lord Talbot. 'You saved us all.'

'How did you get into this room?' said Longshot.

'I climbed the palace walls,' said Young Lord Talbot. 'It's not too hard after you taught me to climb a ship's rigging. I've been climbing the walls at home ever since.'

'You'll get a medal for this,' said Longshot.

'Iron cross, I reckon,' said Quicksilver.

'I don't want an iron cross,' said Young Lord Talbot, his bottom lip trembling. 'Just want my men back. They're all dead. One of them fell on top of me when the orange fire went off, or I'd be dead too.'

'I'm so sorry,' said Crutch. What could he say? He couldn't even tell him, 'We live for the men we bring back alive,' like Cedric had told him after the Kona Track. None of the boy's men would be coming home alive. He must be consumed with pain.

Chapter 49
If You're Reading This

'This looks like it's for you, Crutch,' said Sergeant Zander, handing Crutch a rough envelope from a piece of paper folded together. The envelope had Colonel Crutch written on the front and was stained with the blood of Captain Travis.

Crutch opened the envelope and looked inside. Another piece of paper with writing in charcoal. The first line at the top was *To my dear Tilly*.

Crutch knew he shouldn't read it, but once he'd seen the first words he couldn't stop.

To my dear Tilly,

I know you can read this since you're the one that taught me how to read and write.

If you're reading this letter, that means I won't be coming back to Ironbay. After we lost all those boys at Papageenar, you know better than most how hard it can be for us soldiers to get back home alive after a big battle. There's only so much someone like Colonel Crutch can do to keep us safe.

There's nothing I would have loved more than to come home to you and Timothy, our handsome son. Know that wherever I've gone, I'll be watching over you and loving you and Timothy until the day comes that you get to be with me again.

Even though I would do anything to be home with you, I'm proud I was a soldier. Ironborn forged from steel. Soldiering gave me my life, gave me the nice cottage you and Timothy can stay in.

Having you as my wife and Timothy as my son was way more than a street urchin from the sewers of Ironbay could ever ask for.

Teach Timothy to be brave and to stand up for the innocent people who are too weak or too old to stand up for themselves. Teach him there's no greater thing you can do in life than to be strong for others. Except for loving someone like you loved me.

I know you'll cry when you read this, but don't cry too long. You're still young and so beautiful it would take any man's breath away. I fought so you and Timothy and all the people of Ironbay could live in peace without having to worry about tyrants like Igor Solokov.

When you're ready, you should marry someone kind and make the most of your life. Move on, and leave me and the rest of the past in the past. Knowing you're living your life is what will make me happier than anything.

I love you and Timothy forever.
Travis

A droplet fell on the paper. Then another. Crutch realised the drops came from him. He cried softly at first, hunched over with the letter in his hand. Then he wept. Deep, hard sobs.

The walls he'd built so he wouldn't feel anything were down, and now he thought of the blood of all the men from here to the docks. Good men like Travis, who'd never see their families in Ironbay again. Injured men who'd lost arms and legs and would have to find a way to beg or scrabble when they got back home, their lives changed forever.

He thought of everything he'd lost. Of Abagail, most likely promised to some young lord by now. A prissy young lord who never got a drop of blood on his hands defending the island that gave him his fancy, upbred life.

The pain of knowing he could never be with Abagail again ripped through him and added to his misery. Young Lord Talbot joined him, and Crutch put his arm over the young lord's shoulder as they sobbed together. They cried until they didn't have any tears left in them.

Boulder came to them and put his arms around them both without saying a word.

Solokov was ended but their pain was just beginning.

Chapter 50
We Have A Problem

After a few long moments, Crutch regained his composure.

'I don't want to interrupt,' said Longshot softly as he looked out the window of Solokov's room, 'but we have a problem.'

'What is it?' said Crutch, coming to the window, the weight of loss making it hard to move.

As soon as he looked down to the street, he could see it. Anton, the komitav, and hundreds of the Estovian soldiers had set up positions with crates, doors from buildings, anything they could find. They were ready to fight.

'Looks like they're ready to pick us off as we come out,' said Sergeant Zander. 'Smart. That's what I'd do.'

Crutch looked down at the street, at Anton and the Estovians, and it compounded his grief. More coffins to nail shut. More good men like Captain Travis to turn into corpses in one final, bloody battle between two sides who would literally be deep friends if the situations were different.

More men driven by one tyrant or one privileged noble to fight each other for the betterment of nobody but the rich.

'Not today,' said Crutch under his breath.

'What's that?' said Sergeant Zander.

'Not today,' said Crutch, walking to Solokov's body. He took out his dagger and hacked off Solokov's head. It felt right to watch the lids of the lifeless eyes shake as he cut through this fucking tyrant's neck.

When it was off, he put his dagger back in his belt, held his cane in one hand, held the head by the hair in the other, and headed for the door.

'Where are you going?' said Sergeant Zander.

'To end this, one way or another.'

'You can't go out there,' said Sergeant Zander. 'They'll shoot you full of arrows.'

'If we fight them, we're all dead anyway,' said Crutch. *And I've had enough of living. Without Abagail, I don't have anything to live for.*

'You can't, Crutch,' said Sergeant Zander, grabbing Crutch by the arm.

'I can. And it's *Colonel* Crutch.'

Sergeant Zander looked at Crutch in surprise.

'Yes, sir,' he said, getting out of Crutch's way.

Crutch looked at Sergeant Zander and saw the shock, and the pain, and the concern in his eyes. This man who'd always been a rock for the world to crash over, a man he'd never seen show any fear, was now worried for him.

'I'm sorry,' said Crutch. 'You know this is the only way we all have a chance of getting out of this alive.'

'You're right,' said Sergeant Zander. 'I just don't want to see you put your life at risk one more time. If it goes bad…you've done enough.'

'I haven't done enough until we're all back safe in Ironbay,' said Crutch.

'That's why you're the colonel,' said Sergeant Zander. 'And the best damn leader I've ever seen in my life.'

'Thank you, Sergeant Zander. I learned everything I know from you.'

For a second, they embraced.

'Get out of this alive,' said Sergeant Zander, wiping away a tear as they pulled apart.

Crutch nodded. He didn't tell Sergeant Zander that he didn't care either way.

When he came out into the street, Crutch could see at least a dozen bowmen with bowstrings back and arrows ready to fire.

'I'm unarmed,' yelled Crutch.

'We've seen you fight,' yelled Anton. 'We know that's not true.'

'There's been enough fighting,' yelled Crutch. 'I just want to talk.'

'Walk over here slowly,' yelled Anton. 'If this is trick, you will die.'

'It's not a trick,' said Crutch, slowly walking towards Anton, his crutch in one hand and Solokov's head in the other.

Then they were face-to-face. They'd been face-to-face so many times before, but this time was different. In the past he was disguised as Crujge. This time Crutch was the leader of the Ironborn forces who'd killed Anton's compatriots. Crutch could feel the tension, feel the hate. Feeling that hate from Anton churned his guts. All Crutch wanted was for all of this killing to end.

'Solokov is dead,' said Crutch, nodding at the head.

'I see that,' said Anton. 'Many Estovians are dead. Some good and some not so good.'

'Teevilgrad is yours now,' said Crutch. 'You can make the city, Estovia, the place you want.'

'You say this, but how can I trust Ironbay after you invade and kill my people.'

'You have the advantage here,' said Crutch. 'You outnumber my troops now. We could fight, but we both want the same thing. An Estovia without Solokov. Peace between Estovia and Ironbay.'

'Hard to believe you want peace,' said Anton. 'When you kill your way from docks to city, and stand there holding dead man's head.'

'You've lost good men,' said Crutch. 'I've lost good men. Too many good men.' Crutch dropped the emperor's head to the street. 'Solokov is dead. No more deaths. Can we please stop fighting?'

The tears came again. Crutch stood there in front of Anton with his head down, sobbing for a long, long time.

When he looked up, tears were running down Anton's face.

'Okay. No more deaths,' said Anton.

Chapter 51
Now We Are Brothers

The Estovians and the Ironborn buried their dead together in a park near the palace. Hundreds of men laid into the ground side by side in rows that stretched the entire width and length of the park. Fathers, brothers, sons, consigned to the earth.

All the love and care that went into raising them, now just lowered into a hole with dirt piled over them. Not even the resources to make gravestones for each soldier.

Crutch had three gravestones made. One for Captain Travis, one for Young Lord Talbot's unit, and one to represent all the Ironborn soldiers who'd died. Anton had two gravestones made. One to represent the brave Estovians who'd died and one for the civilians who died.

Crutch had sent word back to Cedric that they were okay and to bring back something from his personal belongings on the Auld Faithful. He also sent word to General Talbot that his son was unharmed. That was true physically, at least. And that the Ironborn troops should stay on the docks. He didn't want to give Anton and the Estovians any reason to get nervous and start fighting again.

By mid afternoon, the graves were filled, and the marines stood at attention with Anton and a handful of his best men. Behind them were hundreds of Estovians. soldiers and komitav.

Anton spoke first, his voice ringing over the park.

'Too many good men died. Too many are now buried here with Ironborn soldiers they fought. They were enemies, but now they lie together, shoulder to shoulder. Like them, maybe now we can stop fighting and find a way to live together.'

Anton turned to Crutch and nodded.

'Ironbay was never at war with Estovia,' said Crutch. 'We were at war with Emperor Solokov. We killed Solokov so that we could all live in peace together. Some of the finest men I've ever known now lie under your soil. I know you'll take good care of them.'

Crutch took his iron cross the messenger had brought back from the Auld Faithful, kneeled, and laid it on the gravestone of Captain Travis. When he stood and turned around, Anton was there, watching him.

'Never again,' said Crutch.

'Never again,' said Anton, and embraced him. 'Now we are brothers.'

Chapter 52
The Scourge

When Crutch and the marines got back to the Auld Faithful with Queen Astrid, Cedric looked busy supervising repairs to the sails and rigging. He paused to speak to Crutch.

'I'm so glad you're unharmed,' said Cedric.

'Captain Travis was killed,' said Crutch, a knot forming in his throat as he said it.

'That's a terrible thing,' said Cedric. 'He was a good man.'

'The best,' said Crutch.

'You brought someone with you,' said Cedric.

'I didn't think she'd be safe in Teevilgrad. She was royalty once.'

'Just an old woman now by the look of her,' said Cedric. 'She can sleep in the captain's cabin with Larney, the young woman you had placed under my protection.'

Crutch had forgotten about Larney. He'd have to have her escorted to Anton in the morning. Right now, he needed rest. He felt like crawling up in a corner and sobbing his heart out, but he knew that wouldn't help ease the pain inside him.

'Thank you for looking after her,' said Crutch.

'I need to get these repairs finished,' said Cedric. 'Perhaps we could talk over the evening meal. We have plenty of food thanks to… we have plenty of food.'

Thanks to Abagail. At least Cedric didn't say it, but being reminded was one more knife in his guts.

'I can see you're hurting,' said Cedric, putting his arm on Crutch's shoulder. 'Get some rest if you can, Crutch, and we'll talk at dinner.'

'Thank you, Cedric,' said Crutch. He gave the orders to have Queen Astrid escorted to the captain's cabin and then headed below.

Crutch woke with Boulder gently shaking his shoulder. He was in his hammock in the marines quarters with no memory of how he got there.

'Food's ready,' said Boulder. 'Do you want me to bring you some?'

'No, I'll come with you,' said Crutch, crawling out of the hammock, his feet dropping to the boards of the lower deck.

'That's good,' said Boulder with a worried smile. 'You're sad, Crutch. 'I don't like it when you're sad.'

Crutch looked at his friend. The best friend he'd ever had. Over the past months, he'd taken Boulder for granted, but Boulder hadn't wavered an inch. He'd literally stood between Crutch and death over and over, risking his own life without hesitation.

For the first time, he wondered what it must have been like for Boulder when Crutch quit the marines and joined the navy supply office. He was so consumed with his own problems he'd never even thought about how his true friend must have felt.

'I'm so sorry,' said Crutch. 'I haven't been much of a friend to you lately.'

'It's okay,' said Boulder. 'Sergeant Zander told me you were busy.'

'I should have made time for you, Boulder. You deserved much better.'

'You're here now,' said Boulder. 'I knew you'd come back.'

Boulder knew he'd come back when Crutch didn't know it himself.

'You're a true friend, Boulder.'

'You're my best friend,' said Boulder.

Crutch thought about how he couldn't be with Abagail and what he had left in his world. What was really valuable to him.

'You're my best friend too,' said Crutch.

Why had it taken him so long to remember that? He'd been so consumed with anger, he'd forgotten what was really important.

'Thank you for saving my life,' he said.

'You saved my life too,' said Boulder. 'With the bluefire.'

'I don't think that makes us even,' said Crutch.

'That's okay,' said Boulder. 'I'm not counting.'

'Thank you, Boulder.'

'Crutch?'

'Yes, Boulder.'

'Can we eat now? I'm hungry.'

Crutch laughed.

'Yes, we can eat.'

'I like it when you laugh,' said Boulder.

When Crutch and Boulder entered the mess, all the sailors and marines and a handful of soldiers stood at attention and saluted.

'Please sit and eat,' said Crutch. 'I should be saluting you. Every one of you is a hero.'

'It's you who killed Solokov,' said one soldier.

'It's you who talked the Estovians into standing aside and letting the army through to the palace,' said another.

'And it was you and your marines who got the gates of the palace open,' said Sergeant Rogund to the murmurs of agreement of all the men in the mess. 'Three cheers for Colonel Crutch and his marines! Hip hip.'

'Hooray!' went up the cheer from the whole mess.

'Hip hip.'

'Hooray!' They were louder now.

'Hip hip.'

'Hooray!'

Crutch didn't think it was possible, but the last cheer was louder still.

'Thank you, men,' said Crutch. 'Thank you all for everything.'

As they sat, Cedric appeared at the door of the mess, then joined the marines and Crutch.

'I assume all that cheering was for you,' said Cedric. 'Well deserved. You and the marines have made history again.'

'A lot of good men died to make that history,' said Crutch. 'We didn't do it alone.'

'War always takes a terrible toll,' said Cedric. 'But you should all be very proud. From the stories the men told me, you pulled off the impossible more than once.'

'We're royal marines,' said Sergeant Zander. 'Ordinary obstacles we take in our stride. The impossible just takes us a little longer.'

Cedric smiled at that.

'Is it true you convinced the Estovians to stand aside and let you through?'

'Crutch did that,' said Sergeant Zander. 'All by himself.'

'Astonishing,' said Cedric. 'How?'

'The Estovians didn't want war any more than we did,' said Crutch. 'And they wanted Solokov dead. I just convinced them the easiest way to achieve that was to let us do it for them.'

'That must have been quite the conversation,' said Cedric. 'Is it true you went down the sewers and through the dungeons to get the gates of the palace open?'

'We had some help there,' said Sergeant Zander.

'The old woman?' said Cedric.

'Yes, Queen Astrid,' said Sergeant Zander. 'She told us she built the palace. She knew exactly how to get to the control room for the gates and how to get to Solokov.'

Cedric's face went pale.

'Did you say Queen Astrid?'

'Yes,' said Sergeant Zander. 'She helped us navigate our way through the palace.'

'That was Queen Astrid you brought on the ship?' said Cedric.

'She wouldn't have been safe in Teevilgrad,' said Crutch. 'They're not too fond of royalty there, or any of their past leaders.'

'You don't understand,' said Cedric. 'Have you ever heard of the Scourge?'

'The Scourge,' said Sergeant Zander. 'That's just an old fairy tale to scare children into behaving themselves.'

'It's no fairy tale,' said Cedric. 'Queen Astrid is the Scourge.'

'You can't be serious,' said Crutch.

'I'm deadly serious,' said Cedric.

'You're telling us she's some kind of creature of dark magic who commanded armies of wraiths and called down storms and lightning from the skies?'

'That and worse,' said Cedric. 'When I was a young lieutenant, I crewed a ship that transported a powerful mage to battle the Scourge. He fought that beast off but paid a terrible cost. He was a shrivelled shell. He died soon after we got him back on the ship.'

'But how do you know Queen Astrid is the Scourge?' said Cedric.

'It's not in the history books, but officers at the time relayed stories about the old queen who tinkered with dark magic and was taken by it. Some had seen her when she was younger before she became a thing, some kind of foul monster.'

'She looks like an old woman now, not a beast,' said Damen. 'Are you sure about this?'

'I'm certain,' said Cedric. 'We need to put her in irons now. Before she has a chance to use her powers and wreak vengeance on Ironbay or any other living person she can get her hands on.'

Crutch and the marines sat there, stunned. This was not a conversation they expected.

'Now!' said Cedric.

'Yes, captain,' said Sergeant Zander. 'Let's get the manacles from the brig, men.'

Chapter 53
Search For Mists

Crutch felt like he was in some kind of weird dream as he followed Sergeant Zander. Or some kind of nightmare. The stress of the last few days and the emotional upheaval of the burials were already more than he felt he could bear.

Now he had to deal with some kind of magical beast that, according to legend, had the power to conquer Ironbay and its territories, and what was left of Estovia, and bring down an age of darkness.

Sergeant Zander handed Crutch a set of leg irons.

'We'll get her hands fastened, and you can put those around her ankles,' he said. 'Unless you want one of the other men to do it.'

'I can do it,' said Crutch.

They made their way up to the captain's cabin and crowded round the door.

'On the count of three,' whispered Sergeant Zander.

Crutch held his breath. He had no idea what to expect fighting something evil borne of dark magic.

'One...'

If the shadow wraith he'd stabbed on the way to Yavenland was anything to go by, it would not be an easy fight.

'Two...'

A blade had passed right through that thing like it was made of mist.

'Three!'

Sergeant Zander pushed open the door, and they rushed inside, heading for the bed. Crutch was ready for anything.

'She's not here,' said Longshot.

'Search under the bed,' said Sergeant Zander. 'Search everywhere.'

'She could be a mist,' said Crutch. 'Like the wraiths we encountered sailing to and from Yavenland.'

'Search for mists too,' said Sergeant Zander.

'That doesn't sound crazy at all,' said Longshot.

They searched everywhere, even for mists. Crutch saw a cabin window was open, so he peered out that too. Nothing.

Cedric came to the cabin door.

'Did you secure her?' he said.

'She's not here,' said Sergeant Zander. 'I think she escaped out the cabin window.'

'Have the crew search the whole ship for her,' said Cedric. 'Every plank and every board to be sure. And tell them to ready the ship to sail.'

'Where are you going?' said Crutch.

'To see the harbormaster,' said Cedric. 'She might have escaped on a ship.'

'I'll come with you,' said Crutch. 'The harbormaster will be more likely to answer your questions with a colonel there.'

'Thank you, Crutch,' said Cedric as they headed for the gangplank. 'You must think I'm crazy,'

Crutch had been thinking about the strange way Queen Astrid acted and how she kept touching dying men. None of them lived. Was she draining the life out of them the same way the spirit keeper in Papageenar had? The same way the wraiths in the sea near Yavenland had?

'No,' said Crutch. 'I'm starting to think, in my haste to get to Emperor Solokov, I was careless, even reckless.'

'You did what was necessary to kill Emperor Solokov and end this war,' said Cedric. 'No one can judge you for that.'

'Yes, but if you're right, I might have put the entire kingdom of Ironbay at risk. And every other living man, woman, and child in this part of the world.'

'I'm glad you understand the gravity of the situation,' said Cedric as they came to a building on the docks that had been commandeered by the navy. Two guards stood in front of the door, barring their way.

'Colonel Crutch and Captain Beaumont of the Auld Faithful here to see the harbormaster,' said Crutch.

'Right you are, sir,' said the guard standing aside. 'It's an honour to meet you both. An honour indeed.'

'Thank you, corporal,' said Crutch, walking past into the building with Cedric right behind him. Crutch's cane echoed on the wooden floorboards as he came to the desk of the harbormaster.

'The hero of the day, Colonel Crutch,' said the harbormaster. 'This is a surprise. What brings you here?'

'We'd like to know which ships have left the harbour in the last five hours,' said Crutch. 'It's a matter of the most grave importance.'

'Most grave,' said Cedric.

The harbormaster's eyebrows shot up.

'Really? Well, I can answer that without checking my logs. The only ship that's left this harbour in the last few hours is an Ironbay supply ship, the Black Gull.'

'There were no other ships?' said Cedric.

'Not since yesterday,' said the harbormaster. 'The Black Gull left four hours ago.'

'Where was she headed?' said Cedric.

'Ironbay.'

'Damn it,' said Cedric. 'We need to leave now.' Cedric ran out of the harbormaster's office with Crutch close behind, using his walking cane to keep up.

As they approached the Auld Faithful Cedric shouted orders, the ship's bell began to ring, and crewmen swarmed over the deck. By the time Cedric and Crutch came onto the ship, the deckhands were already unfurling sails.

'We should be able to catch the Black Gull,' said Cedric. 'The Auld Faithful is a much faster ship.'

'And if we don't?' said Crutch.

'Then heaven help Ironbay,' said Cedric as he took the wheel of the Auld Faithful and pulled her away from the docks.

Chapter 54
Prince Damen

After a days sailing Crutch and the crew scanned the ocean ahead of them and around them, but the Black Gull was nowhere to be seen.

'We would have caught her by now,' said Cedric. 'If she was headed to Ironbay.'

'Do you think she headed somewhere else?' said Crutch.

'I think that's likely. You told me Queen Astrid was a weak old woman. If Emperor Solokov had her chained in his dungeons for decades, she may have lost most of her power.'

'So she might not be such a threat?' said Crutch.

'The Scourge is always a threat,' said Cedric. 'But she might need to go somewhere and rebuild her strength.'

'By sucking the lives out of innocent people?' said Crutch.

'Yes, it would seem so,' said Cedric. 'She might also build an army of wraiths, if the stories are true.'

That was a terrifying thought. Crutch thought about the struggle they had fighting just one of the wraiths on the Auld Faithful. He had no idea how they could stand against an army of them.

'In the old stories, the Scourge builds its power and waits until men are weak from warring against each other, then takes the opportunity to attack before they can regain their strength,' said Cedric.

'It will take years for Ironbay to rebuild its army,' said Crutch. 'Estovia too.'

'Let's hope she's too weak to attack in the near future,' said Cedric.

'There's something else that's playing on my mind,' said Crutch.

'What's that,' said Cedric.

'Queen Astrid kept calling Damen, *Prince* Damen. She insisted on getting him to help her walk. When Solokov used his dark magic on us it was only Damen and me who were able to move against him. At least until Young Lord Talbot snuck up behind him.'

Cedric stood silent for a few long seconds, as if he pondered exactly what to say.

'This is dangerous talk,' he said. 'You mustn't repeat what you just said to anyone. Remember what King Vargus did to Prince Alderon. If he hears whispers that Damen is a prince, he'll give him the noose too, just to be sure.'

'Of course,' said Crutch. 'But why would Queen Astrid call Damen a prince? At the time, I thought she was a crazy old lady who'd lost her mind, but now I'm not so sure.'

'It's safer for you and Damen if you don't know some things,' said Cedric. 'The most important thing is that you keep this to yourself and tell the marines to do the same.' The tone of Cedric's voice had a finality to it. Crutch got the message that the conversation on this topic ended here.

'I'll tell them,' said Crutch.

'Thank you,' said Cedric. 'I wish I could tell you more. That day will come. The good news is it looks like Ironbay is safe from the Scourge. For now. Heaven help whatever island she lands on though.'

The spirit of the crew was joyous after Crutch and Cedric told them they were no longer chasing after Queen Astrid and they were heading straight for Ironbay. They were excited about seeing family again, about getting home alive and safe when so many wouldn't be coming home at all.

Crutch tried to be excited for them, but his soul was filled with sorrow.

This time, Abagail wouldn't be waiting for him with her arms open. And he was the colonel who led the invading forces. It was his job to tell the families of all those soldiers that their fathers, their sons, their husbands wouldn't be coming home.

Wherever he went on the ship, Boulder was close by. Boulder didn't speak much, but he made sure Crutch always had a plate of food at mealtime and waited until Crutch fell asleep before going to sleep himself.

'You don't have to follow me around everywhere,' said Crutch. 'If you don't want to.'

'I'm your bodyguard,' said Boulder. 'And you're my best friend.' That was all he needed to say.

'Thank you, Boulder,' said Crutch.

'When we get to Ironbay, you can come eat with grandma,' said Boulder.

'Thank you,' said Crutch. 'I won't have time the first day. I have to talk to the families of the dead. Let them know how their soldiers died.'

'I'll come with you,' said Boulder.

'Thank you,' said Crutch. 'But you should go eat with grandma. She'll be worried about you and want to see you. I can talk to the families by myself.'

'Okay,' said Boulder.

Chapter 55
Can't Stay On My Knees

It was barely dawn when they first caught sight of Ironbay. As they got closer, Crutch saw civilians milling around the docks, waiting for them to arrive. So many families and so much bad news he'd have to deliver.

As the Auld Faithful pulled in and the deckhands slid out the gangplank, Abagail was there, as close to the docks as she was allowed.

When Crutch saw Abagail, he didn't feel anger, just a profound sadness for everything he'd lost. She stood there awkward. He wasn't sure if he should hug her, if that was the right thing to do now they could never be together.

'Captain Travis is dead,' said Crutch.

Abagail put her hand to her mouth. 'Oh no.'

'Can you help me tell Tilly, his wife?'

Crutch and Abagail searched through the crowd, looking for Tilly. There were at least two hundred civilians milling around, waiting to welcome their men home. For some, this would be a happy reunion. For many, it would be the worst day of their lives.

They found Tilly higher up on a walkway, where she could see over the crowd to the Auld Faithful. Her boy, Timothy, now a toddler, clung to her leg, peering out at the mass of moving, talking people.

'Colonel Crutch, Abagail,' Tilly said. 'I'm so glad you're here. I was hoping Travis would see me from up here. Timothy is afraid of that big crowd of people. Makes me a bit nervous too, if I'm honest.'

Timothy saw Abagail and held his arms out, hoping to be picked up. Abagail obliged, lifting him onto her hip.

'Timothy always liked you,' said Tilly.

Crutch looked at Tilly, full of hope, full of relief that the war was finally over. It felt like the height of cruelty to snatch that away from her. There was no easy way to do this, and it had to be done.

'I'm sorry,' said Crutch as gently as he could. 'Travis is dead.'

Crutch caught Tilly as her knees buckled from under her. He lowered her till her knees were on the boards of the docks. Abagail turned Timothy away and distracted him by pointing to the ships and people in the crowd.

'How?' said Tilly.

'He was there right to the end of the invasion,' said Crutch. 'He died helping to kill Emperor Solokov. He saved my life and many others.'

Crutch didn't add that Travis was a hero. He knew from his time with the widows of the Kona track that glorifying war by calling their boys heroes could make the pain worse. Just the plain truth, without any talk of the blood, or the guts, or the horror, was as much as they could bear.

Crutch knelt down with Tilly and put his arms around her as she sobbed. After a long moment, she wiped her eyes and regained her composure, looking up to see that Timothy was with Abagail and was blissfully unaware that his mother had been crying.

'Can't stay on my knees all day,' said Tilly. Crutch and Tilly got back to their feet. 'Thank you for telling me quick.'

'He wrote you a letter,' said Crutch.

'He wasn't one for writing much,' said Tilly, surprised.

Crutch thought about that as he gave the letter to Tilly.

'It's a long letter. He must have taken quite some time to write it.'

Tilly clutched the letter to her chest as if it were all she had left of Travis. That and her son Timothy.

'If there's anything I can do, you just let me know,' said Crutch.

'Thank you.'

'Let me walk you home,' said Abagail.

'Thank you,' said Tilly, her eyes red from crying.

Abagail looked into Crutch's eyes and nodded. Crutch looked back and felt the pain of loss even worse than ever. If it wasn't something a colonel does, he would be on those boards on his knees, sobbing his heart out too. But if he started now, he knew he'd never stop.

Crutch spent the next hours with Captain Travis's man, Sergeant Rogund breaking the sad news to the families of soldiers who'd died. Sergeant Rogund had made a list and knew the men well. That made the process as smooth as doing something so brutally heart wrenching could be.

By the time he was finished, all Crutch had the strength for was walking back onto the Auld Faithful and curling up in his hammock. Cedric checked on him every few hours but knew better than to try to talk.

Cedric must have performed the same task many times. He would know Crutch was beyond talking.

CHAPTER 56
EMBROIDERY

Crutch crawled out of his hammock the next day, ate in the galley with Cedric then remembered he had one important task that had to be completed. He set off for the city in full-dress uniform.

Crutch passed the huge wooden doors of the navy office and wound his way through the corridors until he got to the supply office. The door was open, and Abagail was there, hunched over, hard at work, with a pile of papers on her desk.

Magpie sat at the desk next to her. He was the first to look up. Then he stood and saluted. Crutch saluted right back.

'Colonel Crutch. It's an honour to see you again, sir.'

'No need to stand at attention, Magpie,' said Crutch.

At the sound of his voice, Abagail looked up, and Crutch saw those ocean blue eyes. For a second, there was that look of happiness he'd seen so many times. But it lasted just an instant, then it changed to a look of sadness, hopelessness.

'Crutch,' she said. 'Have you come to take back your job?'

Even hearing her voice was a sweet kind of torture, like being jabbed in the stomach with a knife.

'Not at all,' said Crutch. 'I've come to say thank you, to both of you.'

'Thank you?' said Abagail.

'When I was in Teevilgrad, you and Magpie ran the supply office so well it helped us get to Emperor Solokov without having to fight the komitav and a good portion of the Estovian army. We would never have killed Solokov without your help. You should both be very proud of what you accomplished.'

A look of fierce pride fell on Magpie's face. He stood a little taller.

'Thank you, Colonel Crutch,' he said.

'Yes, thank you,' said Abagail. 'It has been an honour to do our duty for Ironbay.'

'I do have a question for you,' said Crutch. 'Where did you get the coin to buy the food and supplies you sent to Teevilgrad.'

'Magpie and I set that up before you left Ironbay,' said Abagail. 'You taught Magpie to stockpile some of the food he collected from the restaurants of Ironbay just in case the supply stopped unexpectedly.'

'So you did the same with the bolts of cloth from Saldoria?' said Crutch.

'Exactly,' said Abagail. She smiled, but it wasn't the smile Crutch was so familiar with. There was a deep sadness to it. 'I never planned to rely on Chudwell Mercantile to feed the navy.'

'I'm glad I put you both in charge of warehousing the fabric,' said Crutch.

Abagail got up and came to Crutch from behind the desk. Standing in front of him, Crutch could feel the awkwardness, feel the desire to take Abagail in his arms and hold her. But holding her was in the past.

'Thank you,' said Abagail. 'It's the first time anyone trusted me with something so important.' She put her hand out as if she were about to touch his chest, then stopped herself.

'That trust was well deserved,' said Crutch, his body aching for the touch that would never come. 'General Talbot has recommended you both for an exemplary service medal. He said he'd give you both an iron cross, but you have to be in combat to get one of those.'

'Thank you, Colonel Crutch,' said Magpie. 'That's a great honour.' If Magpie pushed his chest out any further, Crutch was fairly certain it would explode.

'It is a great honour,' said Abagail. 'Thank you.' She was so close to him he could smell her, sense the shape of her under her dress. It seemed impossible, but he wanted to be here next to her more than anything in the world and wanted to be anywhere else and stop this torture at the same time.

'The thanks belong to you,' said Crutch. 'I've authorised dress uniforms for both of you. You'll have to get them today so you'll be ready for the parade tomorrow.'

'I don't need a uniform,' said Magpie. 'I still have the one my mom made for me.'

Crutch remembered the uniform Magpie wore to dine with Lord Counsel Chudwell. The collar was too high on one side, the hem too low on the other, but Magpie was so proud of what his mother had made for him Crutch couldn't take that away from him.

'That would be perfect,' said Crutch.

'Could we talk alone?' said Abagail. 'There's something you should know.'

'Of course,' said Crutch.

Abagail led Crutch through the corridors of the navy office, outside, then to the park with the fountain, where they'd spent lunchtimes talking and dreaming. Back when they had dreams that involved being together. Those were gone now.

They sat on a wooden bench near the fountain.

'I'm so glad you made it back unhurt,' said Abagail. 'It's terrible what happened to Captain Travis and the other soldiers. Tilly cried for two hours when I got her home.'

Captain Travis was one of many good soldiers who never made it back to Ironbay. It just added to the sense of loss Crutch felt when he was with Abagail. His feeling over losing her seemed so inconsequential, so petty, compared to the loss the families of the dead must be suffering now. But his own feelings were there, and they wouldn't go away just because he could see they were relatively minor.

'This isn't easy to say,' said Abagail. 'While you were gone, mother insisted I keep seeing Young Lord Chudwell. She says he's the only young lord who's shown an interest and I should be grateful. At least he's been more of a gentleman. I think you had something to do with that.'

Holding the deadly-sharp blade of a walking cane an inch from his face and threatening him with dismemberment can have a profound effect on a young lord's behaviour, thought Crutch.

'I would have thought Lord Counsel Chudwell would be penniless with the kapok plantations in Saldoria burned,' said Crutch.

'I don't know where he's getting his money from, but the Chudwells seem to have more of it than ever.'

'So Young Turd Chudwell is still a worthy suitor,' said Crutch, the words bitter on his tongue.

'Yes. Mother has arranged a meeting for me and the young lord tomorrow night at our home. She's very excited about it and won't say what it is. I think Jerry is going to give me his promise ring.'

First a promise ring, then marriage. Once a young lady was promised to a young lord, there was no turning back. She was his.

'I don't want to be promised to anyone,' said Abagail, tears filling her eyes. 'Unless it's you. I finally found something I'm good at, that helps people in the supply office. Now mother wants to marry me off to this young turd so I can sit around doing embroidery and order servants around with the other ladies. I can't stand it, but I don't know how to get out of it. I don't know what to do.'

Crutch sat there with her, wanting to hold her, to tell her everything would be alright. But everything wouldn't be alright. It was all he could do not to burst into tears himself.

So they sat as Abagail sobbed, awkwardly avoiding touching each other.

Chapter 57
Splendid Beyond Words

The Ironbay city square was full of people for the medal ceremony. The crowd was happy. They'd all experienced loss, but there was a sense of joy and relief that the war was finally over.

Crutch and the marines stood near the stage in their navy dress uniforms. Young Lord Talbot stood with them resplendent, standing at attention in his army officer's uniform with its gold braids and silver epaulettes.

Right next to Crutch were Abagail and Magpie, there to be recognised for their exemplary service medals. Crutch tried not to look at Abagail but it was impossible. Whenever she was near him, he couldn't look anywhere else. She looked back at Crutch.

'I'm worried about my uniform,' she said.

'Why?' said Crutch.

'Mother said the ladies of Ironbay will be scandalised that a young lady is wearing navy trousers.'

'If the ladies are scandalised, it's only because they could never hope to approach the vision of loveliness you are today in full navy dress,' said Crutch. 'You look magnificent.'

And she did. Her blonde hair falling over her white navy coat, and gold buttons shimmering in the sunlight. She looked like she owned the navy.

'You always have the perfect words,' said Abagail. She beamed and pulled Crutch into a hug. 'Thank you, Crutch.'

The feel of her body pressed against his felt like the burning of a fire that ran from his skin right through him. It had been so long since they touched, and now he wished that they could stay like this forever, her body against his, the smell of her hair next to his face, the beating of her heart so close he could feel it.

Over Abagail's shoulder, Crutch could see the special raised and roped area for nobles and their families. And there he saw Lord Counsel Chudwell with his son, Young Turd Chudwell, both looking right at them. Crutch made eye contact with the young turd, and the cowardly little shit immediately looked down to avoid his gaze.

Abagail pulled away. Too soon. She looked into his eyes, and in a flash her joy changed to a sad longing. 'I'm sorry,' she said.

'It's alright,' said Crutch. 'It's not your fault. You do look splendid, almost beyond words.'

Abagail smiled again, but this time there was a sadness to it.

'Thank you, Crutch. I wish…'

'I know,' said Crutch. He didn't know what to say. How could you explain that you felt like your life was ripped from you and every reason you had for living was about to end with a little ceremony where a young lord she didn't even like would give her a ring.

Their exchange was interrupted by the voice of the city crier.

'Welcome, citizens of Ironbay, to our celebration of victory over the vile empire of Estovia,' boomed the crier in a huge voice. The crowd roared and cheered.

'Today we celebrate peace and recognise the heroes of Teevilgrad.' The crowd cheered again, even louder when they heard the word *peace*.

'Ladies and gentlemen, show your appreciation for the marines who need no introduction. Your siege breakers, heroes of the Kona Track, and now heroes of Teevilgrad, including double iron cross winner Colonel Crutch.'

The crowd in the city square clapped and cheered as Crutch and the marines walked on to the huge wooden platform in the city square. Nearly everyone in that crowd knew someone who'd lost their life at Teevilgrad, but today was about celebrating peace after years of war. Their joy at the war finally being finished overwhelmed any loss they might feel.

Crutch looked at Boulder, smiling happily, then he looked at Damen and immediately thought of Prince Alderon hanged in this same city square, just a few feet from where they stood.

Why did he torture himself with these thoughts? Cedric had told him a man who isn't swept away by the moment and can see all sides of a situation has a rare gift.

With the picture of Prince Alderon swinging by his neck on a rope filling his mind, it felt more like a curse than a gift.

The city crier continued. 'The marines, your marines, have asked that instead of honouring them with medals, that you give honour to the brave Ironborn men who fought and died at Teevilgrad.'

The crowd went silent for a few seconds, then a warmer, softer applause started and kept going on and on. It seemed like a good two or three minutes of clapping before the city crier started speaking again.

'For the first time in history, we award medals to two workers from the navy office. Young Lady Hastings and Sergeant 'Magpie' Rennar are awarded the exemplary service medals of the navy. Their tireless work helped win over the Estovians in Teevilgrad and avoid unnecessary bloodshed.

'Young Lady Hastings asked that their medals should symbolise the work and the sacrifice that everyone in Ironbay made for the war effort. She says this is your award for your years of selfless dedication to the cause.'

The crowd roared their approval, cheering and clapping as Abagail and Magpie stepped forward, Abagail beaming and Magpie's chest puffed out in the off kilter navy dress uniform his mother had hand-sewn.

'Finally, Young Lord Talbot,' said the crier. 'Scaled the palace walls in Teevilgrad without a rope or assistance, made his way into Emperor Solokov's inner sanctum, and struck the blow that led to the emperor's death. For his bravery, Young Lord Talbot has been awarded the iron cross.'

Young Lord Talbot stepped forward sombre to begin with, then the crowd yelled and cheered. There was nothing Ironbay crowds loved more than an iron cross winner. Crutch knew the mix of emotions that medal would bring for Young Lord Talbot. Proud of the honour but struggling with the adulation when he knew that so many of the real heroes died in Teevilgrad.

When the cheering and the clapping ended, the crowd milled around a long set of tables where the king had catered thousands of candied sweet potatoes, free to everyone. Crutch saw some of Bram's black knives, taking as many as they could before the guards shooed them away.

Before he could leave, Crutch talked to Young Lord Talbot.

'Congratulations on the iron cross,' said Crutch.

'Thank you, Colonel Crutch,' said Young Lord Talbot. 'I always thought if I got a medal, I'd feel proud. It doesn't feel like that at all. I just feel…'

'Guilt,' said Crutch. 'That you're still alive and so many better men aren't.'

'Yes,' said Young Lord Talbot, a deep sadness in his eyes.

'I felt the same way. It took me a long time after the Kona Track to start feeling normal, like I could start living again.'

'How do you move on?' said Young Lord Talbot. 'I can't stop thinking about Teevilgrad, about everything I saw.'

'Look around you,' said Crutch, motioning to all the people in the city square, happy, eating their candied sweet potatoes, laughing, and talking. 'We fight so that all these people and their children can live their lives in peace. We give them the gift of life.'

Young Lord Talbot stared at the happy crowd for a long moment.

'That does help,' he said. 'But it still hurts so bad.'

'I know,' said Crutch. 'It will hurt less with time.'

'Thank you, Colonel Crutch,' said Young Lord Talbot. He held out his hand for a handshake, and Crutch pulled him into a hug.

Crutch never said what he was feeling. That some things you get over, but some loss stays with you forever, eating at your insides like maggots chewing on dead, decaying flesh.

Chapter 58
Use It Wisely

Cedric and Crutch sat together in the galley of the Auld Faithful for their evening meal. With most of the sailors and the marines on shore leave, they had a table to themselves. For the first time, Crutch realised that Cedric must have sat here eating by himself all those years when Crutch was off with Abagail on shore leave.

'I'm sorry,' said Crutch.

'Sorry for what,' said Cedric.

'All the times we had shore leave, and I left you here by yourself.'

'Never apologise for living your life,' said Cedric. ' I enjoy the times when the ship's nearly empty and I get to be by myself for a while. And nothing gave me more pleasure than knowing you and Abagail were together.'

Just hearing her name was like a knife in his guts. Cedric saw his reaction and frowned.

'I'm sorry, Crutch. I shouldn't have mentioned her.'

Crutch tried to keep his grief in check, but it overwhelmed him. All the deaths, Captain Travis, now the knowledge that he was losing Abagail forever. It was too much.

'What is it?' said Cedric.

'Abagail. She's to be promised to Young Lord Chudwell tonight.'

'If you feel this strongly about her, then you should tell her,' said Cedric.

'It's not Abagail's doing. Her mother won't let her be with a commoner.'

'The same mother you saved from the true royals,' said Cedric. 'That's a travesty.'

'Young Lord Chudwell's a slimy little turd,' said Crutch. 'But Lady Hastings likes him because he was born into nobility and his father's a lord counsel.'

'Instead of climbing his way out of the sewers and earning everything he has,' said Cedric. 'This is outrageous.'

'Outrageous or not, Young Lord Chudwell will be promised to Abagail tonight, and I'll have lost her forever.'

Cedric sat there in silence, looking at Crutch for a long moment. Then he stood up.

'I wish you'd told me this sooner,' he said. 'Will you be staying on the ship tonight?'

'I have nowhere else to go,' said Crutch.

'I'll be back shortly,' said Cedric. 'We can talk more about this then.'

'Okay,' said Crutch, surprised Cedric would leave him alone.

Cookie served up Crutch a cake made with sweet potato and dried mango as he sat in the galley by himself. It helped a little to fill his belly, but there was a hole deep inside him that nothing could fill.

Less than an hour later, Cedric returned, sweat on his face and slightly out of breath. By his side was a skinny man wearing spectacles and carrying a thick piece of parchment. His face was red, and he was breathing heavily.

'Were you both running?' said Crutch when they came and sat at the table in the galley with him.

'We were,' said Cedric. 'This is Gilbert. He's a clerk from the records office. It's closed at night, but he opened up the office to get what we needed.'

'The least I could do for you and Colonel Crutch,' said Gilbert. 'Ironbay owes you everything.'

'I don't understand,' said Crutch.

'I know you grew up an orphan in the streets and sewers of Ironbay,' said Cedric. 'You don't even know who your mother and father were. You've lived your whole life with something simple the rest of us take for granted. A surname. I'd like to remedy that. If you'll have me, I'd be proud to adopt you as my son.'

Crutch looked at Cedric, stunned.

When Crutch eked out a living as a street urchin, he dreamed of what it would be like to have a mother or a father who cared for him. He dreamed of having a roof over his head, his own place to sleep, regular meals, and someone who always looked out for him, protected him.

Cedric had given him that all those years ago, when he first came on to the Auld Faithful. Cedric had lied and convinced Captain Featherstone to let Crutch stay on the Auld Faithful as Cedric's assistant. Cedric had introduced Crutch to history, philosophy, his library of books, and opened up worlds to him that he didn't even know existed.

Cedric had fought a deadly duel against Wyld Dog, the pirate, to save Crutch from a flogging that most likely would have killed him. He was like a rock to Crutch, waiting every time he came back to the Auld Faithful, giving him guidance, just being there for him.

His relationship with Cedric was something else Crutch had taken for granted in his anger over the situation with Abagail. How could he have shown such indifference to someone who'd treated him with such kindness?

A lump formed in Crutch's throat, and a single tear ran down his cheek.

'I'd be honoured to be your son,' he said. 'More than honoured.'

'And I'll be more than honoured to have you as my son,' said Cedric, unable to hold back his own tears.

'Well, that's touching,' said Gilbert, visibly moved by their display of emotion. 'You need to sign on that line there,' he said, sliding the thick piece of parchment over the table in front of Cedric, dipping a quill into a small pot of ink, and handing it to him. Cedric signed with a flourish.

'Now you,' said Gilbert, sliding the parchment over to Crutch and handing him the quill. 'Right on that line there.'

Crutch signed, unable to read the parchment with the tears filling his eyes.

'Now I sign to witness the document.' Gilbert added his own signature, then looked up and handed the parchment to Crutch. 'Congratulations. By order of his majesty's records office of Ironbay, you're officially father and son.'

'You have my name now,' said Cedric. 'I know you'll use it wisely.'

Crutch sat there, momentarily speechless, wiping the tears from his eyes.

'Thank you,' he said, struggling to get back his composure. 'I'll be forever grateful. But I still don't understand why you needed to do this in such a hurry.'

'The secret lies in the name,' said Cedric. 'I'm *Lord* Beaumont. Since you're now my adopted son, that makes you…'

'Young Lord Beaumont,' said Crutch, springing to his feet and hugging Cedric. 'Thank you, Cedric. Thank you!'

'One more thing,' said Cedric, pushing a gold ring into Crutch's palm. 'It's a long story, but I never got to use this promise ring my mother gave me. Perhaps you'll have more luck than I did.'

'I don't know what to say,' said Crutch.

'I believe you have a young lady to see, Young Lord Beaumont,' said Cedric, grinning. 'Best not keep her waiting.'

Chapter 59
I Put Up A Good Fight

Crutch flew out of the galley, his cane clacking on the boards of the lower deck, then up the ladder, across the upper deck, and out onto the docks. He ran down King's Way as fast as he could go, pushing off with his good leg, then with his walking cane.

Over and over in his mind he kept telling himself, *Please don't let me be too late.*

Then he started thinking about what he'd say if he did get there on time. The words went round and round his head. None of it sounded right. A jumble of words that tried to say something that could never be adequately expressed with mere words.

He thought about Admiral and Lady Hastings. Would they even let him see Abagail? Would that little turd, Young Lord Chudwell, be there, smiling triumphantly with his promise ring safely on Abagail's hand?

He came down the street of the admiral's residence and realised he might have a more immediate problem. Would the guard let him inside?

As he got closer, he recognised Corporal Levi. The corporal stood at attention and saluted as Crutch came up the stairs. Crutch saluted right back, faking a calm demeanour he certainly didn't feel.

'A pleasure to see you, Colonel Crutch,' said Corporal Levi. 'You're cutting it a bit fine. Young Lord Chudwell's been in there with Young Lady Hastings for at least half an hour.'

'You're not going to try to stop me from going inside?' said Crutch.

'Oh hell no.' Corporal Levi spoke as if he were explaining himself to the admiral. 'I'm sorry, admiral, I tried to stop him, but we all know Colonel Crutch is a master in hand-to-hand combat. I put up a good fight, but the colonel was just too strong for me.'

Corporal Levi opened the door to the admiral's residence and called out, 'Colonel Crutch, here to see Young Lady Hastings.'

The admiral came to the door with Lady Hastings following behind, an annoyed frown on her face. Behind them in the living room, Crutch could make out Young Lord Chudwell standing in front of Abagail. Was he holding a ring?

'What is this?' said Admiral Hastings.

'I'm sorry, admiral. I tried to stop the colonel, but he's a master in hand to hand combat…'

'Yes, yes,' said the admiral. 'You put up a good fight, but he was too strong for you. I'm glad you're unhurt. I wonder why I keep you on as a guard. What brings you here, Crutch?'

'I came to inform you my status has changed.'

'What do you mean?' said the admiral. Young Lord Chudwell and Abagail were now behind Lady Hastings. Abagail looked at Crutch, a glimmer of hope in her eyes.

'I'm not a commoner. Today, I was formally adopted by Lord Cedric Beaumont. I'm now Young Lord Beaumont.'

'I assume that parchment you're carrying is the official documentation?' said Admiral Hastings.

'It is,' said Crutch. 'From his majesty's records office.'

'Let me see,' said the admiral, taking the parchment from Crutch. The admiral read it carefully, then smiled. 'Nicely played,' he whispered to Crutch.

The admiral turned to his wife. 'This document clearly shows that Colonel Crutch is now Young Lord Beaumont,' he said.

'He's still a street urchin from the sewers,' said Lady Hastings. 'He's not fit to be a match for Abagail.'

'Not fit?' said the admiral. 'He saved our lives. Twice! He's the most decorated officer in the history of the royal navy. He's honest, smart, brave, reliable, and he's treated our daughter with kindness and respect. He's never tried to lay a hand on her once. That's more than I can say for this gropey turd you're trying to match her with.'

'I would never…' said Young Lord Chudwell.

'You should keep your mouth shut, Chudwell,' yelled the admiral. 'Do you think I'd let my daughter out with you without having you followed? You're lucky I don't have you flogged!'

Lady Hastings stood with a hand over her mouth in shock. Abagail tried in vain to suppress a grin as she locked eyes with Crutch.

The admiral calmed himself, then spoke softly to his wife. 'I let you have free rein with this because you're my wife, but it's time for me to put my foot down. You've done a magnificent job raising Abagail, and she's more than a good enough judge of character to choose the men she courts. And if one of those men is Colonel Crutch, now Young Lord Beaumont, then I, for one, am thrilled with her choice.'

'But he has no family estate, no inheritance,' said Lady Hastings. 'How will they survive?'

'Crutch found a way to fight off an army of Estovians on the Kona track and found a way to kill Emperor Solokov in Teevilgrad and end the war. I'm quite certain he'll find a way to house and care for Abagail's needs. If she chooses to marry him.'

'But he's really a commoner,' said Lady Hastings.

'Not any more,' said the admiral, shaking the parchment. 'He's a young lord.'

'Only in title and only because a pirate adopted him.'

'Enough of this,' said the admiral. 'This is my house, and I have spoken.'

'Thank you father,' said Abagail, beaming.

'You're welcome Abagail. I wish I'd spoken up sooner. Do you have any more interest in being courted by Young Lord Chudwell?'

Abagail shook her head.

'You heard her Chudwell,' said the admiral. 'Out of my house and out of our lives. If I ever see your snivelly arse again, I'll kick it across the street.'

Young Lord Chudwell looked at the admiral in shock.

'Out!' yelled the admiral and went to draw the dress sword on his belt.

Chudwell ran, slipping on the wooden floor, got up and scrambled out of the door. Admiral Hastings, Abagail, Corporal Levi, and Crutch smiled as they watched him go. The admiral turned to Crutch.

'I expect you and Abagail have plenty to talk about. Come inside to the living room. Lady Hastings and I shall leave you alone together.'

'But I...' said Lady Hastings.

'Come, darling,' said the admiral as he took her hand and led her away. 'They have a lot of catching up to do.'

Chapter 60
Wooing Maidens

Abagail slid her hand into Crutch's and guided him into the living room. Crutch let go of her hand as they turned to face each other. Crutch looked at Abagail, and she looked right back at him, both frozen for a moment.

Crutch knew what he had to do, but that didn't stop his hands from trembling. The hero who fought off the Estovians on the Kona Track and in Teevilgrad shaking like a leaf.

'There's something I need to ask you,' said Crutch.

'You can ask me anything,' said Abagail.

'When you told me your mother wouldn't let us be together, it hurt more than anything ever hurt in my life. It was like someone had reached in my chest and crushed my heart.'

'Me too,' said Abagail.

'And when I was in Teevilgrad, all I could do was think about you. I tried to find a way to live without you. Without the thought of being with you, of seeing your smile, of taking you in my arms.

'It left me angry and bitter. The person I became without you was an ugly, angry shell of a man. It was a torture I hope I never endure again.

'Every day, when I wake up, I think of you. When I go to sleep, I dream of you. You are my world, my reason for living, the light that leads me out of the darkness. With you, I have hope. Without you, I have nothing.'

Crutch dropped to one knee and pulled the ring out of his pocket.

'Young Lady Abagail Hastings, would you take my promise from this day until the end of days? Would you promise to be mine?'

Crutch's hands shook so hard he lost his grip on the ring, and it flew onto the polished wooden floor and slid away under a large sofa. He scrambled on his hands and knees after it. He stuck his hand under the sofa, but couldn't feel it, so he stuck his head under there to find it.

He finally spotted the ring in the corner under the sofa, right against the wall. He slipped on his stomach under the sofa to retrieve it. When he had the ring in his still shaking hand, he turned and Abagail was right there on her stomach next to him.

'Yes,' she said.

'What's that?' said Crutch, caught by surprise that she was lying next to him under a sofa.

'Yes, I give you my promise. From this day till the end of days.'

'You said yes?' Crutch could hardly believe his ears. His hands shook even harder than when he dropped the ring.

'Yes,' said Abagail. 'Now put that ring on my finger before you drop it again.'

Crutch went to put the ring on Abagail's finger, but his hand shook so hard he couldn't line it up. Abagail put her free hand on his and looked straight in his eyes. A calm swept over him as he gazed at that wonderful crooked face and into those ocean blue eyes.

He slipped the ring over her finger, and she smiled at him. He leaned his head towards her, and their lips met in a long, soft kiss. Then they lay there, looking into each other's eyes.

'In all my fantasies of being promised, doing it under a sofa was never one of them,' said Abagail.

'I wanted to make it memorable,' said Crutch, laughing. As he laughed, he lifted his head and banged it on the sofa above him. Abagail laughed too, then banged her head on the sofa too.

'Ow. That hurt,' she said, still laughing. 'You take me to the nicest places.'

'Nowhere is too good for you,' said Crutch.

'Let's get out from under the sofa before mother and the servants start wondering what we're doing,' said Abagail. 'I have something I want to show you.'

After they crawled out, Abagail took Crutch by the hand and led him out a side door of the residence. They walked until they came to a wall with a wooden trellis.

'Follow me,' said Abagail as she began to climb the trellis. Crutch remembered the first time Abagail climbed a ladder onto a roof and how scared she was. Now she climbed like she'd spent her life as a deckhand in the rigging of the Auld Faithful.

Crutch slid his walking cane into his belt and climbed after her until they reached the roof of the admiral's residence. Abagail took his hand and led him to the other side of the building. From here, they could see the navy office, see the city, see the other mansions around them, see the stars filling the night sky.

They'd looked over the city so many times before, but this time it was different. This time, they were promised forever.

'So you're a young lord now?' said Abagail, smiling.

'Young Lord Beaumont in the flesh,' said Crutch.

'You're full of surprises, Young Lord Beaumont.'

'Just call me Crutch.'

'I don't know. I kind of like Young Lord Beaumont. It sounds dashing and romantic. Young Lord Beaumont, wooing maidens under the sofas of the Ironborn territories, no young lady safe from his hand-trembling charms.'

'Stop,' said Crutch, laughing.

'I'm just getting started,' said Abagail. 'We're just getting started.'

'I just realised something,' said Crutch.

'What's that?' said Abagail.

'This is the best night of my entire life.'

Abagail looked into Crutch's eyes, then she kissed him. A long, sweet kiss that made his body tingle and his heart sing with joy.

'Mine too,' whispered Abagail softly as their lips parted.

Crutch knew the world was filled with pain and suffering, and even with the war over, that pain and suffering wouldn't end.

But right now, standing on this roof, holding Abagail's hand, with the roofs of the other buildings around them and the lights of lamps and torches flickering like tiny stars across the city, his world was about as perfect as it ever could be.

Thank you Please Read

As an author, I want to thank you from the bottom of my heart for reading my novel. Without you, the reader, there would be no novel. You make it possible for me to practice the craft I love.

If you enjoyed this novel please consider rating and reviewing it on Amazon. Leaving a review on Amazon is the single most powerful thing you can do for an author with their novels listed there. It helps the novels become more visible on the site which leads to more sales and downloads.

My genuine thanks again for reading this novel.
Andrew Cavanagh

Novels by Andrew Cavanagh available on Amazon include:
Ironborn: Book #1 in The Ironborn Saga
Our Blood Our Land: Book #2 in The Ironborn Saga
Igor's Kitchen: Book #3 in The Ironborn Saga
True Royals: Book #4 in The Ironborn Saga
Black Tide: Book #5 in The Ironborn Saga
Coming Soon:
Wyld Kingdom: Book #6 in The Ironborn Saga
With more to come after that.

Download Your FREE Novella:
Wyld Vengance: Prequel to The Ironborn Saga
is available FREE at <u>andrewcavanagh.com</u>

Printed in Dunstable, United Kingdom

66476981R00145